# Citizen Vince

Also by Jess Walter

**FICTION**

LAND OF THE BLIND

OVER TUMBLED GRAVES

**NONFICTION**

RUBY RIDGE: The Truth and Tragedy
of the Randy Weaver Family
(originally released as
EVERY KNEE SHALL BOW)

# Citizen Vince

JESS WALTER

Author of *Over Tumbled Graves*
and *Land of the Blind*

10 ReganBooks
Celebrating Ten Bestselling Years
*An Imprint of HarperCollinsPublishers*

HarperCollins books may be purchased for educational, business, or sales promotional use. For information please write: Special Markets Department, HarperCollins Publishers Inc., 10 East 53rd Street, New York, NY 10022.


FIRST EDITION

Designed by Richard Ljoenes

Printed on acid-free paper

Library of Congress Cataloging-in-Publication Data
Walter, Jess, 1969–
    Citizen Vince : a novel / Jess Walter.—1st ed.
      p. cm.
    ISBN 0-06-039441-2 (acid-free paper)
    1. Police—Washington (State)—Spokane—Fiction. 2. Spokane (Wash.)—Fiction. I. Title.
   PS3573.A4722834C57 2005
   813'.54—dc22
                                                    2004046828

05 06 07 08 09 BVG/RRD 10 9 8 7 6 5 4 3 2 1          ·

For Anne

"A great nation
is like a
great man...

He thinks of
his ENEMY
as the shadow

that he himself
casts.

—Tao Te Ching

Spokane, Washington

1980 / October 28 / Tuesday / 1:59 A.M.

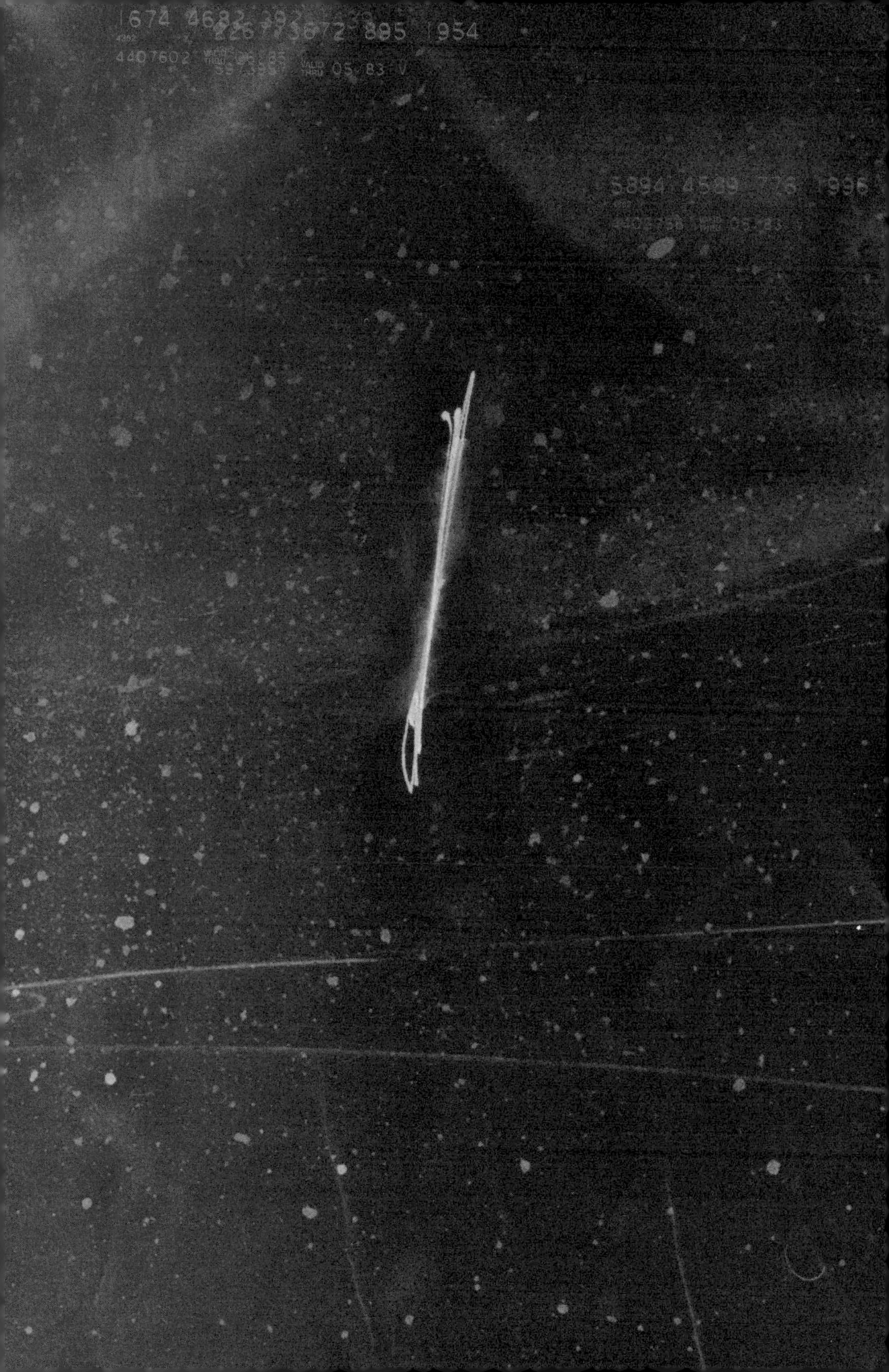

# chapter 1

One day you know more dead people than live ones.

The thought greets Vince Camden as he sits up in bed, frantic, casting around a dark bedroom for proof of his existence and finding only props: nightstand, dresser, ashtray, clock. Vince breathes heavily. Sweats in the cool air. Rubs his eyes to shake the dust of these musings, not a dream exactly, this late-sleep panic—fine glass thin as paper, shattered and swirling, cutting as it blows away.

Vince Camden pops his jaw, leans over, and turns off the alarm just as the one, five, and nine begin their fall. Each morning at 1:59 he sits up like this and turns off the clock radio in the split second before two and the shrill blast of alarm. He wonders: How is a thing like that possible? And yet . . . if you can manage such a trick— every morning waking up a few ticks *before* your alarm goes off— why couldn't you count all the dead people you know?

START WITH GRANDPARENTS. Two sets. One grandfather had a second wife. That's five. Vince runs a toothbrush over his molars.

Mother and father. Seven. Does a stillborn sister count? No. A person has to have been alive to be dead. By the time he finishes his shower, blow-dries his hair, and gets dressed—gray slacks, long-sleeve black dress shirt, two buttons open—he's gone through family, neighbors, and former associates: already thirty-four people he knows to be dead. Wonders if that's high, if it's normal to know so many dead people.

Normal. That word tails him from a safe distance most days. He opens a drawer and pulls out a stack of forged credit cards, looks at the names on the cards: Thomas A. Spaulding. Lane Bailey. Margaret Gold. He imagines Margaret Gold's lovely *normal* life, a crocheted afghan tossed over the back of her sofa. How many dead people could Margaret Gold possibly know?

Vince counts out ten credit cards—including Margaret Gold's—and puts these in the pocket of his windbreaker. Fills the other pocket with Ziploc bags of marijuana. It's 2:16 in the morning when Vince slides his watch onto his wrist, careful not to catch the thick hair on his forearm. Oh yeah, Davie Lincoln—retarded kid used to carry money in his mouth while he ran errands for Coletti in the neighborhood. Choked on a half-dollar. Thirty-five.

Vince stands in the tiny foyer of his tiny house, if you can call a coatrack and a mail slot a foyer. Zips his windbreaker and snaps his cuffs out like a Vegas dealer leaving the table. Steps out into the world.

About Vince Camden: he is thirty-six and white. Single. Six feet tall, 160 pounds, broad-shouldered and thin, like a martini glass. Brown and blue, as the police reports have recorded his hair and eyes. His mouth curls at the right corner, thick eyebrows go their own way, and this casts his face in perpetual smirk, so that every woman who has ever been involved with him eventually arrives at the same expression, hands on hips, head cocked: *Please. Be serious.*

Vince is employed in midlevel management, food industry: baking division—donuts. Generally, there is less to making donuts than one might assume. But Vince likes it, likes getting to work at 4:30 in the morning and finishing before lunch. He feels as if he's gotten one over on the world, leaving his place of employment for lunch and simply not coming back. He's realizing this is a fixed part of his personality, this desire to get one over on the world. Maybe there is a hooky gene.

Outside, he pulls the collar of his windbreaker against his cheeks. Cold this morning: late October. Freezing, in fact—the steam leaks from his mouth and reminds him of an elementary school experiment with dry ice, which reminds him of Mr. Harlow, his fifth-grade teacher. Hanged himself after it became common knowledge that he was a bit too fond of his male students. Thirty-six.

It's a serene world from your front steps at 2:20 in the morning: dim porch lights on houses black with sleep; sidewalks split the dark dewed lawns. But the night has a grimmer hold on Vince's imagination, and he shivers with the creeping sensation—even as he reminds himself it's impossible—that he's on the menu tonight.

"SO, WHAT . . . YOU want me to do this thing or not?"

The two men stare across the bench seat of a burgundy Cadillac Seville. The driver asks: "How much would something like that cost?"

The bigger man, in the passenger seat, is impatient, restless, but he pauses to think. It's a fair question. After all, it is 1980, and the service industries are mired in this stagnant economy, too. Are the criminal sectors subject to the same sad market forces: inflation, deflation, stagflation? Recession? Do thugs suffer double-digit unemployment? Do criminals feel malaise?

"Gratis," quotes the passenger.

"Gratis?" repeats the driver, shifting in the leather seat.

"Yeah." And after a pause: "Means free."

"I know what it means. I was just surprised. That's all. You're saying you'll help me out with this guy for free?"

"I'm saying we'll work something out."

"But it won't cost me anything?"

"We'll work it out."

And it says something about the man driving the Cadillac that in addition to not knowing what the word *gratis* means, he also doesn't realize that nothing is free.

EIGHTY-SEVEN BARS in greater Spokane, serving three hundred thousand people. One taxicab company: eight cabs. So on a Tuesday morning just past two A.M., last call, the economics are clear: more drunks than the market can bear. They leach out onto the sidewalks and stagger and yawn to their cars—those who own them and remember where they're parked. The rest walk from downtown to the neighborhoods, scattering in all directions across bridges, through underpasses, beneath trestles, up hills to dark residential streets, solitary figures beneath thought bubbles of warm breath and cigarette smoke. Rehearsed lies.

Vince Camden concentrates on his own thoughts as he walks sober and rested among the drunk and tired. Stout downtown brick and brownstone give way to low-rent low-rise strips—karate dojos, waterbed liquidators, erotic bookstores, pawnshops, and Asian massage—then a neighborhood of empty warehouses, rail lines, vacant fields, and a solitary two-story Victorian house, an after-hours cards and rib joint called Sam's Pit. This is where Vince hangs out most nights before his shift begins at the donut shop.

Vince was only in town a few months when Sam died. Thirty-seven. The new owner is named Eddie, but everyone calls him

Sam—it being easier to change one's name to Sam than to change the faded Pepsi sign on the old house from SAM'S to EDDIE'S. Just as old Sam did, new Sam opens the Pit when the rest of the city closes, after Last Call. The place works like a drain for the city; every morning when the bars close, the drunks and hookers and lawyers and johns and addicts and thieves and cops and cardplayers—as old Sam used to say, "Evergodambody"—swirls around the streets and ends up here. It's why the cops don't sweat the gambling and undercounter booze. It's just nice to know that at three A.M., everyone will be gathered in one place, like the suspects in a seamy British drawing room.

The Pit lurks behind high, unkempt shrubs, the only thing on a block of vacant lots, like a last tooth. Behind, a rutted dirt field functions as a parking lot for Sam's and a factory showroom for the half-dozen professional women who gather here each night for last tricks. Inside, pimps play cards and wait for their cut.

Gravel cracks beneath Vince's shoes as he angles for Sam's Pit. Six cars are parked randomly in this weed-covered field, girls doing business in a couple. A car door opens fifty feet from Vince, and a woman's voice skitters across the weedy lot: "Let go!"

Vince stares straight ahead. *Not your business.*

"Vince! Tell this guy to let go of me!"

Beth's voice. At the door, Vince turns and walks back across the lot toward a tan Plymouth Duster. Inside, Beth Sherman is wrestling with a guy in a white turtleneck sweater and a navy sport coat. As he walks up to the car, Vince can see the guy's pants are open and that he's trying to keep Beth from getting out of the car. She swings at him with the frayed, dirty cast on her right forearm. Barely misses.

Vince leans down and opens the car door. "Hey, Beth. What's going on?"

The guy lets go and she pulls away, climbs out of the car and past Vince. He is amazed again how pretty she can be, triangular face and round eyes, bangs cut straight across them. She can't weigh a hundred pounds. Odd for a woman in her line of work to actually look younger than she is, but Beth could pass for a teenager—at least from a distance. Up close—well, the lifestyle is tough to hide. Beth points at the guy in the car with her cast. "He grabbed my ass."

The guy is incredulous. "You're a hooker!"

"I'm in real estate!"

"You were blowing me!"

Beth yells around Vince at the man: "Do you grab your plumber's ass when *he's* working?"

Vince steps between Beth and the john, and smiles disarmingly at the guy. "Look, she doesn't like to be touched."

"What kind of hooker doesn't like to be touched?"

Vince can't argue the premise. But he wishes the guy had just kept his mouth shut. He knows how this will go now, and in fact Beth steps around him, fishes around in her pocket, and throws a twenty-dollar bill in his face.

The guy holds up the twenty. "I gave you forty!"

"You got half," she says. "You get half your money back."

"Half? There's no such thing!" He looks up at Vince. "Is there such thing as half?"

Vince looks from Beth to the guy and opens his mouth without the slightest expectation that anything will come. He looks back at Beth and their eyes catch long enough for both of them to note.

About Beth Sherman: she is thirty-three, just leaving "cute," with brown hair and eyes that dart from attention. Her dislike of contact notwithstanding, Beth is well respected among the working women at Sam's, mostly for one big accomplishment—she quit heroin without methadone, cold fucking turkey, exactly nineteen months and two weeks ago, on the very day she found out she was pregnant. Her boy, Kenyon, is a little more than a year now and he seems fine, but everyone knows how she watches him breathlessly, constantly comparing him to the other kids in the park and at his day care, looking for any sign that he is slow or stunted, that her worst fears are realized, that the junk has ruined him, too. And while she is clearly on her way out of this life—she fired her pimp, *in writing*—Beth continues to turn tricks, maybe because there are so few ways for a high school dropout to support herself and her son. Anyway, she's not the only hooker at Sam's who introduces herself as something else. It's a place full of actresses and massage therapists, models, students, and social workers, but when Beth says she's in real estate, people actually seem to believe it.

When he first arrived, Vince purchased Beth's services (he tried a few of the girls) and found himself intrigued by her cool distance, the way she bristled under his hands. Then one night six months ago, she and Vince drank two bottles of wine and spent a night together *without* the exchange of money. And it was different—alarming and close. No bristle. But since then everything has been out of sorts—Beth not wanting to charge him, Vince wary of becoming involved with a woman with a kid. And so they haven't slept together in three months. The worst part is that it feels like cheating to be with the other women, and so Vince is in the midst of his longest stretch of celibacy that doesn't involve a jail cell. The whole thing has proven to him the old axiom among the professional class: *Free sex ruins everything.*

In the parking lot, Beth stalks away from the angry, unsated john—her tight jeans beneath a coat that stops midriff. Vince watches her go, then takes one of the bags of dope from his pocket, bends down, and holds it up to the window. The Bible says that even the peacemaker deserves a profit. Or it says something anyway.

After a second, the guy shrugs and holds up the twenty. "Yeah, okay," he says. As they exchange dope for money, the guy shakes his head. "Never heard of a hooker who didn't want to be touched."

Vince nods, although in his estimation the world is made of only such people, pot-smoking cops, thieves who tithe 10 percent, society women who wear garters, tramps who sleep with stuffed bears, criminal donut makers, real estate hookers. He remembers a firefighter in the old neighborhood named Alvin Dunphy who was claustrophobic. Died when a burning apartment building collapsed on him. Thirty-eight.

**"YOU CAN'T HAVE** half. You either get one or you don't."

"Bet a buck. I'm with Jacks. What good's the job if you don't get to blow?"

"I don't know, I think I got a half the first time."

"How old were you, Petey?"

"The first time? Thirteen. Bump a buck."

"Thirteen? No shit? Wish I had a sister."

"It *was* your sister."

"So what do you think, Vince?"

He has been quiet, lost in thought, hungover from a night of disquieting dreams. He sits perfectly still, leaning forward on his knees, staring off to the side, his cards stacked neatly in front of him. Sam's Pit is dark and carpeted—the old dining room and living room of the Victorian decorated with velvet wall hangings of men with mustaches and Afros screwing huge-hipped women. Light comes from a couple of bare bulbs hanging from the ceiling and a lamp behind the bar. There are six tables in two main rooms—poker games going on at two of the tables; at the other four, people are eating ribs. Four women, including Beth and her best friend, Angela, sit at the bar, swirling drinks made from the bottles Eddie keeps under the counter.

Vince sits up and pushes the hair out of his eyes. "I'm in." Snaps a five into the pot without looking at his cards. Eventually, they all know Vince will hold forth: "What do I think? I think you could reasonably have a half. Honestly, the first part is the best part anyway, and some people say that the end is the death of the thing. Or at least when it all goes downhill. No, I think the real value might be in those first few minutes . . . just getting someone's full attention."

The players look from their cards to Vince's, stacked neatly on the table, and try to remember if he's even looked at his hand. Vince looks up to the bar, where Beth is staring at him; she gives him a half smile, then looks to the ceiling, as if she's just let go of a nice thought and is watching it float away like a kid's balloon.

GAME OVER AND Vince is flush, counting a roll of bills as big as a pair of socks. The other guys exchange glances. Everyone has heard the whispered talk about Vince—the sudden appearance, the New York accent, the proficiency at cards, women, and crime. It is a reputation that Vince has been able to sustain without ever acknowledging—his past in winks and nods. "Where'd you learn to play like that?" Petey asks.

"Baking school." The guys laugh. Vince tosses two fives on the table for the drinks. Stands. Four-thirty A.M., and he's starting to get over whatever was gnawing at him this morning. "Fellas," he says, and taps the roll of bills.

Having finished their ribs and settled with their pimps, the hookers are standing in a clutch at the door. They know not to bother Vince until after he's either won or lost, but tonight, since he's won, they hit him hard. Arms trail his sleeves, lacquered nails riffle his hair. Vince moves through like an aging idol.

"Some a' this, Vince?"

"Got cards for us, Vinnie?"

"Take you 'round the world, baby."

"Smoke? You got any smoke?"

At the door, he exchanges lifted credit cards and lids of pot for cash and fleshy hugs. Although he rejects the offers of freebies and trade-outs, he'd be lying if he didn't admit this was his favorite part of each day, this bit of stage business outside Sam's, when the guys envy him and the women make their plays for him and he holds them off with pinched credit cards and at-cost dope.

When his cards and pot are gone, Vince continues out the door. Outside, he hears his name. He turns and sees Beth looking at her shoes. She glances up at Vince, all eyes, her chin still pointed down; it's a sweet, demure move, and the fact that she has no idea she's doing it makes it that much sweeter. "Thanks for earlier, Vince," she says. "I don't know why I get so . . ."

"It's okay," Vince says. "You been studying?" As long as Vince has known her, Beth has been studying to get her real estate license. She studies, but never actually signs up to take the test.

"Yeah." She shrugs. "I get to run an open house next week. Sort of a trial run. Larry's having three, and he needs someone to run one for him. If I sell it, he'll give me half a percent commission under the table."

"Yeah?" Vince asks. "I'll come by."

"Really?"

"Yeah. Maybe I'll even buy the house."

"Very funny." She squeezes his arm, does that thing with her eyes again—up and down, a flash of release—then turns to go back inside.

CARS LEER ON the street behind Vince; headlights trace his back. Who was that girl from junior high school? Got drunk with some older kids and stepped in front of a car. Angie Wolfe. Thirty-nine.

Vince's hands are in the pockets of his windbreaker, and his shoulders are hunched up around his ears. Only six blocks to the donut shop and he likes the walk fine in the crisp cold, sun still a rumor on the Idaho border, his shadow slowing up for him as he nears the next streetlight. What about old Danello, whose body was never technically found? Doesn't matter. That's forty.

The donut shop is regrettably named Donut Make You Hungry, and is owned by Ted and Marcie, an old gray couple who come in for a few minutes every day to smoke cigarettes and drink coffee with their old gray friends. It works fine for Vince; he gets to manage the place, and Ted and Marcie give him all the space he needs.

He approaches the building—fever-colored stucco on a busy corner a mile from downtown. Lights on inside. That's good. Vince walks down the alley to grab the newspaper, slides the rubber band off, and stands beneath a flickering streetlight to make out the front page: Carter and Reagan in a dead heat, with the debate tonight. The Iranian parliament is meeting to look for a solution to the hostage crisis. He glances at headlines but doesn't read stories, flips instead to the sports page. Alabama plus fifteen at Mississippi State. Seems heavy. Vince closes the paper and starts for the front door when something moves in his periphery.

He cocks his head and takes a step deeper into the alley, clutching the paper to his chest. A car starts. Cadillac. Its lights come on and Vince reflexively covers his eyes while the old voices tell him to run. But there is no place to dive in this alley, nowhere to hide, so he waits.

The burgundy Cadillac Seville inches toward him and the driver's window sinks with a mechanical whir.

Vince bends at the waist. "Jesus, Len. What are you doing here?"

Len Huggins's face is a conference of bad ideas: baby corn teeth, thin lips, broken nose, pocked cheeks, and two bushy black capital-*L* sideburns ("For Len, man! Get it? *L?* Len?"). Len runs a stereo store where Vince uses the phony credit cards to buy merchandise, and get cash advances. Len removes the aviator sunglasses he wears even at night, and slides them into his shirt pocket. "Vincers!" He extends his hand out the window.

"What are you doing here, Lenny?" Vince repeats.

"I came for my credit cards, man."

"It's Tuesday morning."

"I know that."

"We do this on Friday."

"I know that, too."

"Then why are you here on Tuesday?"

Finally, Len withdraws the unshaken hand. "So you ain't got my credit cards, that what you're saying?"

"I'm saying it doesn't matter what I have. We do this on Friday. I don't understand why you're even here."

"I just thought you might have cards today."

"Well, I don't."

"Okay." Len nods and checks his rearview mirror. "That's cool."

Vince straightens up and cranes his neck to see down the alley. "Why are you doing that?"

"Doing what?"

"Looking down the alley."

"What do you mean?"

"Is someone down there?"

"Where?"

Vince points down the alley. "Back there. You keep checking your rearview."

Len puts his sunglasses back on. "You're paranoid, Vince."

"Yeah. I'm paranoid." Vince starts to walk away. "I'll see you Friday."

"I won't be there Friday. That's what I had to tell you. I'm sending a new guy."

Vince turns back—cold. "What do you mean, a new guy?"

"I mean a guy who's new, as opposed to a guy who's old."

"Yeah, I got that part. Who is he?"

"Just a guy to help out on my end. His name is Ray. You'd like him."

Vince walks back to the open car window. "Since when do you have an *end*, Lenny? You buy shit with my credit cards. Since when is that an *end?*"

"Hell's the matter with you? Just meet with this guy, Vince. Relax." Len presses the button to roll up his window. "You're losing it, man." It's the last thing Vince hears before the Cadillac drives away. The car pauses at the corner—a wink from the brake lights—and turns, Vince alone in the alley, watching his own breath. He looks down the alley once more, then starts for the donut shop.

Vince hates alleys. Jimmy Plums got piped in an alley outside a strip club when he went off to piss. They made it look like a robbery, but everyone knew that Jimmy got taken off for a deep skim on some jukeboxes in Howard Beach. So what's that? Forty-one? Or forty-two? Oh, great. Now you've lost count.

**AND THE DONUTS?** It works like this: Vince gets to Donut Make You Hungry at 4:45. He goes to the basement first and puts whatever side money he's made in a lockbox he hides down there. Back upstairs, his assistant, Tic, has been at work an hour already, turning on lights, mixing up doughs according to Vince's recipes, firing the oven and deep fryers, taking frostings out of the walk-in to thaw. Tic is eighteen or nineteen—Vince isn't sure—with long thin hair he constantly throws back—Vince has never seen him use the big-handled comb in his back pocket—droopy eyes, and a jittery sort of energy that never seems to flag. Every night, Tic drinks and smokes pot until three in the morning, has breakfast, goes to the donut shop, finally goes to sleep when he gets off work at ten A.M., wakes up at six P.M., and starts the whole thing over.

The second Vince walks through the door, Tic starts talking.

"Love me some maple bars, Mr. Vince. Love 'em like a naughty girlfriend."

Vince has a locker in back. Inside are his work clothes and the paperback book that he reads on his break—he's struggling with a novel called *The System of Dante's Hell.* He opens the book, reads a couple of cryptic sentences, and puts it back. Slips out of his slacks and black dress shirt and into white coveralls.

"Wanna go steady with a maple bar," Tic is saying. "Wanna take a maple bar to the prom. Wanna take a maple bar home to meet my folks."

Vince washes his hands.

"Wanna marry a maple bar and have little maple-bar babies and go to their little donut baseball games, have slumber parties with all their little bear-claw, cinnamon-twisty friends . . ."

Vince used to track Tic's rants and even to contribute, but it only confuses and irritates Tic when someone else talks and so Vince has learned to treat his young assistant like dissonant background music.

"Hate the apple fritters. Hate the whole fuckin' fritter family. I don't want pesticides in my weed, and I don't want fruit in my donuts."

Four years ago, if someone had told Vince he'd actually enjoy the routine of a job like this, he would've laughed his ass off. You spend your first thirty-six years trying to avoid this kind of life. Then you find yourself plunked right down in the middle of it and it's more than bearable—it's thrilling in a way you could never explain to your old self. And yet Vince wonders if a person like him is capable of change—real change, the elemental parts, the hungers and biases.

The donut shop warms to morning, and at ten till six the waitress Nancy comes in without a word, spends ten minutes on the toilet, then comes out in a waitress shirt and slacks and a lit Virginia Slim and starts humming songs off-key. They are a symphony of irritation, these two. Tic brings Vince a tray of cinnamon rolls that Vince looks over without disrupting Tic's newest rant, about a government program to—

"—perform experiments on monkeys and people and shit underground probably at the poles or in Canada or Greenland which is smaller than it looks on maps explain that to me Mr. Vince why they always make Greenland look bigger on maps unless they're doing something they don't want us to know about so you want me to frost the holes or just powder 'em?"

"Powder."

"See with the dead humans they gotta be careful obviously so they burn the bodies to get rid of all traces of the disease and the implants and shit but do you know what they do with the monkeys, Mr. Vince? Do you? Do you? Do you know?"

Vince keeps his mouth shut.

"With the monkeys they grind 'em up and put 'em in the meat supply so you don't even know. You get a taco at half the restaurants in this country you got any idea what you're eating?"

Vince knows better than to answer.

"Monkey, man. Mother. Fucking. Monkey."

SO YOU CONSTRUCT a life from what's there. Patterns emerge—fry, frost, and fill with jelly—and comfort comes from order, especially on a day when you can't stop counting dead people. (Ardo Ginelli. Forty-eight.) Fry, frost, and fill. No reason such a sequence should be any less satisfying than some other sequence—say, scalpel, suction, and suture. Load the cases, seal the boxes, and greet the guy from the wholesale van, who always, *always* says how good it smells in here, as if he's forgotten since yesterday.

The "Open" sign comes on with a spark and then the lights in the dining room snap on white-hot. The first wave is men: garbage guys, cops, widowers, and drunks—blowing on their hands, removing knit gloves and stocking caps. Vince abides with warm fritters and maple bars and steaming black coffee and awaits the next wave of regulars—deeper sleepers: men with wives, retired guys, office workers with regular donuts and regular coffees with regular amounts of creamer and sugar, sitting in their regular spots at the Formica tables, smoking their regular cigarettes. Vince likes the sameness of their chatter even as he ignores the content, a trick he learned from his old girlfriend Tina, who was an actress when she wasn't working as a paralegal for her brother Benny. Tina got most of her acting jobs in old rat-and-roach houses in the Village and SoHo, but one time she landed a small role in a big off-Broadway thing, in the background of a couple of scenes. Vince was so proud he went every night; loved that play more each time he saw it, loved the predictability and the small differences within the sameness—an actor might pause before a line, or change the inflection, might come in a second earlier or later. One night one of the regulars came in with a cup of prop coffee. Just like that! Coffee! And while the action unfolded (the play was about a family that owned a restaurant; there was a gay brother, a brother studying to be a priest, and a sister who was unmarried and pregnant), the extras just talked and talked, oblivious. Vince asked Tina what she and the other extras talked about when they were in the background of a particularly crowded restaurant scene. She said they were just supposed to mutter nonsense to make background noise and make their lips move. Vince's girlfriend said, over and over, *Banana, apple, strawberry.* Or she changed the order: *Strawberry, apple, banana.*

So that's what Vince began imagining the people on the street were saying all those years: Banana, apple, strawberry. It seemed to confirm what he'd always figured: that normal people, regular people—schoolteachers, firemen, accountants—were simply extras in the lives of guys like him. That's what the straight life always seemed like, a collection of meaningless words and concepts: job, marriage, mortgage, orthodontist, PTA, motor home. How are you? Fine. How are you? Fine. Nice weather we're having. Banana, apple, strawberry. Fry, frost, fill. Banana, apple, strawberry.

But today he *listens* to the conversations of the regulars—two guys on their way to the dump to look for a washing machine; a man advising another man to put his money in gold; a woman showing pictures of her grandchildren—and he thinks that there might be serviceable washers at the dump, that the woman's grandchildren must be adorable, that gold is a great investment. It takes a sort of courage to live a quiet life.

There used to be an inspirational poster on the door to the library at Rikers. It showed a night sky, and across the bottom were the words: *The community of men is made of a billion tiny lights.*

The community of men . . . at night on the ward (institutional sleep is like morphine, dreamless and cold) Vince imagined a real place, a town somewhere that he could actually see, like the old TV shows *Leave It to Beaver* and *Ozzie and Harriet,* a 1950s city where there were always two parents and houses had picket fences, where policemen smiled and tipped their hats.

And now . . . here he is. Spokane, Washington.

Tic has finished the dishes and is putting them away. Vince goes to his locker and grabs his paperback book—he always reads on his coffee break—but he walks to the sink instead, sets his book down, puts one foot on a stool, and lights a smoke. Stares at his young assistant. "I ask you something, Tic?"

Attention makes Tic uneasy.

"How many dead people would you say you know?"

The young man takes a step back.

Vince shifts his weight. This is not what he meant to ask, necessarily. He takes his foot off the stool. "I don't mean, specifically, how many dead people. What I mean is, you ever get some crazy thought stuck in your head—like today, I just kept thinking about how many dead people I know. Anything like that ever happen to you?"

Tic leans forward seriously. "Every fuckin' day, man."

NEVER LET YOUR job get in the way of work. That might be Vince's motto, if he believed in mottos. By noon, he has finished his job at Donut Make You Hungry, and closes the place. Outside, in the blue cool daylight, he feels better—although he still finds himself counting. The whole thing is like some pop song he can't get out of his head. Fifty-seven at last count (Ann Mahoney's father). He walks south, crosses the river, and glances once more over his shoulder. Finally he steps inside a small brick storefront with a stenciled sign that reads DOUG'S PASSPORT PHOTOS AND SOUVENIRS.

A college kid is getting his picture taken. Vince sits at the counter, grabs a magazine, and waits for Doug—fat, white-bearded, and red-faced Doug, like Santa's bad seed—to finish making the guy's phony ID. "How she hangin', Vince?"

Vince ignores him as he reads a story about the new Ford Escort, which is supposed to get forty-six miles to the gallon, but is roomier than the Chevette. Cars all got so small and boxy. When did that happen? They look like lunch boxes. Must be tough on car thieves. Where do you fence a four-cylinder lunch box?

Doug seals the kid's new driver's license, waves it in the air to cool, and hands it to him. Takes twenty bucks for his trouble. "Some bartender grabs that thing, you tell him you got it in Seattle, understand?"

The kid doesn't look up from his new ID. Finally, he grins—all braces and dimples. When he finally leaves, Vince sets the magazine down on the counter.

"You got numbers for me?" Doug asks. He hoists his big haunches onto a stool behind the counter. Vince hands him a sheet of paper filled with names and numbers from the latest run of stolen credit cards.

Doug runs his finger down the list. "Monday okay for these?"

"Fine."

Doug shifts his considerable weight, opens a drawer, and removes a handful of phony credit cards—made from Vince's last batch of numbers.

"So where do you get all of these? You can't be stealing all these credit card numbers from the donut shop."

Vince doesn't answer.

"Is this the way they do it Back East?"

Vince doesn't answer.

Doug sulks as he looks over the numbers. "Shit, man, why are you so edgy?"

"I'm not edgy."

"Then why can't you tell me where you get the numbers?"

There is a hint of forced nonchalance in the question. Vince takes the phony cards and hands Doug a small roll of bills.

"Come on," Doug says as he counts. "I got a right to know."

Vince puts the cards in his pocket.

"I mean, I got a pretty good idea how it works," Doug says. "I haven't been asleep the last six months, you know."

"Okay," Vince says. "Why don't you tell me how it works?"

"Well, you steal these cards *somewhere*. You write down the numbers and then you give the cards back so the owners won't report them stolen. I make copies of the cards. You take the cards I make you, buy shit with them, sell the shit, and then sell the cards. So you get paid twice. Am I right?"

Vince doesn't answer. Turns to leave.

"Come on"—Doug laughs—"we're partners. What do you think, I'm gonna go against you?"

Vince stops, turns back slowly. "Someone want you to go against me?"

Doug straightens. "What are you talking about?"

"What are *you* talking about?"

"I'm not talking about anything. Jesus! Lighten up, Vince. Don't be so paranoid."

That word again. Vince stares at him a moment, and then

walks outside. He looks back in through the front window. Doug mouths the word *paranoid* again.

There was this old guy named Meyers who ran a chop shop back in the world. This Meyers worked only with recent Vietnamese immigrants, because he could pay them less and, according to Meyers, they were too unsettled by America to backstab him. Used to sit in this big rocking chair while the Vietnamese kids stole cars for him, stripped them down, and hauled the parts all around New Jersey. And he paid them shit. Then, one day, Meyers just disappeared. Next day, some old Vietnamese guy is running the chop shop, sitting in that rocking chair. There's a lesson in there—something about condescension. Or maybe rocking chairs. And what is that? Fifty-eight?

VINCE CAMDEN WALKS everywhere. In two years he still hasn't gotten used to all of the cars; everyone drives everywhere here, even the ladies. In this town, five guys drive to a tavern in five cars, have a beer, then get in their five cars and drive three blocks to the next tavern. It's not just wasteful. It's uncivilized. People say it's because of the harsh winters in Spokane, which are a cross between upstate New York and Pluto. But outside a few places in Florida and California, the weather is shitty everywhere. Every place is too hot or too cold or too humid or too something. No, even in the cold Vince prefers walking—like now, strolling away from Doug's storefront toward downtown, which looms ahead, a couple of newer twenty-story glass-and-steel slabs surrounded by brick-and-stone stumps. He likes the cluster of buildings from a distance like this—the suggestion of cornices and pillars; imagination fills in the blanks.

Vince stops at a little diner, orders coffee, and sits alone at a table, staring out the window, chewing a thumbnail. Twice in one day: that word. *Paranoid*. Still, how could you possibly tell if you're paranoid when worrying about being paranoid is a symptom of paranoia? It's not the fact of Doug asking where he gets the credit cards, necessarily, or of Lenny showing up in the alley two days early—although either one of those things would have made him suspicious. It's this feeling he's slogged around with since he woke up—this sense of being herded along, that his time is coming. What if death is just *out there*, at some fixed point, waiting for you to walk under it like a piano suspended above the sidewalk? He feels like a chess piece, like a knight that's come out with no support and is being chased around the board by the other side's pawns. He can escape the pawns, but he senses other pieces, larger pieces, more significant pieces—a move, two moves, three moves away. After a minute, Vince goes to the front of the diner and drops a quarter into the pay phone. Dials.

"Hey. Is he in?"

Waits.

"It's Vince. You up for a game of chess?"

Listens.

"Oh, come on. Why do I gotta do it like that?"

Listens.

"Jesus. Okay, okay . . . This is twenty-four-fourteen. I need to come in. There. How's that?"

Listens.

"I need to see you now. Today."

Listens.

"Of course it's an emergency. What do you think?"

He hangs up, walks back to his table, and finishes his coffee. He zips up his windbreaker and steps outside. He walks with his head tilted forward, toward downtown. It's cool and sunny and the combination thrills him in a way; he pulls a deep breath through his nose and takes in the bare, skeletal trees, the strip of black avenue leading downtown. It really is a beautiful city in its way. Not so much architecturally, but in contrasts: glimmers of style against those drastic hills and urban trees, and through it all the river cut—a wilderness very nearly civilized with a few tons of concrete, blacktop, and brick. A real place. He walks without looking back, uncharacteristically.

If he did look back, he wouldn't like what he saw. Two blocks behind him, Len Huggins's burgundy Cadillac sits in front of Doug's Passport Photos and Souvenirs.

DOUG RUBS HIS jaw. "How much?"

"He said for gratis." Lenny takes off his sunglasses. "Means free."

"I know what it means. Who is this guy?"

"Just a guy. Name's Ray."

"Where's this Ray from?"

"Back East, like Vince. He just got into town."

"What's he doin' here?"

"I don't know, man. He didn't say."

"But he does this for a living?"

"Oh yeah. He pushes buttons."

"Buttons?"

"That's what they call it."

"Buttons?"

"Yeah, that's what he said. He works for some serious guys back there."

"And you're sure he ain't a cop?"

"He ain't a cop, Doug. Not this guy."

"I don't know."

"Look. This guy wants to do it for gratis. How can we say no?"

"It's not *for gratis*, Len. It's just gratis."

"Whatever. Look, this Ray says they do the whole credit-card thing different Back East. Vince is making a lot more money than he's paying us. That ain't right. And he won't tell us where he gets the cards? That ain't right, neither. We're supposed to be partners and he's holding back on us, man."

"It's just . . . I like Vince."

"I like Vince, too. Everyone likes Vince. It's got nothing to do with Vince."

"So what would we have to do?"

"Nothing."

"Nothing?"

"Just show him where to point the gun."

**WALK ANY BLOCK** in Spokane and you can see in the city's design the way it was settled—a slow, 150-year flood of homes, filling the river gorge first, west to east, and then rising onto the ledges, ridges, and hills: outward and onward, north, south, east, and generally up. The downtown, seven blocks by fifteen blocks of brick and block and terra-cotta, covers the first ledge, and beyond and above that are neighborhoods of Victorian, Tudor, and Craftsman, and beyond that Deco, cottage, and bungalow, and beyond that rambler, rancher, and split level, neighborhoods that have begun to spill over the far sides of the facing hills.

At the center of this sprawl are the pearly waterfalls that the city oystered around, and two blocks above the falls sits the Federal Courthouse, a bland new box of a building, ten stories tall. In an office on the sixth floor, on either side of a chessboard, sit Vince Camden and a chunk of a deputy U.S. marshal named David Best. Vince has moved one pawn out, and Deputy Marshal Best has his hand on his queen's knight and is considering putting Vince's pawn in jeopardy. He looks all around the board, under and over his own arm, eyes darting from piece to piece.

"You moving that horse or grooming it?"

"Just a sec," says David. He is fifty and looks it—overweight and gray, his cheeks and nose flushed with blood, a bald circle at the peak of his scalp. He wears wrinkled slacks, a herringbone jacket, and a thick knit tie pulled into a knot that would choke the very horse he's contemplating moving. Finally, David brings the knight out and threatens Vince's pawn.

Vince quickly moves his own knight out to protect his earlier move. Slaps an imaginary chess timer. "How about Christensen?"

"Vince Christensen?"

"Carver?"

"Vince Carver?"

"Claypool?"

David rests his hand on a pawn and takes in the entire board again, looking under his arm in both directions as he considers his move. "Look, you can't just go changing your name every six months. It doesn't work that way."

"Does it work better if someone kills me?"

"Come on. Who's going to kill you, Vince?"

"I told you. Camden is a city in New Jersey. Right? Vince *Camden?* Might as well call me Vince Capone. You don't think they'll figure that out?"

David looks up from the chessboard. "Who?"

"What?"

"*Who* will figure it out? You come in here every six months thinking someone is out to get you. Last time—"

"Yeah, but this time—"

"Last time, you almost killed that poor guy from the phone company."

"He was on the pole outside my house for forty minutes! You tell me what a guy's doing up on a phone pole for forty minutes."

"Fixing the phone?"

"I'm just saying, this time—"

"This time!" David spreads his hands. "Who are these people

out to get you, Vince? I looked up your case. There's no one after you."

Vince just stares at him.

"The crew you testified against doesn't even exist anymore. Bailey's dead. Crapo's dead. And the only guy who was even connected ... what's his name? The old guy, Coletti? He was nothing—a soldier. An old man. Didn't even do a year after his conviction. And he's retired now. Frankly, I'm shocked they put you in the program. I don't really see the protection part of this witness protection." David stares at Vince, his thick nightcrawler fingers resting on the pawn.

"You keep moving your fingers up and down on that thing, it might get excited and grow into a bishop," Vince says.

Finally, David moves the pawn. Sits back and pushes his glasses up on his nose.

Vince moves a knight into position. "Just put it in your little book that I came in," he says. "That way, when I get planted, you can explain to your bosses why you did nothing."

This finally pisses David off. His face goes crimson. He sits back and looks across the board unhappily. After a moment, he pushes his chair away and rises with some trouble, goes to a filing cabinet, opens a drawer, and returns with a manila folder. The file reads WITSEC. "There are thirty-two hundred people in this program, Vince. You know how many we've lost? How many witnesses have been killed after we relocated them?"

Vince looks up.

"Zero. Not one." David opens the file. "Every month we get intelligence reports from wiretaps and informants and correspondence. Every time we get a threat, or a contract goes out, we record it. Every time one of our witnesses is mentioned, it is noted and cataloged and a report goes out to the field office. Each witness is assigned a number corresponding to this ongoing assessment of the danger they face, one to five. Know what your assessment is, Vince?"

Shrugs.

"Zero. No pertinent threat. You know how many times your name has come up in intelligence reports since you went into the program?"

Looks around the office.

"Zero. Zip. In four years: nothing. You haven't shown up on one wiretap. Not even *That guy could sure hold his beer.* Vince, no one is out to kill you because no one remembers you anymore. No one cares. Frankly, to them, you're not worth killing. They got bigger fish." David sits back down. His chair groans and David breathes heavily.

The room is quiet.

"Look," David says. "I'm sorry."

Vince shrugs. "Maybe you're right. It's just . . ." Lifts a pawn to move it, then picks it up and stares at it. "All day, it feels like someone's watching me, manipulating me. You ever feel like that, David?" He cocks his head. "Like they know what you're going to do before you do it?"

"No. I don't feel like that. Sane people don't feel like that, Vince. Sane people don't change their names because they had bad days." David considers Vince's face, then pushes his glasses up and leans forward. "Maybe you should see Dr. Welstrom again. Just to talk about—"

"No."

"These sound like the same issues you had before, Vince, irrational fear, anxiety—"

"David—"

"Adjusting to a new life is not easy—"

"No."

"Especially when you leave everything behind. Way of life. Friends. Your girlfriend. What was her name? She was an actress, right? Tina?"

"Is this necessary?" Vince throws his arms in the air. "Can't we just play chess?"

"Okay." David nods. "Sorry." He looks around the board. "So how's the job?"

"It's fine."

"Because sometimes, it can be hard to give up a more interesting life for, you know . . . donuts. Do you see what I'm trying to tell you?"

"That you play chess like my grandmother?"

David smiles in spite of himself, puts his hand on his bishop, and begins looking around the board again. "Maybe you need hobbies, Vince. You should learn to play golf. What do you do with your free time, anyway?"

"I play cards. I read some."

"What do you read?"

"Beginnings of novels."

David looks up. "Why don't you finish them?"

"I don't know," Vince says.

He leans back in his chair and stares over David's head, to a portrait on the wall behind the big deputy marshal. In the portrait, President Jimmy Carter, somber in a gray suit, stares down at Vince, the president's blond hair gone to silver, his lips pressed tight, suppressing that oft-mocked toothy smile—his face revealing a softness, a give, that wasn't there four years ago. *The most powerful man in the world?*

Vince can't look away. There is something about Jimmy Carter's face, the quality of an outsider lost on the inside, something familiar that Vince has never considered before—and something about this man, this president, about the limits of power and the weight of responsibility—but just as the thought is forming in his head, Vince loses it and hears David's voice: *No one cares.*

Bailey and Crapo are dead. Of course. He can still see them at trial, sort of bored, not really surprised that Vince was testifying. Not even angry. Just tired. The prosecutor: *Are the men who conspired with you to use stolen credit cards to purchase this merchandise in the courtroom today?* Vince pointing at Bailey, and then Crapo. Jesus, and now they're both dead. Bailey had a heart attack. And Crapo got shivved breaking up a fight. How could he have forgotten those two? That's sixty. And sixty-one.

Vince looks down at the board, where David's hand still rests on his bishop. "You planning to marry that bishop, or are you two just living together?"

**AFTER FIVE AND** already getting dark when Vince gets home from the Federal Courthouse and a bowl of tavern soup. He opens the door and sees the day's mail below the door slot, on the foyer floor in front of him. There's a manila envelope with no return address. From the mailman. Right on time. Thank God for that at least.

The house he rents is small and warm, a 1930s pitched-roof one-story, leaning forward over a porch the size of a casket, supported by a couple of pine four-by pillars—the whole thing a fair definition of lowered expectations. The living room is carpeted, and Vince steps out of his shoes and clicks on the TV. It fades up close on the face of President Carter, behind a podium, weary, eyes deep in sockets: *The best weapons are the ones that are never fired in combat and the best soldier is one who never has to lay his life down on the field of battle. Strength is imperative for peace, but the two must go hand in hand.*

Oh yeah. The debate. Cool. Vince turns the volume up and heads for the kitchen. He sets the mail on the table and grabs an Oly from the fridge. He opens it, reads the puzzle on the bottle cap—*Eye th-ink, there-4 eye yam*—and takes a long pull. Then he sets the beer down on the small kitchen table next to the mail and opens the cabinet under the sink. He takes out a produce box and sets it on the table next to the beer.

Inside the box is his latest project, the best idea he's ever had; it has the potential to finally get him out of the credit-card business forever. Vince sets out six Kerr jelly jars, a scale, a large bucket of ash, and a cigar box filled with marijuana leaves and stems. He weighs two ounces of pot and puts it in one of the Kerr jars. Then he takes a soup spoon and fills the rest of the jar with the gray ash, packing it around the dope. When it's full, he screws a lid on the jar and seals on a purple-and-white printed label that reads:

**MOUNT ST. JELLY**

**Real Volcanic Ash from Mount St. Helens**

**In a decorative jelly jar**

**Packaged and shipped in Spokane, WA**

Below, in even smaller print:

**Not for consumption. A souvenir novelty item only.**

He plans to ship the volcanic ash to Boise and Portland, where two guys he knows will sift the dope out, stomp it, and sell it. Then the beauty part: they'll actually sell the ash to tourists! That part always makes him smile. Usually you have to hire mules to drive the shit, and you just live with them undercutting you— selling some off, smoking more. And you always have to worry that they'll get busted and give up your name. No: if you can get the U.S. government to mule it for you, it cuts your shipping costs to about eight cents per ounce of pot, which the ash more than pays for. Vince had thought about shipping his pot in smoked salmon, but this is far cheaper and easier, and the customers can't complain about the fishy smell of their weed. Best of all, there is an almost endless supply of ash along the roadsides; even now, five months after the eruption of Mount St. Helens, a thousand crappy little souvenir shops sell the shit in pens and Coke bottles and ashtrays. So why not jelly jars?

When two jars of Mount St. Jelly are full and his beer is finished, Vince goes to the fridge and gets another beer.

He sits back at the table and looks at the television. Reagan is talking now, dark-suited, breathy, and theatrical, almost reading, but not quite: *I stood in the South Bronx on the exact spot that President Carter stood on in 1977 . . . a bombed-out city—great, gaunt skeletons of buildings. Windows smashed out, painted on one of them "Unkept promises," on another "Despair." They are now charging to take tourists there to see this terrible desolation. I talked to a man just briefly there who asked me one simple question: "Do I have reason to hope that I can someday take care of my family again?"*

*Do I have reason to hope?* That's good. He tries to imagine some mope from the Bronx actually saying, "Do I have reason to hope"—no fuckin' way. Vince reaches for his mail, the manila envelope from the mailman, two bills, two campaign solicitations, and a small envelope from the county auditor. Vince opens that one first. It is empty except for a small paper card, the size of a driver's license. On top, it reads: *Certificate of Registration.* Vince turns it over in his hand:

*This is to certify that Vincent J. Camden . . . is a registered voter in 100342.00 Precinct, Spokane County of Washington.*

The card also has the address where he's supposed to vote, a small Catholic school near his house.

So just like that he can vote. Or, at least, *Vince Camden* can vote. He sets the card down, then picks it up again. The marshals said something about getting Vince's record cleared and his voting rights restored if he cooperated with the government. But there was so much other shit going on, and he was so worried about getting whacked, that honestly he didn't give it a second thought. What's voting to a guy who's lived the life he's lived, a guy trying to save his own skin? But now here it is, almost three years later, and he gets a voter's registration card in the mail.

He can't help but wonder what it means, if there aren't quiet omens, too.

Vince opens his wallet and slides the registration card in beside his crisp social-security card.

Next he opens the mailman's manila envelope. The deal works like this: The mailman watches for new credit cards in the mail, and drops them in a manila envelope for Vince, who steams them open, writes down the numbers, then puts the cards back and seals the envelopes with a glue stick. The cards are delivered to their owners, and it's usually a month or two before they realize that someone else is charging the shit out of their account. By then, Vince has dumped the cards.

This load is light: six unopened MasterCard and American Express envelopes slide out. He can feel the hard credit cards inside. Then a white folded note falls from the envelope and flutters to the table, almost the same size as his voter's registration card. He stares at the note from the mailman. No, this isn't right.

Dread takes up very little space.

Vince looks down at the note and has the urge to ignore it. He doesn't need this. Not after the day he's had. Finally, he picks it up and reads it.

*I need to see you. Tomorrow. Three. Regular place.*
*Important.*

No. All wrong. Vince meets the mailman on *Mondays.* They just met yesterday. He paid the mailman and gave him some cards to put back in the mail. Mondays. They've never met any other day. Tomorrow is Wednesday. This is wrong. And just like that, the misgiving, the fear, the paranoia—whatever it is—is back.

Maybe it's being back in his house, where this day started with such unsettling thoughts, or maybe it's the combination of getting the voter's registration and the mailman's note, but Vince can feel darkness in front of him, and he can taste the dread that he woke with this morning, and he knows with certainty: They've found him. They're going to kill him.

When you're dead, the world goes on without you, swallows you up like a stone in black water. So, there's that.

He looks up to see a stern Barbara Walters at the debate moderators' table, the others deferring to her huge head, which is cocked and serious: *Mr. President, the eyes of the country tonight are on the hostages in Iran. I realize this is a sensitive area, but the question of how we respond to acts of terrorism goes beyond this current crisis.*

Vince thinks of Lenny—*You're paranoid, man*—and Doug—*think I'm gonna go against you*—and David—*No one cares anymore.* They are right. All of them. He is paranoid. And they are going against him. And no one cares. Coldness moves up his ankles into his calves. Jimmy Carter bites his lip and cocks his head in sympathy.

*Barbara, one of the blights on this world is the threat and the activities of terrorists . . . we committed ourselves to take strong action against terrorism. Airplane hijacking was one of the elements of that commitment. But ultimately, the most serious terrorist threat is if one of those radical nations like Libya or Iraq, who believe in terrorism as a policy, should have atomic weapons.*

While we watch the small patterns, the big movements elude us. We are so intent on incidental waves of *news* and *memory* that we miss the larger tides of history.

Vince stands and feels his own pulse in his ears. Okay. Think. *Think.* Who is behind all of this? Who has the most to gain? The problem with conspiracies is that only crazy people can find them. That's why conspiracies work, because they shatter the truth into shards and only crazy people can look at shards and see the whole. And who is going to believe a crazy person, anyway? Are you losing it? Vince rubs his temple. You're losing it, aren't you?

Ronald Reagan can't wait to answer: *You've asked that question twice. I think you ought to have at least one answer to it. I have been accused lately of having a secret plan with regard to the hostages . . . Your question is difficult to answer, because, in the situation right now, no one wants to say anything that would inadvertently delay, in any way, the return of those hostages.*

Okay, let's assume David is right, and it's not someone from his old crew out to get Vince. Could one of Vince's own guys be trying to get a bigger cut, or increase the number of credit cards in play? The mailman? No way. Clueless. That leaves Doug and Lenny. He can't imagine Len has the brains, or Doug the balls. They both seem harmless. Still, there's an old Sicilian proverb that Coletti used to quote: *The smiling enemy is the one to fear.*

President Carter doesn't need to be told this: *This attitude is extremely dangerous and belligerent in its tone, although it's said with a quiet voice.* And perhaps it's that last phrase—*a quiet voice*—that finally forces Vince to snap out of his own head and register the low hum he's been hearing for the last thirty seconds. A car is idling outside.

Among certain groups—political operatives, criminal gangs, middle school girls—every breath is conspiracy. And so it should come as no surprise that Reagan's people have gotten their hands on Jimmy Carter's debate notes and used them to coach their candidate. Or that Reagan may be working behind the scenes to make sure the hostages aren't released until *after* the election.

And what about Vince—crouched in front of the parted curtains, looking around his house for some kind of weapon? What plots swarm around him, what currents of malevolence and greed and dark chance? And more important: Who's in that car idling outside his house?

                                          *     *     *

**VINCE CRAWLS ON** his hands and knees across the frosted lawn. He
doesn't recognize the car—an early 1970s Impala. He grips the narrow lead pipe, cold in his hands. Found it under the sink. Grass
crunches beneath him. Vince crawls away from the car, toward his
neighbor's house, then along a shrub line, until he emerges directly
behind the car and breathes in carbon monoxide. There's a bumper
sticker on the car: I BRAKE FOR SASQUATCH! Vince crouches and side-
steps, hefts the pipe one more time, exhaling in small bursts. Okay.
Okay.

He reaches the back bumper without the driver seeing him.
Okay. Deep in his crouch. The driver is smoking, staring down the
block. Vince closes his eyes, counts three and rushes the driver's-
side door, opens it and pulls the guy out by his hair, throws him
down in the grass, and his cigarette sparks and flies across the lawn
and he crab-crawls away on his back.

It's just a kid, maybe eighteen, long stringy red hair and a blue
letterman's coat with a big yellow *M*. "I'm sorry!" he says, and covers his head.

Vince holds the pipe up, but doesn't swing it. "Are you alone?"

"Yeah. Jesus. Don't hit me."

"Someone tell you to park in front of my house?"

"Yeah. She said to wait here."

"What's your name?"

"Everett."

"Everett, I'm going to bust open your head unless you tell me
who sent you."

"Nicky. Nicky said to wait down the block."

"Who's Nicky?"

"What?"

"Nicky. Who the hell is Nicky?"

"Please, sir. Don't do this. I'll leave."

"Who . . . is Nicky?"

"Well, I'm assuming she's your daughter, sir."

Vince sees her then, a girl from the neighborhood. Fifteen, sixteen tops. Climbing up from a window well in the basement of a house three doors down. She wipes the grass off her jeans and starts toward Vince and this boy. But she sees Vince holding a pipe and her stealth date lying on the ground, and she stops and, without changing her expression, turns and climbs back into her window well.

After a moment, Vince helps the kid up and they watch together as the pretty girl shimmies back into the basement window.

*I'VE BEEN PRESIDENT* now *for almost four years. I've had to make thousands of decisions. I've seen the strength of my nation, and I've seen the crises it approached in a tentative way. And I've had to deal with those crises as best I could.*

Vince stands in his dark house with another beer, two feet from the television set, staring into Jimmy Carter's hooded eyes as he delivers his closing remarks: *I alone have had to determine the interests of my country and the degree of involvement of my country. I've done that with moderation, with care, with thoughtfulness.*

Sometimes you just get tired. And maybe there are forces aligned against you, maybe they have stolen your debate notes and maybe they're even making deals with terrorists and maybe the minute you're out of office, the hostages will come home. Then again: maybe not. Maybe you're just too tired to go on. And maybe *that* is defeat, in the end . . . simply giving in. Maybe it's no worse than going to sleep.

Yes, that's it, the president says. *It is a lonely job. The*

*American people now are facing, next Tuesday, a lonely decision.*
*Those listening to my voice will have to make a judgment about the*
*future of this country. And I think they ought to remember that one*
*vote can make a lot of difference. If one vote per precinct had*
*changed in 1960, John Kennedy would never have been president of*
*this nation.*

One vote . . . See, you're not afraid of Lenny. Or Doug. Or the mailman. Or even all three of them together. The conspiracy itself is not what gets you; *it's the idea that they're conspiring.* The unknown. It's not one snowflake, one vote; it's the idea of a landslide. That's what's so scary. How many times have you imagined that life would be easier if you knew the future? Well, you know the future. We're all walking dead.

The sun's going to explode one day . . . so don't get out of bed? Fifteen billion years or fifteen minutes . . . does it matter? Does anything matter?

And then, of all people, Ronald Reagan offers an answer: *Next Tuesday is Election Day. Next Tuesday you will go to the polls, stand there in the polling place, and make a decision. I think when you make that decision, it might be good if you would ask yourself . . .*

*Are you better off than you were four years ago?*

Vince drops his beer. It thuds on the carpet. Bleeds foam.

A single thought is nothing; combined, the thousands of separate electrochemical, synaptic sparks that went into creating this sentence wouldn't fire a ten-watt bulb. And yet here is Vince Camden, at the peak of technology and development, at the crest of a remarkable wave of human achievement, in a world created by piling these single thoughts together, strung out over millennia— here is Vince Camden, himself a technological and legal creation, standing alone in a heated, wired, insulated shelter, witnessing a thirteen-inch box beaming a mash of electrons that when unscrambled depict two men vying for the most powerful position in the history of the world at a time when the push of a button can effectively end civilization. Here is Vince Camden, overwhelmed by his own significance and by his desire to change, by the undertow of history, and by the weight of so many choices, undone by this miracle of being and by all of these strands connected in the thread of one simple thought:

*Which of these stupid fucks are you supposed to vote for?*

Spokane, Washington

1980 / October 29 / Wednesday / 2:25 A.M.

674 4682 992 436
4407602 26 785 VALID 05/83 V

5894 4589 776 1996
9305788 VALID 05/83 V

# chapter 11

Hookers arguing about bras.

If he'd known, Vince would've just kept walking. He was deep in thought about this election business, and something about it was making him feel better—or distracted anyway—but now he's outside Sam's Pit, and Beth and her friend Angela are waving their hands in the cold air, making points with little bursts of steam.

"Vince can settle it," says Angela, and she toddles over in a pair of heels that make her lean dangerously far forward and transform her ass into a shelf. "Beth thinks guys like bras, but I said you all would just as soon see the bare titties."

Vince looks from Angela, all brown and curvy, to Beth, skinny, pale—frayed cast behind her back. "I don't think I'm the right guy to ask."

Angela takes Vince's arm in hers and bunkers it with boobs. She flutters her eyes and he can feel the dusting of her long lashes on his cheek. "Oh, come on, Vince. Which would you rather see? Beth's bra . . . or these?"

"Well, those are nice." Vince glances down at the dark crease of Angela's cleavage. "Then again, a bra has a . . . certain sensuality."

Angela pushes him away. "You'd like balls if Beth had a pair."

Beth laughs uncomfortably. "Angela!"

Vince escapes into Sam's, already crowded with cigarette smoke and poker games, ribs, and beneath-the-counter booze. Eddie comes up from the basement with a pan of coated chicken wings.

"Vince Camden. Hardest-working man in donuts. How she goin', Vince?"

"Good. How you doin', Sam?"

"Fat, tired, and diabetic." Eddie is sixty, black, with a gray beard and black-rimmed glasses.

Vince stops and turns to face him. "Hey, can I ask you something?"

Eddie shrugs. "What's on your mind, Vince?"

"I was just wondering, who do you think won the debate?"

"Two whores arguing about bras? Ain't no winner in a goddamn thing like that."

"No. No. I mean the presidential debate."

Eddie just stares.

"You know. Carter and Reagan? Last night on TV?"

Eddie thinks for a minute, and then shrugs. "Like I said, Vince: ain't no winner when a couple of whores start arguing."

"COLOR HAS A lot to do with it. Bet a buck."

"You mean like black or red?"

"Yeah, those are good. Or even white. Just not that flesh color."

"Color don't matter long as they ain't all wired up. Call."

"No, see, that there's a support bra, your twenty-four-hour model. That's a good thing. A little wire in the cage means they's plenty a' booby inside."

"Booby? Did you just say *booby?*"

"The wired ones are too hard to get off. Bump a buck."

"Then maybe you shouldn't wear one."

"I mean hard to get off the woman."

"Maybe you should try it when she's awake. Call."

"I'm okay with the front clasp, but that back clasp . . . shit oh day."

"That's right. That's flyin' blind, undoing that back clasp."

"What do you think, Vince?"

He looks up. It always comes to this—their deferral to him. The guys are staring, holding their cards like a bunch of kids playing Go Fish. Behind them Angela is sitting on her pimp's lap, sharing a drumstick. Next to them an off-duty uniformed cop is signing Beth's cast. Vince checks his watch. Quarter to four.

"All right," Vince says, and straightens. "I'm going to tell you what it is, but then we're done talking about this. Okay? We talk about something intelligent for a change. Like politics. Agreed?"

Guys nod and listen intently. Jacks swills champagne from a magnum in his lap.

"Okay. First thing you have to realize is that a bra is a symbol for male anxiety. It's, what do you call it . . . a surrogate for the clitoris. You know? That fear that we're all thumbs—it's dark and confusing and we don't know what we're doing down there. Sometimes we get lucky, but even then we don't know exactly what we did. Ten to eighty, all we think about is girls—and when we finally get one, turns out we don't know shit about 'em." He shrugs. "So that's all a bra is—one more thing about women we're afraid we don't know how to work."

The guys stare.

"But you get past that anxiety? Well . . . For example, there's that point in the middle of foreplay; just before the fun starts? You're both half undressed . . . could still go either way. She could change her mind. And you're out of your head for her. Kissing and chewing her neck. Your hands are wrestling around, trying to figure out if it's a hook clasp or a bend-and-twist.

"And right then, at that moment—she stops you. Pulls your hands away. Stands up. Smiles down at you. And then, as slowly as she can . . . watching your eyes as she does it . . . she lowers the straps, unhooks her bra . . . and lets it fall to the ground."

No one breathes. Angela and her pimp stare. Beth, too. The whole room.

"So yeah. I think a bra is sexy. Now"—Vince straightens up and tosses a five into the pot—"am I the only one here who watched the goddamned debate?"

FOUR-THIRTY IN the morning. The girls hit Vince at the door, but he's distracted today. He has no credit cards and he sells weed without ceremony, before they can bestow hugs and innuendo. Tonight even Beth waits at the door, biting her bottom lip, waiting until the other girls leave. "I like what you said about bras, Vince."

"How you doing, Beth?"

She shifts her weight. "I can't sleep I'm so nervous."

"About what?"

She looks at him as if it should be obvious. "The open house. Remember? I told you about it last night. I'm running an open house for Larry."

"Oh, sure, sure." Vince had totally forgotten. "When is that again?"

"Saturday, Sunday, and Monday. You're coming, right?"

"Of course I'm coming."

"It's just . . . I have these dreams where some old trick comes in, or the cops arrest me, or I say something completely retarded."

"Beth—"

"Just tell me the truth. Do people laugh at me?"

"Laugh at you?"

"For trying to get my real estate license? It's stupid, isn't it?"

"No," he says. "It's not stupid."

"Tell me the truth."

"It's not stupid."

"You know how every stripper says she's saving for college? But it's just something they say to make the guys feel better about watching a girl take her clothes off—like their hard-ons are contributing to a better world.

"Well, I think, maybe at the beginning, it was like that for me. I just liked to hear myself say it: 'I'm studying to be a real estate agent.'" She leans in and practically whispers. "But now . . . Shoot, Vince—I mean, they might actually let me do this. And what if I can't? What if I'm not smart enough?"

"Beth—"

"It hurts my head to think about. It's stupid how much I want this."

Finally Vince reaches out and grabs her broken arm. "Look: don't ever feel stupid for wanting something better!"

They're both a little surprised by the force of his answer, and Vince knows he's also talking to himself. They stand across from each other, staring, until Vince lets go of her cast and looks away, embarrassed. "So tell me about this house."

Maybe it's wrong, winding her up like this on real estate ("It's one of those forties north-side stucco bungalows with no yard, no garage, and no charm") since he suspects that the realtor she works for, this guy Larry, is just stringing her along for sex ("They're asking thirty-two, but if they get twenty-five I'll shit buttermilk biscuits") and that she will likely never sell houses for a living ("If this thing passes FHA inspection, I will literally blow the inspector . . . Okay, not literally"), and yet he really does believe what he said about how you can't apologize for wanting to be better.

Still, he's beginning to realize that there's another part to it, something he didn't consider before last night.

"How's Kenyon?" he asks.

"He's great, Vince," Beth says, and looks down. "Thank you." She squeezes his arm, takes a step toward Sam's Pit, turns to say something else, then breaks into a smile and goes into Sam's.

Jacks passes Beth on the way out, and holds the door for her. Vince is lighting a smoke. Jacks blows on his cold hands.

"I ask you something, Jacks?"

Jacks takes a step closer, four hundred pounds packed into a running suit like nylon sausage. "What's on your mind?"

"Are you better off than you were four years ago?"

"Four years?" Jacks stares at the ground. "Four years ago I was married to Satan. So, yeah, on the whole I'd say I'm better off. What about you? Are you better off?"

Vince shrugs. "See, I never thought about it before last night. But I think a guy could move across country, change his name, job, his friends—change everything . . ."

A car trolls by slowly and Vince watches it pass.

". . . and not really change at all."

VINCE IS IN love.

Okay, that might be a little strong since he's never said more than a few dozen words to this woman, and those words have only been about two subjects—donuts and books—and since he only knows her first name, Kelly, and since he only sees her once a week, when she buys a dozen to take to the nursing home where her mother lives.

But if Vince were going to be in love, this would be it. Kelly is a legal secretary who comes in at 10:50 every Wednesday morning, on her way to see her mother. And so, every Wednesday at 10:40, Vince sneaks to the bathroom to check his hair in the mirror. He takes off his apron and sits at a table with a cup of coffee and a paperback book—a different paperback each week. He was reading a book when he met Kelly four months ago; he had taken a coffee

break with a worn copy of *The Milagro Beanfield War* that someone had left in the donut shop. Vince has always liked reading. In
jail he went on nonfiction jags, reading a book a day: Lewis and
Clark, Greek mythology, architecture. But he'd soured on novels
years earlier and hadn't read one until that day, when he found *The
Milagro Beanfield War* on a chair.

He was on page 16, enjoying the description of some old Mex-
ican guy's troubled life, when he looked up and saw two long
smooth legs leading up to a pair of shorts and, eventually, two elec-
tric eyes.

"Isn't that a great novel?"

Vince looked down at the paperback and managed to mutter,
"Yes."

"Don't you love the characters?"

"Yes."

"Do you read a lot?"

"Yes."

"Fiction?"

"Yes," he managed to say to the legs and eyes.

"Me, too," she said. "There's nothing I love more than curling
up in front of a fire with a good novel."

Love. There it was. That was the word that did it for Vince.
Love. From that moment on, he had vowed to love novels, too, to
find himself curled up in front of a fire with Kelly. So now every
Wednesday after work he goes to the used bookstore in his neighborhood and trades the novel he was reading for a new one. During
the week, he leaves the book in his locker at work and gets as far as
he can on coffee breaks so that by the following Wednesday morning he can talk intelligently about a new book when Kelly comes
in. He rarely gets halfway through them, just far enough to understand what the book is about, enough to talk to her about it. Then
he trades the book for a new one.

He'd like to finish some of the books, but he needs to get a new
one each week—so they have something to talk about, but also

because he superstitiously believes he might find the novel that causes her to fall for him. But there's another reason he never finishes, if he's honest with himself. He's afraid of being disappointed by the endings, which is the reason he stopped reading fiction. He'd read *Great Expectations* at Rikers and had loved it—this story of a criminal secretly sponsoring some poor kid's life—until the jail librarian pointed out that Dickens had written two endings. When he found the original ending Vince felt betrayed by the entire idea of narrative fiction. This story he'd carried around in his head had two endings? A book, like a life, should have only one ending. Either the adult Pip and Estella walk off holding hands, or they don't. For him, the ending of that book rendered it entirely moot, five hundred pages of moot. Every novel moot.

So he only reads the beginnings now. And it's not bad. He's even begun to think of this as a more effective approach, to sample only the beginnings of things. After all, a book can only end one of two ways: truthfully or artfully. If it ends artfully, then it never feels quite right. It feels forced, manipulated. If it ends truthfully, then the story ends badly, in death. It's the reason most theories and religions and economic systems break down before you get too far into them—and the reason Buddhism and the Beach Boys make sense to teenagers, because they're too young to know what life really is: a frantic struggle that always ends the same way. The only thing that varies is the beginning and the middle. Life itself always ends badly. If you've seen someone die, you don't need to read to the end of some book to learn that.

Vince's sampling of the beginnings of novels was going fine until a few weeks ago, when Kelly failed to ask about a book he was reading (*Cancer Ward* by Solzhenitsyn) and Vince panicked, ran to the dotty old clerk at his used bookstore, and asked for help. The clerk, Margaret, theorized that perhaps Vince's reading list was becoming too prosaic and linear ("Too plotty") to duly impress a twenty-six-year-old woman in the year 1980. Since then Margaret has been sending Vince in some strange directions, toward modernism, metafiction, and the avant-garde. And Vince has been pleasantly surprised. Last week he read *Pricksongs and Descants,* a book of short "fictions" by Robert Coover, and found himself explaining to the seemingly refascinated Kelly the way Coover fractured the world into not only different points of view, but into different realities. ("It's like there are all these pieces on the ground and we can pick them up and make the world we want.") He was thrilled when she expressed interest and peppered him with questions.

So now he's gone even further into experimental fiction with this *System of Dante's Hell,* an angry, concentric, metaphoric, poetic guidebook to hell by the militant black author LeRoi Jones. Vince isn't sure he gets it, but he's enjoying the language and some of the images as he starts in on the fourth circle of hell—*"A summer of dead names. Early twilight of birds beyond the buildings . . ."* and that's what he's reading when Kelly walks in and comes directly to his table.

About Kelly: she is five feet ten inches tall, a former college volleyball player, twenty-six, white. Soft clear skin. She irons creases in her tight blue jeans, and wears her long blond hair in a perfect feather, middle-parted, falling away from her face like angel wings. Tic calls her Farrah. "Oh, here comes Farrah," he says.

Even the oldest men look up from their donuts.

"Hi, Vince." She smiles. "Don't tell me that's another new book?"

He nods.

"You're amazing."

Smiles.

"What is it today?"

Vince holds it up and tries not to sound rehearsed. "It's about how we create our own version of hell right here on earth."

"Huh," she says noncommittally, and Vince keeps going.

"For this guy, hell is Newark, New Jersey. You ever been to Newark, Kelly?"

"No," she says. Is that distraction he reads? "I guess I haven't."

Vince stands. "Yeah, Newark is bad, but me, I'd put hell closer to Paterson. Compared to Paterson, Newark is Sea World."

Yes, she is definitely distracted: smiles and nods but doesn't laugh at his joke. "Huh," she says again, and turns toward the donut case. That's it? That's all he's getting today? He follows, crushed, puts on his apron and walks around the case. LeRoi Jones. Stupid. Vince curses himself and the bookstore clerk. I'm too far out there, he thinks, and wonders if he ought not to go to another John Nichols book. He thinks *Milagro* might be part of a loose trilogy. That seems smart: when in doubt, go with a trilogy.

"Today, I need . . ." and Kelly describes a dozen donuts, including five jellies.

"That's more jellies than usual," Vince says quietly as he fills the box. He crouches and watches her through the glass case, the symmetry of tight jeans on toned legs. *God.* As he fills the box, Vince notices a white political button pinned to Kelly's coat. It has red and white stripes, and in blue letters: *Grebbe* and *GOP.*

He stands and faces her. "Gre-e-e-eb?"

"Greb-*eee*. Aaron Grebbe. He's a lawyer at the firm where I work . . . and a friend of mine. He's running for state legislature."

"You gonna vote for him?"

She smiles. "Yes. I am. He's a good man." She looks down at the donuts.

Vince nods, seals the box, and puts it on the counter. "Then you're a Republican?"

She flinches. "No. Well, maybe. When I was young I was a staunch Democrat. Everyone was. But now . . . I just think the country is so screwed up that we need a change. That's what Aaron's campaign is about. *Returning America to its glory.*" She shrugs, a little embarrassed. "At least that's what Aaron always says."

"What's he think about the hostages?"

"He says it's not really an issue for state legislature."

Vince nods.

"But he wants them to come home, I'm sure."

"Goin' out on a limb, isn't he?"

She laughs. "You should vote for Aaron. You'd like him. He reads a lot. Like you."

"Yeah?"

"But he likes nonfiction, mostly. Hey, are you going to hear Reagan's son tonight?" Kelly asks. "Aaron's going to be there. You could meet him."

"Yeah," Vince says. "I was thinking about going to Reagan's son."

She smiles again, and in that smile Vince has visions of children and country clubs, of creases ironed into his own jeans.

"Then I'll see you there," she says.

"Okay," he says, and watches her leave. He runs to the back, throws his book in his locker, grabs the newspaper and begins flipping the pages, looking for some mention of Ronald Reagan's kid coming to town.

"*I READ A* book one time," Tic says as he lugs a tray of maple bars to the front. "It was called *1984* and we had to read it in school and it was by this French dude Harwell. He wrote it in, like, the 1500s and he predicted that by 1984, there wouldn't be any football or basketball or anything. The only sport would be BMX bike racing. That's why I ride my bike everywhere. Because when we make it back to the Olympics in '84, that shit is going to be an Olympic sport and I'm gonna get me a fuckin' gold medal, guaran-damn-teed. And then, when we go back to a gold standard, that medal is gonna be worth its weight in gold, man.

"This book said that bike racing will be taught like karate, in dojos. I'm gonna be sensei of my own BMX dojo, man. We'll sleep and meditate and smoke weed and screw . . . everything from the seats of our bikes. People will come from miles around to learn from the various masters. Every few months I'll just disappear, wander the countryside, teaching and—"

Vince interrupts. "Hey, Tic? How old are you?"

Shrugs. "I don't measure time like everyone else, Mr. Vince."

"But you're old enough to vote?"

"Yeah . . ."

Vince holds out the folded newspaper. "I need someone to go hear Reagan's son with me and—"

"Whoa, whoa." Tic steps away from the newspaper as if it were a bomb. "I don't vote, Mr. Vince. That's what they want . . . register your ass. So when the shit comes down, they just go to their master list and there's Maxwell Ticman, 2718 West Sherwood Avenue, Spokane, Washington, and *bang!* First thing next morning, you got a fuckin' homing device in your teeth."

He walks away, leaving Vince staring at the newspaper story.

**DEPUTY U.S. MARSHAL** David Best comes out into the lobby, red-faced. "First of all, *do not* come in here without calling first." David looks even older when he's angry like this and Vince can imagine the strain on his heart filling those thick limbs with blood.

Vince throws hands up, pleads guilty to David and his receptionist. "I'm sorry."

"What? Carlisle? Carson? What is it today?"

"No, no. I don't want to change my name. Nothing like that."

"Then what?"

Vince looks from David to the receptionist and back. "Don't you think we should talk about this in private, David?"

David turns and stalks into his office. He has to raise each shoulder to hoist his haunches and legs. He edges around his desk and sits. "You don't just drop by the office. I've told you that. You call, give us a number, and I'll meet you somewhere. Anywhere you want. And if you have to come in, if it's some kind of emergency, you call first. You have no idea who could've been in my office."

"I thought you said it doesn't matter," Vince says. "That I'm not worth killing."

He sighs. "I'm sorry about that."

"I know. I was a little crazy yesterday." Vince laughs at himself. "I went after this kid parked in front of my house."

"For Christ's sake, Vince—"

"No, it's okay. I didn't hurt him. Nice kid, actually. Waiting for his girlfriend. She was just trying to sneak out of her house. But it made me realize that you're right. I have been acting paranoid, like I'm living my old life. But I'm not there. I'm here. I got a new name, new life. I should be . . . I should be better than I was four years ago."

David listens without judgment.

"I mean, there's no reason I can't . . . you know, be a part of things. Maybe go back to school. Or get married. Have kids. Join a country club. That kind of thing. I'm smart. I could do anything I set my mind to, right?"

David smiles. "You got a particular country club in mind?"

Vince looks at the framed picture above David's chair. In the portrait, Jimmy Carter seems even more forlorn than he did yesterday. Vince nods at the picture. "You probably have to go with the guy in charge, huh?"

"What are you talking about?"

"The president. You'd probably get in trouble if you went with me to hear Reagan's kid tonight."

David looks over his shoulder, as if seeing the portrait of Carter for the first time. "I can vote however I want, Vince."

Vince puts a newspaper clipping on David's oak desk. A small headline reads: REAGAN'S SON COMING TO SPOKANE.

"It's tonight, at nine, at Casey's restaurant on Monroe."

David pushes the clipping back. "I can't go with you to this, Vince."

"Yeah, sure." Vince nods, folds up the clipping, and puts it back in his pocket.

"I'm sorry, but it would be—"

"No, it's no big deal."

"I'm glad you're getting involved politically, though."

Vince leans forward. "They don't tell you about that in the program. You get your voting rights restored, but what if you've never—" Vince shifts his weight. "In my neighborhood only the jerks cared about this stuff. Politicians paid unions and churches to deliver neighborhoods, and the aldermen and councilmen were just two more guys with their hands in your pocket. Nobody voted. Why bother? But now—" Vince can feel his train of thought getting away. "See, what I'm tryin' to figure out—" He leans forward. "David, how do you know who to vote for?"

David looks tired. "Go home, Vince."

VINCE SETS *THE SYSTEM OF DANTE'S HELL* down on the counter.

Margaret, the moon-eyed clerk at The Bookend, is in her sixties, white-haired and bird thin, wearing a peasant dress and a glasses chain around her neck. She stands behind the counter—covered with slipcases and homemade bookmarks—behind her a deep, one-story room, books double-filed and stacked to the ceiling in dark rows, more books piled in every corner. Margaret looks into Vince's eyes and seems to know it's gone badly. She covers her heart with her hand. "Oh, no. What happened, Mr. Camden? Did we go too far with the Afro-American literature?"

"I don't know what we did, Margaret. I just know she didn't like this one."

Margaret removes her big round glasses and shakes her head. "Now don't lose heart, Mr. Camden. We're not beaten yet. Remember: Win the mind and the heart will follow." She comes around the counter. "Or is it the other way around?"

He follows her to the stacks of alphabetical paperbacks. "The good news is that there are more books," she says, "always more books. Let's start from the top, shall we?" She makes clicking noises as she looks through the bottoms of her bifocals. "Perhaps the experimental fiction was a bit of a stretch, Mr. Camden. I know just what we need—something romantic and sweeping. An epic!"

"Actually"—Vince steps in behind her—"I want something on politics. You got anything like that?"

She doesn't turn to face him. "Oh, a political novel. Excellent. Perhaps Robert Penn Warren?"

"I was thinking nonfiction."

This stops Margaret short. She turns. "But your girl said she likes novels."

"It turns out she's working for this guy's campaign and I thought—"

"A campaign?" Margaret brightens. "Your girl is an activist? Well. A girl with a social conscience. Excellent, Mr. Camden. This girl sounds substantial."

"She's pretty tall."

Margaret misses his joke as she moves down to the nonfiction stacks.

"Perhaps something on governmental theory? Electoral politics? Maybe straight reportage? Essays?"

"What do you have on presidential elections?"

"Ah, yes. Timely. Easy to talk about. Perfect entrée to a meaningful discussion. Very good, Mr. Camden. Very sly." Margaret is not quite five feet tall and she slides a stool along as she moves through tall, narrow stacks of essays and biography. He follows her and she hands him books: *Fear and Loathing on the Campaign Trail 1972* and *The Making of the President 1960* and *The Selling of the President 1968*.

Vince looks at the books. "Which one of these will tell me who to vote for?"

Again she misses the joke, is concentrating and doesn't answer, just keeps handing him books. Vince considers her, dangling from the stepladder.

"Margaret, are you busy tonight?" When there is no answer he continues. "I'm going to hear Reagan's son tonight. Do you have any interest in going to that?"

She stops and turns, comes down the steps, and hands him Arthur Schlesinger's massive *A Thousand Days*. Then she smiles sweetly. "Reagan? Oh, God no, Mr. Camden. Those Republican snakes scare the goddamned wind right out of me."

ABOUT THE MAILMAN: his name is Clay Gainer. Forty-eight, black, tall and wiry, from Lamar, Texas, face framed with graying sideburns. The son of sharecroppers and the first of his family to get out of Lamar, Clay got married at sixteen, joined the military, and ended up at Fairchild Air Force Base in Spokane, where he settled, re-tired, and started a second career with the post office. Vince met him at the donut shop and, after getting to know him for a few weeks, explained how it could work—Clay keeping an eye out for new credit cards going out to people, then yanking them out of his bag, giving them to Vince, who pays twenty bucks a card, unseals the envelopes, writes down the card number and name, seals them back up, and gives them back to Clay to deliver. He ran a similar operation back in the world, so he knew which cards to steal. At first Clay wanted nothing to do with it, but Vince noticed that he kept asking questions and Vince explained it slowly and clearly, how they weren't stealing from *people*, they were stealing from *banks*. How, if they did it right, the banks would assume the num-bers were being stolen by people *after* they'd been delivered, when they were used in restaurants or stores. Clay started slowly, a credit card from a jerk on his route, then from a guy who refused to shovel snow from the sidewalk. And then they moved Clay to a central processing office and he had access to all that mail, all those new credit cards going out to all those people. And bang, they were in business.

"You being careful?" Vince asks the mailman.

"Just like you said."

"Tell me."

"Ah, Vince."

"Tell me."

Sighs and recites: "Only steal from national banks. Never take more than two pieces per zip. Never take more than five pieces a week. Never take from the same zip in the same week. Look for cards going back in the mail. If I think anyone's watching me, stop for a month."

"You been talking to someone at the post office?"

"No. 'Course not."

"Talking to anyone?"

"What do you think, I want to go to jail?"

Certain as he was yesterday that everyone was conspiring against him, Vince can see today that Clay is telling the truth. And of all the people in Vince's small enterprise—Clay, Len, and Doug—Clay is the only vital one. Maybe everything is okay.

They sit bundled up at an outdoor picnic table at a drive-up burger restaurant called Dicks, each holding a Whammy—two gray hamburger patties, a shingle of cheese, a pickle, and a circle of onion. A flock of tiny french-fry birds scavenges the parking lot and the picnic tables, but at three P.M. Vince and Clay are the only people eating. The birds are impatient.

Vince slides the note across the table. "Okay," he says, "then what's this about? Why'd you need to see me?"

Clay slides a brochure across the table. Vince stares at him for a minute and finally looks down. The brochure shows a 1981 Nissan 300ZX. Personally, Vince doesn't think much of Japanese sports cars.

"I've always wanted one," Clay says. "And this guy will take the Caprice on trade. I'll only have to come up with—"

"Come on, Clay. I told you a hundred times. We can't go flashing money around."

"But, Vince. I really want this car."

"You can afford this?"

"Not yet. But I was hoping you could pay me a little more. I know you got it, Vince. Maybe you could give me an advance on the cards I'm going to steal, or give me a little bigger percentage."

Vince rubs his temple. "You know something like that draws attention. Are the other guys at the post office driving new sports cars?"

"I could say I inherited some money. Or an insurance settlement."

"Clay, there'll be plenty of time for—"

"Please, Vince."

"Let's talk about something else. Who are you gonna vote for?"

"I wouldn't even drive it to work. I can walk to work most days."

"Carter or Reagan?"

"I'll only drive it on the weekends."

"'Cause if you're not doing anything tonight, I'm going to hear Reagan's son."

"Vince. Listen to me. It's not like a Ferrari or a Porsche."

"Clay. It's not a good idea."

"Please, Vince. Just this one thing. I mean, what's the point? What good is all this money we're making if we don't ever get to spend it?"

Another thing about Clay: his wife died two years ago. An aneurysm. Sudden thing. She got up to make Clay's breakfast and he found her slumped like empty clothes in a corner of the kitchen, still holding an egg in her hand. That's why Clay started coming into the donut shop every morning, and how Vince got talking to him in the first place. There was something about him that Vince identified with, like he knew some better part of his life was over.

Vince stares out toward downtown. After a moment, he slides

the brochure back across the table. "Look, Clay, it's just not the right time. Give it a month or two, and then we'll talk again. Okay?"

Clay doesn't say anything, just takes his brochure back and, in the process, knocks a few french fries onto the ground. They've barely hit before the birds are at Clay's feet fighting over them.

**REAGAN'S KID LOOKS** like a bookkeeper approaching middle age, just this side of respectability, even in coat and tie. He is at the podium at the front of this restaurant lounge, maybe eighty people at tables around the room, like they're waiting for a nightclub act—a comic, or some Sinatra impersonator. And that's what Reagan's kid gives them, an act. Vince imagines that this guy has been doing this for weeks, flying around to minor campaign stops like Spokane, Washington, and giving the hard conservative sell while his father tries looking moderate on TV. It's clear he's been sent out to rally the troops for his old man.

... *time we took our country back from the liberal, permissive anti-American forces that have taken over. It's time we returned to the position of world leader. It's time we had a man in the White House who can stand up to the Communists and the socialists and the abortionists and the rapists and the Ayatollah Khomeini. It is time!*

The room breaks into applause, whistles, and cheers. Vince looks around at eager white faces. In the opposite corner, beautiful blond Kelly is sitting next to a youngish guy with short hair, square jaw, and bushy sideburns—a man in full compromise with himself—that Vince guesses must be Aaron Grebbe, the candidate for legislature she talked about. They're not holding hands or anything, and Vince can't tell if there's anything between them. When Grebbe claps, Vince notices a big band on his ring finger. Kelly meets Vince's eyes and frowns, as if Michael Reagan is not quite what she expected. Then she looks at the woman on Vince's left and raises her eyebrows, as if to say, *Way to go, Vince. She's pretty.*

Vince glances over at Beth, who is smiling, and who has been smiling since Vince tracked her down at her apartment, and offered to pay her to come hear Reagan's kid with him. And she does look pretty, in a tight baby blue dress—her real estate dress—open at the top, with big, lacy sleeves, one of which covers most of her cast. Her wrap rests on the back of her chair.

*. . . pride in America. Pride in our products and our armed services and our farmers and our factory workers. Pride in our God. And we are equally bonded in our disdain for the appeasers and apologists, the radical environmentalists and atheists . . .*

In between his enthusiastic bursts of applause, Grebbe leans over and whispers something to Kelly, who nods curtly. Kelly is wearing a red sweater and a sheer black skirt, and when she crosses her legs Vince can see the muscles in her thighs through the material and he wonders if anyone hears the slight whimper he makes.

*. . . coddling and catering to criminals of all stripe, the triumph of fear in our cities. Well, let me tell you something: to the rapists and forgers, to the hippies and the socialists and pornographers, to those who hate this country, your days are numbered. You, who live off the goodwill of the rest of us, who siphon this country's promise, who subvert the very idea of America, who . . .*

Grebbe puts his hand at his side and Vince notices that Kelly puts her arm to her side, and while he can't see it, he can imagine their hands finding each other, squeezing. After a second, Grebbe leans over and whispers again. Kelly shakes her head, pulls her hand away, and frowns again.

*. . . pinko college professors and student agitators, the liberal establishment and their media lapdogs, corrupt union leaders and professional protesters, druggies and commies and hippies and streakers and welfare mothers and hookers and thieves and fetus murderers and . . .*

Evergodambody. Vince feels a hand on his own, and when he looks down he sees that the hand is connected to Beth's unbroken arm. He knows she hates holding hands. He looks up at her small, triangular face: the picture of calm, her neck long and slender, her chin high, taking all of this in, a soft smile at the corners of her mouth, her cast in her lap, her other hand in Vince's lap, squeezing his fingers.

"YOU KNOW WHAT freaked me out?" Beth asks as they wait in line. "How Jimmy Carter said he had lust in his heart. You know? In *Playboy*? I never thought of a president like that before. You know . . . horny?"

"I'm sure they all get like that," Vince says.

"I suppose," Beth says. She seems disappointed.

They edge forward in line to see Michael Reagan. Up close, he's younger than he looked on stage.

"Thanks for coming down," Michael Reagan says in a slightly condescending rasp. "I hope my dad can count on your support."

Vince extends his hand. "You think he's gonna bomb Iran?"

Reagan's kid pumps Vince's hand. "I'll tell you what. The extremists in Iran are shaking in their boots at the thought of a Reagan presidency, just like the liberals in this country. I promise you that, sir. Thanks for coming." And he pushes Vince along with his free hand and extends his hand for Beth's, but Vince isn't done.

"So what does that *mean?* Is your old man gonna send in the Marines?"

"I can tell you that Ronald Reagan's America will be a nation that acts with forethought and resolve, and sometimes with might. Thanks for your support."

Vince just stares at him. "But what does that mean?" Before he can get another answer, someone has taken Vince by the elbow and pushed him through the line.

Meantime, Michael Reagan is looking for more help as he stares at a thin woman in a blue dress offering her cast and a pen. "Can you sign this?"

OUTSIDE ON THE sidewalk, a handful of lesser local Republican candidates—five white men in their late thirties and forties—are blowing in their cold hands, bouncing on the balls of their feet, handing out buttons and brochures to the people leaving Michael Reagan's speech. Vince takes a Grebbe pin. Aaron Grebbe is 1980's idea of handsome, an ascension of squares—square shoulders and square jaw, short hair squared around an honest square face, a news anchor's face, just the kind of guy he'd expect Kelly to be involved with, except for the wedding band on his left hand, the only round thing on the man. He wears shiny new cowboy boots; this is the only city Vince has ever known where lawyers and politicians wear cowboy boots with their suits.

Kelly stands a few feet from him, her hands crossed in front of her. "Aaron, this is Vince Camden, from the donut shop, the guy I told you about who reads everything."

*The guy who reads everything.* Vince covers his smile. "It's nice to meet you."

Grebbe's handshake is fast and firm, all business. "Good to meet you. I trust I can count on your support Tuesday." When they drop their handshake, Grebbe's right hand goes straight to his wedding ring. He spins it on his finger as if he's desperately trying to unscrew it.

"Vince was reading *The World According to Garp* a few months ago." Kelly touches Grebbe's arm. "That's Aaron's favorite book."

"What did you think of it?" Grebbe asks. He shifts his weight from one cowboy boot to the other.

"I liked the beginning," Vince says.

Kelly looks from Vince to Beth, who is standing behind his left shoulder.

"Oh, sorry," Vince says, stepping out of the way. "This is my friend Beth."

"Real estate," Beth blurts, as if she's been repeating it over and over in her head, waiting for her opportunity.

Kelly and Grebbe stare at her.

"Beth's in real estate," Vince explains.

Her face flushes. "I'm studying for my license."

They all shift their weight and agree that it's wonderful. Beth seems sickly standing next to the tall, blond Kelly. "I love your hair," Beth says to Kelly—almost a whisper, an apology.

"Oh, aren't you sweet." Kelly's head drops and she smiles like a person would smile at a sick puppy or a little kid in a wheelchair. "Thank you. It's actually a mess today. It was so windy. But thank you." She looks at Beth's wispy hair and her eyes continue down. "What happened to your arm?"

Beth holds up her cast and stares at it, unsure what to say. "It . . . broke."

"Well," Kelly says, and when no one says anything else, she announces that she went for a long bike ride and that she was up late last night and that she has to be at work at seven and that it's late and that she's exhausted and in general offers far more information than anyone would need to be convinced that she is going home.

"I'll see you in the morning," Aaron Grebbe says, and then he adds, "at work."

Their eyes linger for just a moment and then Kelly turns to Vince. "Thanks so much for coming, Vince."

"It was really nice to meet you," Kelly says to Beth.

"I fell," Beth says, and holds up her cast again. "Down some stairs."

"Oh," Kelly says.

"That's what happened to my arm."

"Oh." Kelly smiles politely, then pulls her car keys from her purse, excuses herself, and walks toward the parking lot.

Vince and Grebbe watch her go. Beth stares at her shoes.

"Wasn't Michael Reagan great?" Grebbe asks.

"You think so?" Vince asks.

"It's exciting to have him here, at the end like this. You can feel a change in the air. Something remarkable is happening in this country. It's palpable, don't you think?"

Vince recognizes the tone of the patter, rote sales, but he can't quite pinpoint. "I'll tell you what I think," Vince says. "I was sitting in that restaurant, thinking that if I was running Ronald Reagan's campaign, and he had this dickhead for a kid, where could I send him six days before the election that was far enough away that he wouldn't be able to screw everything up?"

At first Aaron Grebbe is taken aback, but then he looks hard at Vince. "I'm sorry. What did you say your name was?"

"ALL I'M SAYING . . ." Vince's voice rises above the din of the bar. "All I'm saying is that I've been watching both sides for a couple of days, and I hear differences, sure, but I don't hear anyone saying what's really going to change."

"What's going to change?" Aaron Grebbe slaps his forehead. "What's going to change? Everything. It's all going to change. The 1980s will be the beginning of a new age—a return to American ideals and supremacy. This is a revolution. Government is going back to serving the people, not the other way around. We're halting the decline of this country, fifty years of unchecked liberal erosion."

"That's exactly what I'm talking about. It's like something you read in fortune cookies. What does all of that mean?"

"It means what it means—"

"Yeah, but you won't tell me what's going to change—"

"I *am* telling you: reforming welfare, restoring the rights of gun owners, reversing decades of flawed tax policy. If you would listen—"

"I *am* listening! You aren't saying anything—"

The bartender leans over. "Is there a problem?"

Both men shake their heads. "Sorry," Aaron says. Leaning back in the booth, Beth doesn't even open her eyes.

"Look," Vince says. "All I'm saying is that you can't blame people for getting cynical. It's all a bunch of noise. It's no different than selling cars. Or toilet paper."

Aaron Grebbe's face flushes. "I have humped across this district for eight months trying to get people to turn away from their TV sets so I can tell them what I would do if I'm elected. In"—he checks his watch—"one hundred and twenty-four hours, fewer than half the people in this city will vote. Half of those people will vote because it's a presidential election. They'll have no idea who I am and will vote for the other guy because Grebbe sounds like something their dog coughed up. They'll have no clue about my ideas on economic development, on public works, on schools, on highways. They'll have no idea what I plan to do first if I'm elected, even though I've been talking about it nonstop for months. No one cares."

Vince remembers David saying the same thing: *No one cares.*

"And now some *donut* guy wants to lecture me about all of these poor people waiting for political enlightenment? Okay. Take me to these hungry voters! I'm ready. Let's go. Find me five genuinely interested voters and I'll answer questions all night. But spare me the vague outrage from people too lazy to even know who's running unless a campaign ad happens to run between *Hollywood Squares* and *Family Feud.*"

The two men stare across the small table at each other.

"You were in Vietnam," Vince says.

Grebbe leans back and eyes Vince suspiciously. "What?"

"You just said you humped across the district."

Grebbe stares.

"I had a friend over there," Vince says. "He used to say humped, too."

Grebbe takes a drink, says coolly, "Your friend, did he come back okay?"

"Yeah. Pretty much." Vince holds up a *Vote Grebbe* brochure. "You don't mention Vietnam in here."

Grebbe stares, measuring.

"So what's the thing you're gonna do?" Vince asks.

"What?"

"You said 'the first thing I plan to do.' What is it?"

"The zoo. I want a better zoo in Spokane."

"I can see that," Vince says. "Yeah. I went to that zoo one day. It's pretty bad."

"You didn't like the domestic cat exhibit?"

Vince smiles. "Gophers of the Northwest."

"House of Roadkill."

"Are you sleeping with Kelly?"

Grebbe doesn't flinch, only pauses for a few seconds. "I guess I don't . . . I don't see how that's any of your business."

"No." Vince sighs. "It's not." He sits back and picks up Beth's wrap. He leans over into the booth and puts the wrap over Beth's shoulders.

Beth's eyes pop open and she takes a deep breath, looks around the bar, forests of beer bottles, gardens of cigarette butts. "Mmm. Are we done?"

Grebbe is putting his coat on, too, when Vince looks up at him.

"So were you serious?"

"Serious about what?"

"About talking to voters?"

Grebbe checks his watch. "You mean now? It's almost midnight."

"Yeah," Vince says. "It's early. But we can drive over there and wait."

SOME NIGHTS YOU can't help wondering what's going on out there, beneath all those lights. Some nights you can imagine life happening all at once, piled on top of itself, and you can imagine a city subdivided by regrets—neighborhoods of desire. Even a city this size, a couple hundred thousand people, it can be staggering, the marriage proposals and fistfights, kids stealing smokes from their parents, women praying that their drunk husbands go to sleep. You can see it now, crosscut at midnight, buzzing across town in Aaron Grebbe's brand-new Dodge pickup truck, Beth asleep on your shoulder while you argue politics across the bench seat with this guy who's screwing the girl you had convinced yourself that you loved.

Maybe this is how normal people behave, staring straight ahead, not worrying so much what's happening in the periphery, behind all those doors. At least that's what you convince yourself. And so when Aaron Grebbe's sparkling new pickup truck barrels past Doug's Passport Photos and Souvenirs, you make a conscious effort not to look, to ignore all those things that usually get to you, the lights streaming past your car window, faces in windshields and on street corners. For once, you don't get lost imagining the love affairs and breakups—all that lies behind those window shades, vicious acts of boredom and treachery.

But if you *had* looked—

The lights are on in Doug's place. Doug is seated on a stool behind the counter, and Len Huggins and another man are on the customer side of that counter, a perfect triangle. Lenny has just introduced the new man, finished his little pitch, and replaced his sunglasses on his pinched, pocked face. "So what do you think, Doug? We in business?"

"I don't know." Doug chews on the side of his cheek and leans on the stool, arms across his gut like bandoliers of fat. "When would you want to do this?"

Len checks his watch. "We're gonna meet him at Sam's in an hour."

Doug nods. "What are you going to do?"

Lenny nods. "First we'll"—he glances at the third man—"persuade Vince to give us whatever money he's been holding out. Then we'll ask him for the name of the mailman. And then . . . we'll just have to see."

"I don't know." Doug keeps gnawing on that cheek. "What if he won't give you the mailman's name?"

Len looks over at the third man. "He will."

"I don't know," Doug says.

"Look, that's not your problem. You just have to decide. In or out?"

Doug sighs. "I don't know."

Lenny removes his sunglasses and tries to expand his little black eyes, but they don't open any wider. "What's not to know? Didn't we go over everything?"

The third man just stands calmly, watching, ignoring Len.

"It just seems sort of drastic to me. I don't—"

Of the three, Len is the only one who jumps at the pop. Doug simply slides off his stool and to the ground, the black cheerio in his temple smoking for a moment and then bubbling red and then bleeding outright, no expression on his face at all, just like it's been wiped clean. His eyes are open, but one of them is lolling sideways in his rubber mask of a face.

"Oh my God!" Len stares at Doug's body on the other side of the counter. "What did you do?"

The third man, Ray, simply puts the handgun back in his belt, pulls gloves onto his hands, and begins going through the cash register. He takes two twenties, gives one to Len, and puts the other in his pocket. He doesn't bother divvying up the fives and ones, just puts them all in his pants pockets. Then he takes Doug's wallet from his back pocket and slides it into his coat. He pulls drawers out and throws them on the ground, knocks over a stack of printed brochures.

"What . . ." Len sputters, ". . . the fuck?"

"What?"

"What are you doing?"

Ray looks up. "I'm making it look like a robbery."

"No, I mean, why did you do that?"

"That?" Ray jerks his head toward Doug. His voice comes flat and unruffled, just a trace of South Philly. "Isn't that what you wanted me to do?"

Len can't look away from the body. Already something is

changing inside him, his brain registering unheard-of levels of adrenaline and testosterone, and buzzing somewhere is a new perspective on power. "I . . . I don't know."

Ray looks back at the body as if it were a car he was considering buying. "Look, we don't need this fat fuck. First rule: We only need as many guys as we need."

Len steps closer, watches the blood pearl from the head wound, imagines Doug's heart still pumping, and wonders how long that continues. He says, an afterthought: "But we don't have anyone to forge the credit cards now."

Ray looks from Len down to the body. "Oh yeah. That's right." He scratches his ear. "Honestly? I just couldn't listen to him say *I don't know* anymore."

Len removes his sunglasses, crouches down, and stares into Doug's lolling eyes. So easy. Just like that, like flicking a switch and bang. Gone. Move your right index finger a half inch and you can take away . . . everything. Goddamn. Goddamn.

Above him Ray takes a deep breath and steps in behind the crouching Len. "Yeah, sometimes I go too far." He stares a hole into the back of Len's head. "Live and learn."

Len turns and looks up, wonder in his eyes. "Is it always like that?" he asks.

"Pretty much," Ray says. "Yeah."

"Goddamn," Len says respectfully.

Ray grabs Len's arm and pulls him away from the big pile of flesh on the floor. "Come on, chief. Let's go see your buddy."

Spokane, Washington

1980 / October 30 / Thursday / 2:58 A.M.

# chapter III

"So let me get this straight." Jacks puts his champagne magnum on the table and leans forward on it like a short cane. "You're saying the Ayatollah took our people hostage because America has too many lazy women on welfare?"

Aaron Grebbe laughs and shakes his head appreciatively. "No. Of course not. But I don't think it's ludicrous to imagine that these things are connected, that they might be part of a larger erosion, a loss of confidence that has infected America. Crime. Inflation. Forty years of failed liberal policies. And yes, a loss of stature abroad. A sense that we've lost our way." His back is to the bar and his square, honest face is addressing the poker tables, where Vince's regular game is on hold, the players listening with cocked heads as Aaron Grebbe explains why they should vote for him. "A country is like a woman. Who is going to respect her if she doesn't respect herself?"

Hookers roll their eyes. Guys nod, mumble to themselves.

"What about the zoo?" Petey asks. "What did you say was wrong with our zoo?"

Grebbe takes another drink of his whiskey and points the glass at the questioner like he's made an excellent point. "Well, Petey, let's start with the name. Walk in the Wild? That's not a zoo. A zoo should be called a zoo. The Spokane Zoo. What the hell is a Walk in the Wild? That's a better name for *this* place."

Grebbe pushes his hair off his forehead, but in Vince's estimation it's an unnecessary gesture; his hair hasn't moved in six hours. He makes little karate chops with his hands, emphasizing his points. "Our zoo is *underfunded*"—chop—"*undersupported*"—chop—"and in the *wrong location*"—big chop. "But this isn't just about a zoo. This is about economic development for the whole region. Our lousy zoo is emblematic of a city and a region afraid to succeed."

Vince looks from Aaron Grebbe to the rapt faces of the poker players and hookers, and that's when he realizes that Beth isn't here anymore. He leans over to Angela, who is eating a chicken drumstick. "You know where Beth went?"

Angela shrugs. "Home, I guess."

"Ah shit. How long ago?"

"Fifteen minutes."

Vince looks at the door and then to Grebbe, who has accepted a refill of whiskey from Eddie and moved on to criminal justice issues, his hands slicing in tiny drunken figure eights.

"My opponent claims that gun control will lower crime, but this is simply wrong. Gun control punishes law-abiding citizens, not criminals. It should be easier for an honest citizen to buy a gun for protection, not harder. It should be easier to protect our families, our property, and ourselves, not harder."

Some of the men in the Pit nod in agreement.

"If we really want to stop crime, we must beef up the criminal justice system. Make sure criminals serve their sentences. Strengthen our court system. More prisons."

Everyone in the Pit winces or shakes his head, but Grebbe

doesn't seem to notice. Vince stands and leans into Grebbe's shoulder, and barely misses getting karate-chopped. ". . . *more* jails, *more* prosecutors, *more* cops."

"Hey," Vince says. "This might not be your best issue here. We should go."

"I don't want to go," Grebbe says, his eyes and lips well lubricated. "This is the best audience I've ever had. You go."

"I don't think I should leave you here."

Grebbe turns to face him. "You don't understand. This is exactly why I got into politics, Vince. I'm . . . I'm actually reaching these people. It's invigorating. For the first time, I'm actually connecting with them."

Vince backs away from Grebbe and calls out to the room. "Hey! How many of you are registered to vote?"

Grebbe looks up and sees what Vince sees. Not one hand goes up.

OUTSIDE, THE COLD hits like a hangover. Fog clings to the ground. Grebbe pulls his herringbone jacket up around his neck and squints into the streetlight.

"Time is it?"

Vince checks his watch. "After three."

"Jesus."

Vince imagines this isn't the first time Aaron Grebbe has come home late. And this makes him think about Kelly. He's opening his mouth to ask about her when he hears a car door close behind them. He and Grebbe are halfway across the parking lot and he wonders why he didn't look over his shoulder. Getting soft.

"Slow down, chief." From behind.

It's not so much the voice, but some quality within the voice that he recognizes, some hint of common past—a set of rules. Outer borough. Or Jersey. No . . . Philly. And it's not just East Coast; he hears that often enough in Spokane. No, it's something more, something dark.

He does a slow turn. It takes a moment for him to comprehend that Lenny is the one who has gone against him, and even as he's patting himself on the back for guessing he'd be the one, his eyes swing to the other guy and it's clear: this is not about Lenny. This guy is from the world.

Fifty feet away and closing, Len takes off his aviators. "Hey, Vincers. We need to talk with you a minute. Ray and me, we got a few questions."

Grebbe stops and looks back at the two men, his eyes sticking on Ray—everyone's eyes sticking on Ray—the man's gravity. "Everything okay, Vince?"

Vince does a quick scan of this new man, this Ray. He is a few inches shorter than Vince, and a few inches thicker, with huge black eyebrows, slick black hair furrowed back, and dark-lidded eyes—a face bored cold. He is wearing black slacks like Vince's, a dress shirt without a tie, charcoal overcoat. Right hand in right coat pocket.

"I'm kind of busy right now," Vince says. He doesn't like the precariousness of his own voice, as if he's just learning the language.

They are fifteen feet apart, the distance itself telling: too far for a friendly chat.

"This won't take long," Len says.

Even though Len is doing the talking, Vince addresses the new guy. "How about we do this tomorrow?"

"No, I think we better do this tonight," Len says. The new guy sniffs and his upper lip twitches. The eyes close and open, slower and more measured than a blink.

Vince glances over at Grebbe, who seems to sense that something has gone wrong. "But my friend here—" Vince begins.

"Bring him," Ray says, his first words. Takes a step forward, gravel crunching under his feet.

"No." Vince can't look away from the new guy. "That's okay. I'll come alone." Vince turns to Grebbe. He can feel the sweat ring his hairline. "I'll . . . uh . . . I'll catch a ride with these guys. You go on ahead."

Grebbe doesn't say anything. Vince pats his shoulder and walks toward Len. Ray takes a step back and gives Vince a ten-foot berth and then falls in behind Vince and Len as they walk across the parking lot toward Len's car, parked on a side street.

"It won't take long," Len says again, and tries a smile. "Don't worry."

Vince nods. His mouth is dry. He can't see Ray, who is behind him, but he can hear the gravel crunching beneath Ray's feet. Their shadows bleed out before them as they walk away from the streetlight.

"You win tonight at cards?" Len asks.

"Didn't play," Vince says. There's something different about Len, a confidence he didn't have before, bravado.

"That's too bad," Len says. When they reach the Cadillac, Vince feels Ray's hand on his shoulder, then his waist—a casual pat down. "Front seat, chief," Ray says—as if Vince needs to be told. Vince has never actually seen this part, not in person, but he's imagined it, and it's exactly as he's imagined. A few of those sixty people he counted yesterday would've been told the same thing right beforehand: *front seat.*

As he climbs in, Vince glances over toward Grebbe, but the candidate is already in his truck. He watches the red pickup pull away. That's it, then. Vince sits next to Len on a big vinyl bench seat. Ray is behind Vince, in the darkness. Doors close. Len starts the car and blows on his hands. "Fuckin' freezing, ain't it?" They sit in the dark.

"Look, Len. Whatever this is—"

"I told you. We just need to talk. Don't start getting all paranoid again, Vince."

"Sure. Okay." Vince looks around the parking lot. They are on the dark side street, a good forty yards behind the Pit, far away from the other cars. Nothing on either side of the car for thirty or forty feet. Even if he got the door open, he'd make it about ten feet before—

Len looks to the backseat. "See, Ray, didn't I tell you Vince would be cool? Cool as a cucumber."

Ray doesn't say anything.

Vince stares straight ahead.

"Cool as a glass of water."

Vince and Ray are silent.

"Cool as—"

"What's this about?" Vince turns and catches Ray's eyes.

Len puts his aviators back on and looks over the rims, his sideburns diving toward his chin. "Okay, Vince. Here's the thing. You're out."

Vince looks from the backseat to Len. "Out?"

"That's right. I know you've been holding out on me. You don't pay me half what I deserve. I'm takin' all the risk. It's my stereo store."

"So ask for more money," Vince says. "I'll give you more."

"No, it's too late for that. You're out. And you can be out one of two ways. First, my way: pay me what you owe me for the last ten months. I figure fifteen thousand. Then introduce me to the mailman, give me whatever credit cards you got now, and you're free. You can walk away. Leave town or whatever."

That's typical, too. Leave town. And it's funny; you find yourself wanting to believe: Yeah, I'll just give them the money and the mailman and leave town. They'll let me leave town. But you know better. You're not a kid anymore. "What mailman?" Vince asks, his voice raspy. "What money?"

Len rubs the bridge of his nose. "Goddamn it, Vince. Now

you're just insulting my intelligence. I know you got money stashed away. I fuckin' know it. No way you spend all the money we've been makin' on this. Now come on. I said there were two ways. You don't want Ray's way. Trust me——"

Vince catches Ray's eyes in the rearview and sees that he's not listening to Len either. His eyes say that this has nothing to do with Len, that this is between the two of them. And that's when Vince becomes aware of a car running outside. He looks past Len and sees a pickup truck creeping up darkly on the cross street, on the driver's side of the car. Ten feet away the truck stops, a door opens, the high beams come on at eye level, and the radio blares (*"I believe in miracles! Since ya came along, you sexy thing!"*) All three men jump, instinctively cover their eyes, and turn toward the pickup truck's lights.

"What the——" Len starts.

Ray speaks up from the backseat. "Uh, Len . . ."

There is a light tapping on Ray's window, a clicking, metal on glass. While they were distracted by the high beams on the driver's side, Aaron Grebbe has gotten out of the truck and run around to the passenger side of Lenny's car. There he stands red-faced and slick with sweat, behind the long, slender barrel of a .22 rifle, pointed into the backseat at a spot between Ray's big eyebrows.

"Easy, chief," Ray says. "Easy." Vince hears the thud of something drop on the back floorboard and Ray puts his hands up to show they're empty. "It's okay," he says to his closed window. "Stop shaking before you hurt someone." Then, to Vince: "Does your boyfriend know how to use that thing?"

"Looks like it." Vince opens his car door and steps out. He can't believe how good the cold air feels on his throat. He drinks it. Grebbe is staring down the barrel of the rifle, his feet shoulder width, like someone trained to shoot in the military. Hands are steady. He wipes the sweat from his forehead to his shoulder without looking away from Ray in the backseat, illuminated by the sharp headlights from Grebbe's truck.

"Open the windows," Grebbe says to Len. All four windows come down. "Now turn off the car." The engine dies. "Now toss me the keys."

Len throws the keys through the open window and they hit the ground at Grebbe's feet. Vince looks in the backseat and sees Ray's black eyes watching Grebbe closely, to see if he bends over for the keys. He doesn't. His chin remains above the stock of the rifle. "Vince," he says, but Vince is already bending to grab Len's keys. He tosses them into the vacant field. They clink in the grass.

Grebbe gestures with the gun. "Now put your hands out the windows. Both of you. As far as they'll go."

They do, their arms out the windows to the elbows. Grebbe breathes in deep pulls. "Okay. Keep your hands like that." He glances over at Vince and begins edging back around to his car, keeping the rifle in front of him. "Let's get out of here before I piss my pants."

IT TAKES VINCE only a minute to talk Grebbe out of going to the police ("You really want to go in there and explain what you were doing hanging out with gamblers and hookers at three o'clock in the morning? And why you pointed a gun at someone who's going to say he wasn't armed? And you want to do all of this five days before the election?") When Grebbe finally concedes, Vince sits back in the truck seat and rubs his temples, trying to figure out what to do next.

"I don't want to know what you do for a living, do I, Vince?"

"I make donuts," Vince says.

Grebbe drives down side roads, rubbing his jaw. "You know what the strangest part of it was?"

"What?" Vince asks.

"How badly I wanted to shoot that guy." He looks over. "Who is he?"

"I don't know," Vince says. "I just know he isn't from here."

"It looked like he was frisking you—"

Vince looks back at the rifle behind the bench seat, tennis balls jammed in the rack to keep it from rattling. "So you're a hunter?"

"Not really. I've been bird hunting once or twice."

"Could you have done it?"

Grebbe looks back at the road. "If you had asked me before, I would've said no. But . . . yeah, I could have done it. I *wanted* to do it."

"In Vietnam? Did you ever—"

"It's different. You're watching a line of trees, a puff of smoke, a rise in the ground. You fire at movement as much as people. I was only in one firefight—and it was chaos, coming from everywhere, behind you, in front of you. Tracers and smoke. It doesn't feel like you're firing at anyone, just like you're contributing, like you're . . . spitting into a rainstorm. People fall, but it's not like anyone caused it. It's like you're all in it together, all hiding from the same rain." He shakes his head, snaps out of it. "How about you? You ever—"

"No," Vince says. "Never."

They drive quietly again, Vince staring out the passenger window. He can't go home, so he has Grebbe take him to Beth's apartment in the West Central neighborhood, a few minutes from downtown. They drive in silence, Grebbe rubbing his head every few minutes. They park in front of Beth's building and Grebbe laughs.

"I have this terrible feeling that tomorrow I'm going to wake up and realize that was the best speech I'll ever give." He smiles. "For a roomful of felons."

"It's too bad," Vince says. "You had those guys." He takes in Grebbe's face. "Why are you doing it? Running for office?"

Grebbe stares out the front window. "I'm sure it's mostly ego. But you know what? I really do believe in this. It's corny, but I wake up in the morning sometimes, and I just can't wait to get started fixing the things I think are broken . . . like making a better zoo. It probably seems stupid, but you know what? A better goddamned zoo is a better goddamned zoo."

Vince smiles and reaches into his wallet. He hands Grebbe his crisp, new voter's registration card. The candidate reads it, turns it over, and hands it back. "Well," Vince says, "you got my vote."

"Yeah?" Grebbe tries a smile. "Lot of work for one vote."

HE KNOCKS LIGHTLY, with the knuckle of his middle finger. Beth's apartment is at the bottom of a wrought-iron staircase, in the basement of a five-story brick building. The door cracks. She smiles at the ground. "Hey."

"I woke you."

"No." She opens the door wider. She's wearing a long white T-shirt and plaid pajama bottoms. Her hair is pulled into a pony-tail. Toenails painted red.

Vince follows her inside. Beth lives in a one-bedroom apart-ment, but her mother has the bedroom, so Beth and one-year-old Kenyon sleep in the living room, Beth on the foldout couch. Kenyon is asleep now, in footed pajamas, sprawled in a playpen with a stuffed dog and a foam basketball. There is a cup of tea on the table, next to a booklet: *Getting the Most for Your Home.*

Vince looks down at the boy, sleeping easily, a spit of curly black hair on the top of his head. "He's getting big."

"Seventy-fifth percentile," she says.

"Can I use your phone, Beth?"

She grabs her tea and he follows her into the kitchen. She points to a wall phone next to the refrigerator and sits down at the kitchen table. Vince dials the donut shop, even though he knows Tic would never answer the telephone. "Come on, pick up, Tic. Just this once." He hangs up and dials again. Nothing. He'll have to go down there.

Next he tries Doug's house. No answer. Tries again. No answer. He checks his watch. Four in the morning. No way Doug would be at work. Still, he tries Doug's Passport Photos and Souvenirs. Nothing.

Vince hangs up. Beth is staring at him from the kitchen table, finishing a cigarette. "Is everything okay, Vince?" She offers him the smoke.

He doesn't like the edgy sound of his own laughter. "Do you . . ." Riffles his hair. "Do you have a phone book, Beth?" He takes the cigarette, inhales it.

She brings the phone book, and Vince looks up the taxi company. The dispatcher says that both cabs are out, but they'll have one in about thirty minutes.

Vince hangs up. *Both cabs.* Fuckin' town. He shakes his head, sits down at the table. Beth brings him a glass of water.

"Are you okay, Vince?"

Vince drains the glass and considers Beth, her big, round eyes and thin features. "Look, I'm sorry about earlier. I wanted to walk you home—"

She looks down at her own glass of water. "It's okay. I was tired, and you seemed to be enjoying yourself."

"Still, I could've walked you."

"I didn't want you to. I was afraid you'd try paying me."

Vince doesn't say anything.

"And it's just . . . I told everyone it was a regular date."

"It was a regular date."

"No." She brushes a strand of hair back from her eyes. "No, it wasn't. It might not have been the other thing, but it wasn't a date. You know when I realized that?"

"Beth—"

"When I saw that girl. The blond girl?"

"Beth—"

"I don't blame you. She's pretty."

"Beth, there's nothing going on."

Beth nods. "She's screwing that married guy. The politician. No, it was more the way you looked at her . . ."

"Beth—"

"I realized . . . you could never look at me that way."

"Listen, Beth—"

"No, it's okay. But I could never be something that you wanted like that. Remember what you said last night—that it's okay to want something better? Well, I could never be something better for you."

"Listen, Beth," Vince says, "I'm leaving town for a while."

Her eyes shift, but otherwise nothing. "When?" she asks. Vince feels deflated by her matter-of-factness. Not that she doesn't care, just that they're the kind of people—sitting in her mother's apartment at four in the morning—who don't bat an eye at disappointment, who expect it.

"Now. Today."

The strand of hair falls back in front of her eyes.

"Are you coming back?" she asks.

Vince reaches up to push the hair back from her face and she allows him, watching closely as his fingers brush her temple. "I don't know."

She pulls away from his fingers. "You're going to miss my open house." Then, before he can say anything: "It's okay." She clears the dishes, smiles, and says, in a voice rich with delusions, the voice of real estate hookers and criminal bakers: "Well, you'll just have to come to the next one."

*  *  *

VINCE HAS THE cabbie drive him past Sam's Pit. Len's Cadillac is gone. Then the cabbie drives the block behind his house, and sure enough Vince sees the Cadillac through the gaps in the trees and houses, parked in his driveway. The cab waits down the block as Vince slinks along his neighbor's shrub line. He can see shadows behind the shades of his window, someone tossing the clothes in his dresser, another figure lifting the mattress. Vince returns to the cab and has the driver drop him two blocks from the donut shop. It's already after five—the morning inching toward light. He works his way down the alley and doesn't see anything. At Donut Make You Hungry, Vince peers through the small window in the back door. Tic has finished his prep work and is sitting at a table, talking to himself, arms at his sides, as if he doesn't know what to do next. Vince opens the door and eases into the kitchen. Tic's back is to him. Vince realizes he's never seen Tic quiet before.

He looks up, relieved. "Mr. Vince! You weren't here and . . . I couldn't do the maple bars and . . . I . . . I didn't know—"

It strikes Vince that in the two years since he finished his training as a baker, he hasn't missed a single day at Donut Make You Hungry, Monday through Saturday, for two years. He was supposed to train Tic to work one day a week by himself, but Vince never thought the kid was ready. So six days a week, six hours a day, for close to two years, he has worked every minute of every shift. When the owners hired him, they said something about vacations, but Vince has never taken one. Where would he go?

Tic stands up. "We can make the maple bars now, huh?"

"No," Vince says. "I can't work today. I'm sorry, Tic. I have to go out of town. There's a . . . funeral."

"That's too bad. Somebody died?"

Vince goes back to the broom closet, opens it, and turns a mop bucket over. "That's generally why they have funerals, Tic." He climbs on the overturned bucket and slides a ceiling tile from the broom closet. From there, he takes a key and an empty manila envelope. "Wait here," he says. "I gotta go downstairs."

There is a trapdoor in the back. Vince lowers himself down a ladder, to a close, dark space—something between a basement and a crawl space. He pulls a string and a single bulb lights the dirt floor and foundation walls. The floor is littered with sprung rat traps, concrete bags, and old coffee cans, and in the far corner a pile of empty oil tins, flour crates, and sugar bags. Vince pushes the garbage aside until he finds an old coal chute, opens it, reaches high into it, and pulls out a metal box, the size of a small shoebox, secured with a padlock. He looks over his shoulder, then opens the lock with his key. Fifty-dollar bills are stacked sideways the length of the box. It's been a while since he's counted . . . who is he kidding: $30,550; he keeps the tally in his head. He takes out handfuls of bills and begins counting, sets them in piles of twenty, rubber bands each pile, counts out ten of those piles and then puts the money—$10,000—in the manila envelope and slides it into his waistband. Then he takes another ten fifties and puts these in his pocket. He closes the box, pushes it back into the coal chute, and covers the opening with empty bags again. Upstairs, Tic is standing in the kitchen, right where Vince left him, staring at the balls of dough and the mixing bowls of frosting.

"Listen," Vince says, and he steps in close to Tic's face. "This is important. You're going to have to make the donuts yourself today. You and Nancy. She'll be here in a few minutes. You can do it. Right?"

Tic nods.

"Some guys are going to come in here later," Vince continues, "looking for me. Don't lie. Tell them I was here, but I left. Don't get smart with these guys. Don't tell stories. Just keep it simple. 'Vince was here. He left. I don't know where he went.'"

"Don't worry." Tic's head begins bobbing. "If those fuckers

try to stop me, man . . . I'll pull my balls up in my torso and do some tae kwon do on their punk asses . . ."

"No. Tic. Listen to me. I need you to concentrate. No tae kwon do, no conspiracies, no balls. I need you to concentrate."

Tic settles down and nods earnestly. "Yeah. I'll be cool."

"I know you will," Vince says, and he pats the young man on the shoulder. "Look, I need you to do something else for me." Vince pulls the last bundle of fifties from his waistband, peels off two. "This is for you," he says.

"No shit!"

"And this"—he hands Tic the other eight fifties, four hundred bucks—"is for a friend of mine." Vince writes the address down. "Her name is Beth Sherman. You take her this money. Okay? But you can't tell anyone about it."

He walks to the back door, sticks his head out, and looks both ways.

"You coming back, Mr. Vince?"

"Sure," Vince says. Then he looks over his shoulder and steps into the alley.

THE LACK OF sleep shouldn't be so powerful. It has no quality of its own; it is simply a hole, an absence, like the lack of sex or water or any other hole. Down side streets and alleys, Vince bobs in and out of cars, stopping to look both ways at every intersection. Vince wishes he could just stop and close his eyes. Sleep. Just for a minute. He looks down at the black slacks and red button shirt that he went out in last night. The math is tougher than it ought to be. Let's see: You last went to bed Tuesday night, after the presidential debate. You woke up Wednesday morning at two. It's now . . . 6:40 Thursday morning. Going on twenty-seven hours without sleep.

He's done that a hundred times, gone a day or two without sleep. So why is he so tired? The surge and drain of adrenaline. Or something else? Vince thinks about what Beth said, the willful delusion in her voice—*You'll just have to come to the next one*—and he slams his eyes open and closed as he works his way down the alley behind Sprague Avenue. He finally emerges onto Sprague and stops cold at what he sees in the parking lot of Doug's Passport Photos and Souvenirs—two police radio cars and two detectives' cars, plastic police tape stretched across the front of the business. He edges closer and crosses the tape to get a look at the activity behind the plate-glass storefront. Two detectives gesture with rubber-gloved hands. Vince leans forward onto the cold trunk of a patrol car.

The car door opens. "Returning to the scene of the crime?"

Vince straightens up. Out of the patrol car steps a skinny young guy—mid to late twenties, if he had to guess—wearing a down jacket over a shirt and tie and holding a Styrofoam cup of coffee. This math is easier: Cop. Plainclothes. Detective. His hair is thin on top, but bushy in back. It curls up at the collar. He wears a friendly smile, just this side of cocky. "What did you say?" Vince asks.

The detective champs his gum. "You know, that old saying: 'The criminal always returns to the scene of the crime.' Doesn't that seem stupid? I can't imagine that really happening. Why would you come back? Nostalgia?"

"I guess I don't know."

"Well, would you?"

"Would I—"

"If you killed the owner of this place last night, would you come back here in the morning? I know I wouldn't."

Vince can feel the young cop's eyes on him, and he's careful to show no reaction, no grief or surprise, no lack of grief or lack of surprise, at hearing that Doug has been murdered. Still, Vince thinks back to Ray in the backseat and now he *knows* what was going to happen to him last night. And another thought catches up: Doug is dead. Because of Vince. He feels bad for the man, even as his mind instantly tallies: sixty-one. Vince feels trapped by the expression on his own face—look sad and this detective asks if you knew Doug, show no surprise and maybe it's because you killed him. He tries to look concerned but placid, the way someone would worry about crime going up in his neighborhood. "Maybe I'd come back if I left something behind."

The young cop stares at him for a moment, and then nods appreciatively. "See, I didn't think of that. So let's say you got home and realized that one of your gloves was missing. And you worried that you'd left it next to the body. You might come down early, thinking that the cops hadn't found the body yet, so you could get your glove."

"Yeah, something like that."

"Shit. I should've thought of that." The cop laughs appreciatively. "Guess that's why they got me out here instead of in there with the smart guys, huh?"

"I wouldn't know."

The cop shrugs and flashes a couple of mirthful green eyes. "I'm on loan from patrol. A couple of detectives got transferred for taking free meals at this gambler's restaurant. Brass can't fill their spots for three months, so here I am . . . fetching coffee." He offers his hand. "Alan Dupree."

Vince shakes his hand.

"So did you know the victim? This guy—" He looks up at the sign. "Doug?"

"No," Vince is more comfortable now lying to this rookie detective. "Just happened to be walking by and saw the cop cars."

Dupree nods. "Quarter to seven. You're about the earliest gawker I've ever seen, Mr.—"

"I was on my way to breakfast."

"Yeah? Where you going?"

"Chet's."

"Oh, downtown. Yeah, I've always seen that place but I've never been in there. They got hash browns or home fries there?"

"You know, I'm not sure."

Dupree laughs. "That's a long walk, you don't even know what kind of potatoes you're getting, Mr.—"

"I like 'em both equally." Vince looks back inside at the older detectives, who are gesturing behind the counter, presumably toward Doug's body. "So what happened?"

"In there? No idea. The fellas think robbery." Dupree sips coffee.

"You don't think so?"

"There was a robbery all right. But that's not why he got killed."

"What do you mean?"

"Well, the guy closes his shop every day at six o'clock, right? But we got the shooting at between midnight and four this morning. Who's going to think to rob a guy six hours after he normally closes his shop?"

"Maybe it was spur-of-the-moment," Vince offers. "He surprised a burglar."

"I guess." Alan Dupree drinks his coffee. "But if you're a burglar, would you think you're going to get anything out of a passport photo shop? After they're closed? There's no cash. No stereo equipment. So what—you're just driving by and you think, Cool, I can steal fake ID? It makes no sense. Unless Doug was into something else—something not on the sign. You see what I mean?"

Vince doesn't say anything.

"No, I'll tell you what I think," Dupree says. "Between you and me?" He leans on the hood of one of the patrol cars and begins blowing on his cold hands. "I think Doug was meeting someone here at midnight. And whoever it was, Doug knew the guy.

Trusted him. A friend. Or an associate. Someone he was working with—and probably not on passports."

"Why midnight?"

"Last time anyone saw him alive. Wife says he left the house at 11:50."

Vince stares at the young cop's face, which is maybe not so young. Jesus. The guy's playing him. This whole time, the asshole has been interviewing him. Without a lawyer. *Would you come back here . . . Did you know this guy . . . earliest gawker I ever seen . . . long walk, you don't know what kind of potatoes you're getting . . . wife says he left the house at 11:50.*

See, the thing is, Doug didn't have a wife. Ah shit. Vince remembers finding himself in a backyard with a Doberman once. Move slowly. Don't panic. He sets his face, shakes his head in sympathy. "That's too bad. Did they have any kids?"

"Four." Dupree shakes his head sadly.

"No." Vince covers his mouth and shakes his head. "Four! Jesus, that's sad."

Dupree straightens up from the car he was leaning against. Vince swallows. He's totally screwed this up. Said he didn't know Doug. And now he's standing here with ten grand in his pockets outside the business he used to forge credit cards, on the day when the owner of that business has been killed.

Dupree appears ready to ask something else when the door to the passport photo shop opens and a tall, pale cop—older, in walrus mustache and rubber gloves—leans out. "Dupree! What the fuck are you doing out here?"

Dupree turns.

The tall cop steps out in a tight corduroy jacket with elbow patches; looks like an overgrown philosophy professor. "Where's my coffee?"

"I was . . . interviewing this witness," Dupree says.

At the word *witness*, the walrus mutters to himself and comes outside. "Freezing out here." The older cop walks right up to Vince, stands only inches from his face. The man is big, maybe six feet three inches tall. His arms are tight in the sleeves of his coat. There is a bit of food—egg?—in his mustache. "I'm Detective Phelps," he says when he finally reaches Vince. "So why don't you tell me what you saw, Mr.——"

"Nothing," Vince says, almost too eagerly. He looks back and forth from one cop to the other. "I didn't see anything. Like I told Officer Dupree here, I was walking by for breakfast and I saw the cop cars. I don't know anything about it."

"Uh-huh." Phelps continues to stare at Vince for a moment, and then his face reddens and he turns to Dupree. "We prefer our witnesses to have actually witnessed something, Dupree."

The young cop smiles like someone used to charming his way out of trouble. "Yeah, we hadn't gotten that far."

Phelps turns his thick neck back and smiles at Vince. "Officer Dupree is a little excitable. I'm sorry if he wasted your time."

"No problem." Vince starts to back away.

Dupree opens his mouth to object, but Phelps is in his face. "The fuck's my coffee, rook?"

Dupree looks once more at Vince, then reaches back in his car, grabs another cup of coffee, and hands it to Phelps. Vince turns and begins walking.

He's ten paces away when he hears Dupree call out: "Enjoy your hash browns, Mr.——"

Vince calls over his shoulder: "I will."

THE DOWNTOWN PAN AM office opens at nine sharp, and the first customer through the door is a tall, slender guy in black slacks and a red shirt, with buzzed brown hair crew-cut at the barbershop across the street. He runs his fingers over the stubble in the back; he can't remember when his hair was this short.

The clerk has trouble fitting Vince's travel needs. He needs to leave today, but he has some things to do, so he wants to go in the afternoon.

"You'd be better off waiting until tomorrow morning," says the clerk, shrugging in her robin's-egg poly Pan Am blouse. "That way you won't have to lay over anywhere."

"No," Vince says, "I need to leave today."

While the clerk works the phone, Vince brushes small brown hairs off his shirt. After some work, they get it: a 4:30 P.M. flight to Seattle, followed by a 6:20 P.M. flight to O'Hare. He'll spend the night there and catch an early flight the next morning. Vince pays in cash, calls for a cab, and then waits inside until it arrives.

"Thanks for traveling Pan Am," the clerk says as he ducks out the door. "Have a wonderful time in New York."

VINCE SITS AT Chet's Diner, with two stacks of quarters, a pen and a notebook. He finishes his coffee, glances around carefully, grabs one of the stacks, and steps up to the pay phone. He slides them in one at a time, then begins dialing from memory.

"Banks, Murrow, DeVries." A secretary.

Vince smiles. He writes on the sheet of paper: *Partner*. Benny made partner. No shit. "Benny DeVries please."

"I'll see if he's in."

The call is transferred. "Benny DeVries."

Vince feels warmed by the rapid-fire voice. Benny told him once that he actually spoke quickly on purpose, to give his clients a better deal: *billable by the syllable*.

"I'm looking for a lawyer who represents reformed gangsters."

Benny DeVries is uncharacteristically quiet. "Who is this?"

"You don't know who this is?"

Nothing.

"You represent so many best friends you can't keep us all straight?"

"Marty? Is that—?"

His old name sounds so strange, Vince almost wonders. "Yeah."

"Marty! No shit! How the fuck—where are you?"

Vince looks around the quiet coffee shop. "You couldn't even imagine."

"No shit? The feds treatin' you pretty good?"

"Like a king."

"You staying out of trouble?"

"Same old. I got some stuff."

"You back in the credit cards?"

"Yeah."

"Old Plastic Man."

"And I see you finally got your name on the door."

Benny laughs. "Yeah. Couple months ago. You believe that? One good thing about doing big criminal cases—you do tend to get your name in the paper."

"Listen, Benny. I need to ask you something important. Have you heard anything? About me? Maybe someone knows where I am. Wants to collect the money I owe."

"Like who?"

"I don't know. That's why I'm calling. I thought maybe you could reach out to some people—see if anyone is asking about me."

"Jesus, I wouldn't know where to start. The crew you testified against . . . there's no one left. You heard about Bailey and Crapo, poor fuckers. And Coletti—he's pissing in a bag somewhere. Lives in Bay Ridge now, in his kid's old apartment."

Vince writes *Bay Ridge* on the notebook page.

"All the old guys are dead or busted, Marty. It's these new, slick guys now, picked up all their habits out of the movies. Honestly?

You could probably hump down Mulberry with your pants at your ankles, nobody'd think a thing."

Vince chews his thumbnail. It makes no sense. Somebody sent this guy to Spokane. "How's Tina?" he asks.

"How do you mean?"

"I mean how's Tina? Does she ever ask about me?"

He's quiet for a moment. "You know she got married, right, Marty?"

Vince stares out the window. He writes on his page: *Married.*

"You there?"

"I'm here."

"It's been three years, Marty. People move on."

"Who is he?" Vince asks.

"Her husband? He's a good guy. Clean. Played on our softball team. That's how she met him. We went to districts. Almost won the whole thing."

"What's he do?"

"Outfield," Benny says.

"No, asshole. What's he do for a living?"

"Oh. He's an air-traffic controller at Kennedy."

Vince holds the phone away from his head for a few seconds, then puts it back. "Look, Benny. There was this guy from Philly . . . Ray Something. Stocky, black-haired. A contract guy, real thick-necked type. They brought him in to do Jimmy Plums over some jukeboxes in Queens. Remember that guy?"

"Marty. I do five or six criminal cases a month now. I can't keep all the guys straight. I can't even remember which ones owe me money."

"No, you'd remember this guy. Real hard-ass. Had these big black eyebrows like two mad caterpillars. Called everyone chief."

"Why's it so important, this guy?"

"Because . . ." Vince looks around the diner. "He's here."

"What do you mean?"

"He showed up in my town. Tried to take me for a drive last night."

"A contract guy is there? Are you sure?"

"Yeah. I'm pretty sure."

"What's he want with you?"

"What do you think he wants? To be my friend?"

"Christ. Are you sure?"

"Benny! The guy tried to take me for a drive!"

"Okay. Well, I can ask around, find out who hired this guy."

"What's his name?" Vince asks.

"What's whose name?"

"The guy Tina married. Your brother-in-law."

"Oh. Jerry. His name's Jerry."

Vince writes on the page: *Jerry.* "What's his last name?"

"Come on. Don't do this, Marty."

"Just tell me her last name."

Sighs. "McGrath. Jerry and Tina McGrath."

Vince writes *Tina McGrath* on the page. "They still live in the neighborhood?"

"No. They moved out to Long Island."

Vince writes *Long Island* on the page. "Thanks, Benny."

"Look, Marty . . ."

"I'll talk to you soon, buddy." Vince hangs up. Stares at the notebook page: *Partner. Bay Ridge. Married. Jerry. Tina McGrath. Long Island.* Not exactly the information he was looking for . . . or maybe it was. Vince crumples the page, returns to his table, and stuffs the wad of paper in his empty coffee cup. He looks over at the other stack of quarters on the table, and knows he won't need them.

VINCE DUCKS THROUGH a neighbor's backyard, climbs over the fence, and drops into the window well behind his own house.

When he's sure it's empty, Vince uses his elbow to break the window, uses his foot to clear out the glass, and slides into his basement. He steps on the washing machine and hops down, climbs the stairs, and comes out in his kitchen—at least, what's left of it.

They've done a number on the place, cabinets thrown open, food tossed around. His box of dope is gone from under the sink. He expected that. Volcanic ash is everywhere. The little bit of cash he kept in the kitchen is gone. He steps into the living room: magazines and newspapers tossed everywhere. They even tore off the back of his TV. This is why he keeps his money at the donut shop, and why he keeps the mailman's name, address, and phone number in his head. In the bedroom Vince's clothes are everywhere, bed tossed, nightstand cleaned out. Vince turns the nightstand over. Taped to the bottom is a worn letter. Every bit of information on the envelope has been cut out by an FBI censor, except the name of the person who mailed it: *Tina DeVries.* Vince always meant to answer the letter, but he didn't know what to say. He sets the letter on the nightstand and sits on his bed, looking around at the piles of clothes.

Finally he stands and starts packing his duffel. He is pulling the zipper on the bag when the doorbell rings. Jesus. This day. He looks around. He takes the manila envelope with the ten grand in it and stuffs it in his duffel. Then he reaches for the narrow, eight-inch section of pipe that he used to scare the poor kid in the Impala. He looks through the front window and sees a tall woman at the door, holding a handful of brochures and wearing a button that reads: *Anderson for President.*

Vince opens the front door a crack. The woman is professional looking, tall and blond, with big round glasses and horse teeth.

"Hello, sir. Shirley Stafford. I'm canvassing for John Anderson for President. I was wondering if I could talk to you."

"I'm in kind of a hurry," Vince says.

"I understand. Are you a member of one of the two political parties, Mr.——"

"Camden. No, I'm not a member of either party."

"And are you a registered voter, Mr. Camden?"

"Yes."

"And would you classify yourself as undecided at this point?"

Vince opens the door wider. "Matter of fact, I am undecided."

"Mr. Camden, would you agree that the Republicans and Democrats have a stranglehold on the political process in this country?"

"Well—"

She keeps talking. "By keeping John Anderson out of the debate this week, even though his support was in double digits, Carter and Reagan unwittingly showed just how badly we need someone like John Anderson. Mr. Camden, our system is closed to real political dissent. And John Anderson believes—"

"But he can't win."

"I'm sorry?"

"Well, he's at what, ten percent, four days before the election? I just don't get why you're still out here, doing this."

"Well . . . John Anderson has a chance to poll the highest percentage of any third-party candidate since—"

"But he can't win."

She shifts uncomfortably and slides her lips over the big teeth. "Well, no. But John Anderson believes—"

"Look, I'm not talking about that guy. I'm talking about you. Why go door-to-door trying to drum up support for some guy with no chance?"

She looks down at the brochures in her hand. Deflated. "I . . . Well, I signed up for this week and—"

Two blocks away, Len's Cadillac turns onto Vince's street. He pulls the woman into his house. "Please, come in."

Vince closes the door behind her and looks around for something . . . he doesn't quite know what.

Shirley looks around, too, at the piles of clothes and food, cabinets open, TV taken apart, everything broken and on the floor, dusted with volcanic ash. The pipe in his hand. "I really shouldn't be in here."

Vince waves off the mess with the pipe he was prepared to hit someone with. "I left my dog inside and he chased a mouse."

"Oh. You have a dog?" Shirley smiles. "I love dogs. Can I see him?"

Vince parts the blinds and peers out. "He got hit by a car." The Cadillac eases up to the curb across the street. Shit, shit, shit. Vince backs away from the window and his eyes cast around wildly, landing on the pipe in his hand.

Shirley is not comfortable. "I really should go."

It's a stupid idea. Vince knows it's stupid and yet it must be occupying all of his idea-producing brain cells, because he can't think of anything else. He hands Shirley the pipe and points to the metal mail slot at knee level of his door. "Listen, Shirley. I need you to do me a favor. If you do it, I'll vote for Anderson. I'll even wear a button." Even as he asks her, Vince hears his own words: *Why help some guy with no chance?*

A few seconds later, Vince walks confidently out the front door. Len and Ray are climbing out of the car. They look up and see Vince coming. Len takes off his aviators. "Speak to the devil."

"Speak *of* the devil, you dickhead." Vince strides across the lawn. He meets Len and Ray in the middle of the street. They stop ten feet from one another, in a close triangle.

"How you doin', chief?"

Vince looks at Ray. "A little tired."

"That was stupid what your friend pulled last night," Len says. "No more screwing around. Gimme my money and let's go get the mailman."

"No," Vince says to Ray.

Len makes a show of rolling his eyes. "Damn it, Vince. It's like you're trying to make me an asshole."

But Ray and Vince are staring at each other, ignoring Len. Ray steps toward him.

"I wouldn't do that." Vince turns and points.

Ray and Len follow Vince's eyes to the front door of his house, and what appears to be the barrel of a gun sticking out of the mail slot, pointed right at Ray's chest. Ray moves in the street to get a better view. The gun barrel follows him.

*Nice job, Shirley.* She'd looked at Vince as if he were crazy, but it turned out she loved practical jokes as much as dogs; he explained that all she had to do was crouch down on the floor and watch this guy through the pipe. Now Vince allows himself a moment of self-congratulation. See, it's not the cards so much as the way you play them.

"Is that a pipe?" Ray asks, squinting.

Len is squinting, too. "Was that supposed to look like a gun, Vince?"

Ray grins. "You got us surrounded by plumbers, chief?"

As if on cue, the gun barrel is withdrawn from the mail slot. The door opens and Shirley Stafford comes out, a big smile on her face, waving the section of pipe. "Did we trick your friend, Mr. Camden?"

Okay, so sometimes it *is* the cards. Still, Vince is surprised how calm he feels. Fifteen minutes or fifteen billion years—what does it matter? Or an hour? What do you do with the last hour of your life? You try to think of the best hour you've ever had. Great sex, a run in poker, the time your old man took you to the Natural History Museum? But you can't really separate just one hour like that. Just like you can't take one brushstroke from a painting. You remember everything at once; your memories are impressions made upon layers of fabric. What does the whole know of a single hour or a single minute? Fifteen minutes or a lifetime? What does it matter?

Vince finds himself laughing. At first he thinks his laughter is what causes Len and Ray to take a step back in the street. But then Vince sees they are looking past him, down the block, and he turns to see what they see: an unmarked police car tooling down the street toward them. Vince steps back on the curb and the car stops between the men, Vince on one side, Ray and Len on the other.

The thin young cop from Doug's Passport Photos and Souvenirs—Alan Dupree—steps out of the car, smiling at Vince.

Len and Ray shift their weight and stare at the cop. Vince can see Ray sizing up Dupree—five-foot-seven maybe, 140 pounds— and Vince knows how easily Ray could take care of this wrinkle if it came to that.

"Hey, Hash Browns." Dupree says. "This is quite a coincidence."

Vince just nods.

"You cut all your hair off," the cop says.

"Summer cut." Vince runs his hand over his buzzed head.

"It's the end of October," Dupree says.

"Indian summer."

"It's forty degrees."

"Well, there's always next year."

Ray and Lenny look back and forth, off balance.

Vince rocks on the balls of his feet. "So what can I do for you, *Detective?*"

Lenny takes a short step back. Dupree cocks his head, too, at the way he leaned on the word *detective*.

"Still working on the passport thing," he says. "The victim's Rolodex was open to this name here—" He looks down at his notebook and flips a page, makes a show of looking up a name. ". . . Vince Camden. You fellas know this guy Camden? According to the victim's Rolodex, this is his address." Dupree shows Vince the notebook as if he needs proof of what he's saying.

Vince raises his hands like a magician finishing a trick. "That's me. I'm Vince."

"Really?" Dupree smiles. "You're Vince Camden? Now, this is a coincidence."

Ray and Len stand dumbly on the curb.

"Who are your friends?" Dupree asks.

"Criminals," Vince says.

There is a split second of tension that Vince breaks with laughter. They laugh like dominoes: Vince, then Dupree, then Ray, and finally Lenny, who giggles frantically like a car that won't start. "Ha! Ha, ha. Ha! Good one, Vince." Len says. "We'll see you later." He and Ray walk toward Len's Cadillac.

Vince watches the young cop take note of their license plate. The Cadillac eases out of the neighborhood, comes to a complete stop before turning. Len's hands are at ten and two.

"Mr. Camden?"

Vince and Dupree both turn to see Shirley Stafford, who has been waiting patiently.

"I figured out my answer."

Dupree looks from Vince to Shirley.

Vince rubs his temples.

"You caught me off guard when you asked why I'm still out canvassing when John Anderson has no chance of winning."

"Look, Shirley—"

"No, Mr. Camden," Shirley says. "I'm glad you asked. I should be able to explain why this is so important to me. I know you're right; this time we won't win. But if we can get ten percent, maybe the next outsider will get twenty. And maybe one day, twenty years from now, we'll have more than these two corporate choices and maybe someone outside this corrupt system will become president. For me—for my kids, that's worth it. The chance that someday it will improve." She gives Vince a handful of brochures and a button that reads *Anderson for President*. As Officer Dupree watches with a look of bemusement, Vince puts the button on his shirt, and the smile on Shirley's face makes it all feel strangely worthwhile.

"I'M SORRY." DUPREE shrugs as he drives toward downtown. "I'm trying to understand. I really am. But you have to admit . . . it doesn't make much sense." He looks over at Vince. "I just don't see how, four days before the election, you can still be thinking of voting for Anderson."

Vince is in the front seat with him. "So you think I'd be wasting my vote?"

"The only thing he's running on is the fact that he's not one of the other two guys. He's like the guy in high school who wanted to be student body president so he could abolish student politics."

Dupree turns the car toward the river. "But more than that, I just can't believe you still don't know who to vote for. I hear about people like you, undecided, and I just don't get it. What are you waiting for—one of these guys to walk on water?"

Vince stares out the window as buildings slide past. They roll over the huge Monroe Street Bridge, its arches sided with bleached buffalo skulls. "You've known all along who you're going to vote for?" Vince asks.

"For at least a year."

"You're confident one of these guys can run the country?"

"Run the country?" Dupree laughs. "Who told you these guys run the country? That's not what it's about. It's more like an honorary position. Or like a jockey. He's important, but it's the horse you put your money on, not the jockey. He's just the little guy along for the ride."

Vince is trying to follow the metaphor. "So . . . what's the horse? Congress?"

"No. No. We're the horse." Dupree turns his car in behind the classic Gothic towers of the Spokane County Courthouse—one of Vince's favorite buildings in town—and into the parking lot of the Public Safety Building. The cluster of buildings is built on a shelf above the river, across from downtown, surrounded by clapboard homes and empty fields. Behind the cop shop is the county jail—rectangular and dotted with beady little windows, as dull as the courthouse is ornate. Old habit; Vince always scouts the jail in a town.

"I got this theory," Dupree says. "The presidential election is a big mood ring. Four years ago we were pleased with ourselves. Content. So we elected the sweetest guy we could find, a real outsider, because we were tired of shifty insiders like Nixon and Ford. The only reform president of the twentieth century. But then the lunatics took our people hostage in Iran and the economy went in the toilet, and you know what? We're in a bad fuckin' mood now. And we can only blame ourselves. We asked for this. And we don't want the nice guy anymore. We want Dirty Harry. John Wayne. We want Ronald Reagan, a guy who couldn't have gotten thirty percent four years ago. Now, hell, he's just a good Tuesday from being president.

"See." Dupree puts the car in park, turns and faces Vince. "This isn't really about them. This is about us. The government doesn't change. It's the same buildings, same ideas, same pieces of paper. What happens is, every eight years or so, we change."

Vince stares at the young cop, and the thought flashes that they could be friends if things were different. "So . . . who are you voting for?" he asks quietly.

A smile. Dupree nods at the dark Public Safety Building. "I'm sorry, Vince," he says. "But now it's my turn to ask the questions."

\* \* \*

**FOUR CIGARETTES, TWO** Frescas, a donut, and some Corn Nuts later, Vince shrugs his shoulders. "You know, that's really all I can tell you."

The walrus detective, Paul Phelps, is sitting across the small table from him, rubbing his jaw, unable to shake Vince off what is really a simple story: Yes, he did know Doug. They met at the donut shop. Vince was hoping to sell Mount St. Helens volcanic ash out of Doug's store but they hadn't actually gotten around to it.

Sitting against the wall, Dupree listens with a half smirk on his face, appreciating Vince's cool under questioning.

So why did Vince lie and say that he didn't know Doug? Because Doug's death shook him, and the young cop surprised him. He felt under suspicion. He got nervous. He really didn't know Doug well and he didn't want to answer a bunch of questions because he wanted to get to breakfast. He was hungry. As proof, he offers the receipt from Chet's.

Just then, another detective, gray-haired with glasses, comes into the room, bends down, and whispers in Phelps's ear. Then he hands Phelps a sheet of paper. The big detective reads the page, nods, and the old cop shuffles out of the room. Phelps turns to Dupree and shrugs.

"Sorry, Alan. Mr. Camden's alibi checks out." He looks down at the page. "This . . . Beth Sherman says he did go to hear Reagan's son just like he said and that he was with her until after three A.M." Phelps smiles, like someone working a tough puzzle. He waves the sheet of paper and looks up at Vince. "And, since your story checks out and you don't have a criminal record, I don't think there's anything else we need from you. I appreciate you coming down and clearing this up. Next time, don't lie to a cop."

"I won't," Vince says.

Dupree is still smiling at Vince, as if admiring the expertise with which he handled the interrogation, and even managed to get a small meal out of it.

Phelps stands and hands Dupree the sheet of paper, then pats the young cop on the shoulder on his way out. "It was good work, rook. Don't let it get you down." Dupree never stops staring at Vince, even when the big detective walks out of the room.

Vince looks at the clock above Dupree's head. Quarter after three. His flight is at 4:30. He might just make it after all.

Finally Dupree looks down at the page that Phelps handed him. He stares at it for a long time and then cocks his head and smiles.

Vince is already standing to leave. "What?"

Dupree holds up a nearly blank page. "When Paul said you don't have a criminal record he wasn't kidding. Hell, you don't have any kind of record at all. Not a speeding ticket, nothing. Not a parking ticket. Not even a driver's license. Nothing but a social-security number. How is that possible, Vince? How does a person go through life without a divorce? Or a civil lawsuit? No inheritance. Probate. It's like you were born yesterday. Like you're a shadow." But the young cop doesn't like the image. His eyes are steady, less mirthful. He doesn't look away. "Or a ghost."

Standing across the table, Vince finishes his last Fresca. Maybe those other sixty-two think they're alive, too. "You know what? Sometimes, that's exactly what I feel like."

VINCE OFFERS TO take a cab home, but Dupree insists on driving him, and Vince knows better than to protest. His flight leaves in a little more than an hour. Vince goes to the bathroom and steps into a pay phone to call the taxi company. He gives the dispatcher an address exactly one block south of his house and says he wants the driver to start the meter and wait there, not to knock on the door.

The drive home is quiet. Maybe you *are* a ghost. Maybe those sixty-two are running around, scrambling and scurrying, and no one notices. No one cares. Two days without sleep.

"Got any suspects besides me?" Vince asks Dupree finally, to break the silence.

A traffic light turns yellow as Dupree rolls through the intersection. "Nope. You're it."

"But I didn't kill him."

He looks over at Vince. "That certainly complicates my theory."

Dupree tools through the rough edge of Vince's neighborhood—the flats at the base of the South Hill—and slows when he sees three men lurking on a street corner. Two of the men stare at the ground, their backs to the car, as the third tracks the cop without moving his head. After they pass, Dupree watches them in his rearview mirror. Vince turns to see that once the car is past, all three men look up.

"Drugs?" Vince watches the men fade in the back window.

"Be my guess," Dupree says. "I popped the short guy eight months ago selling speed. Guy's got the worst breath. Like onions and cat shit. Make you think twice about arresting him, that's for sure."

Vince turns back to face forward. "You think a guy like that can change?"

"A guy like that? No."

"Why not?"

Dupree thinks for a moment. "I went two years at the community college. For criminal justice. We were supposed to take a psych class, but it was full so they put me in philosophy instead. Turned out to be one of those great mistakes.

"There's this parable I remember"—Dupree turns down Vince's street—"about a flock of crows—real tough birds flying around all day, stealing corn and crops, always on the lookout for shiny things, you know . . . just living the crow life. One day, the crows are flying around, really happy with themselves, when they happen to fly over a lake and see their reflections in the still water. They spend all day diving and soaring, watching themselves in the water, admiring their own power and grace. But after a while they get bored and start making fun of the lake for having no qualities of its own, for only reflecting the world. The lake says that it can do far more than crows can do: it can freeze solid; it can rise up in great waves and wash away the shore; it can evaporate and fall on the hillsides as rain. 'So do it,' say the crows. But it's a warm, clear day and the lake just sits there, still, until finally the crows move on."

Vince stares at the young cop. "What does that mean?"

"I'll tell you what." Dupree pulls out a business card and writes on it. "When you're ready to tell me what happened to Doug, I'll explain the parable."

Vince takes the card.

"Front is my office number. On the back is my home number."

Vince opens his car door.

"On TV shows, this is the part where the cop asks the bad guy not to leave town without notifying him."

"Yeah," Vince says, "I always liked that part." He climbs out of the car, lost in thought. He walks toward his house and fishes in his pocket for his keys, aware of the cop's eyes on his back.

Vince unlocks the front door, steps inside, closes the door, and dead-bolts it. He walks through the trashed house, flips on some lights, opens his packed bag, runs his finger along the ten grand in the manila envelope, then seals it and zips up the bag. He continues through the house, into the kitchen, and straight out the back door.

From his backyard, Vince can hear the car idling in front of his house; he imagines Dupree watching the front window. He's never met a cop like this, with his ghosts and his shadows and his crows. It makes Vince feel uneasy. He walks through the backyard, hops the chain-link fence, sprints alongside the neighbor's house, and comes out on the block behind his own. He slides into the backseat of the waiting cab. As he settles in, he sees Len's Cadillac glide past on the cross street.

The cabbie starts driving. "Airport?"

"Please."

"So where you headed?"

What happens to the crows after they leave the lake? Where do they go?

Driver won't drop it. "Hey, where you flyin' today, buddy?"

Vince falls back in the seat. "Home."

New York, New York

1980 / October 31 / Friday / 10:43 A.M.

# chapter 4||

And then you're back here, of all places, at another airport, staring into the dreadlocks and hack license of another cabbie in the scratched glass that separates you, while outside the car horns play and voices sing in that unending New York chorus of praise: *Hey, move ya fockin' cah arready!*

And that's when it hits you: maybe you're not the crow, flying above all the shit—the people and the traffic and the straight life below—full of self-admiration, occasionally drawn by shiny, worthless things on the ground.

"Hey! You deaf?" The cabbie turns. "Where we goin', mon?"

No, back here, it comes to you in a flash that while you were capable of doing anything when you left the city three years ago, in theory at least you couldn't really break out of patterns that were beyond your control. Maybe a person can't change his own nature—not in any important way—any more than a lake can cause itself to evaporate.

"Fuck's a matter with you, mon? Where to?"

"Greenwich Village," Vince says.

The driver turns forward. "You got a address? 'Sa big place."

Patterns you aren't even aware of— "Washington Square."

"You lookin' for smoke? Junk? I know a closer place."

Maybe you've never had control. Not really— "Park's fine."

"Is your dime." The cabbie cranks the meter and begins driving and Vince settles back. Dog-tired; he flew from Spokane to Chicago the day before, then spent the night not sleeping on the plastic furniture at O'Hare. To get his mind off everything, he bought a new paperback book in the airport store, *The Ghost Writer* by Philip Roth, about two Jewish writers, one young and full of potential, the other old and famous. Vince liked the book the way that he likes science fiction, for creating a world that he could never have imagined himself, but which seemed real enough. Then, at two in the morning, on page 88, the older writer, E. I. Lonoff, said, "Sometimes I like to imagine I've read my last book. And looked for the last time at my watch." And just like that, Vince set the book down and knew that he was done with it. In the morning he caught the first flight to LaGuardia, and when the jet touched down he felt himself tingling, anticipating.

In the cab, he slides over on the bench seat and cranks the window to get a little air. He drifts in and out, and the ride takes on this dreamy quality—the tractor trailers and buses (more brands of diesel stink in New York City than the sum of all the smells in other cities) and people on corners, waiting to cross, leaning into traffic; you don't see that in Spokane, people surging across streets, perched against lampposts and sitting on car hoods, everyone outside, on stoops of row houses and brick Queens storefronts where the world merges and flows onto the Grand Central Parkway, and the horns—he can't remember when he's heard so goddamn many horns—and then *bam!* He jolts awake and comes to the window like a kid at the first sight of the silver-trussed spans of the Fifty-ninth Street Bridge and below, Roosevelt Island, what they called Welfare Island when he was a kid and the island was all sanitariums and smallpox hospitals, before the developers got their hands on it and built apartments where even the swimming pools have views (the swimming pools!) and he peeks across the bridge and sees Manhattan, the ivied, old-money town houses of Sutton Place holding back the army of glass and steel crowded onshore and behind—the needles of Chrysler and Empire and the sulking twin towers, a full skyline, a riot of buildings, a revolution of brick and steel and stone and glass, crawling with people, sick with people, cars surging down long gashes of avenues and short, packed cuts of cross streets and . . . the world. The fucking world. It's all Vince can do not to laugh and clap his hands. And why he's so surprised when he feels the smooth trace of tears sliding down his cheeks.

AFTER HIS FATHER died, Vince used to walk from the apartment on Elizabeth Street to Washington Square, duck between the trees, lean against the marble arch, and watch the world. He was fourteen. He was dreamy and he walked through the city like a tourist, like a mark—always gazing up, taking in the architecture—unlike most natives, who kept their eyes level or pointed slightly down, affecting alertness without eye contact. But Vince had looked up at the world as long as he could remember, always searching the skyline for some sign of his father at a job site. By the time a crane guy wire snapped and cut the old man in two, it was the only way Vince knew to look.

In the park he learned to play chess and poker, to pick out the scams and pickpockets, the shooters swapping dice or shuffling shells, the ball rolling off the table. He learned to get out of the way of knives and barefoot women and people on smack, to drift-not-run when the cops came. Everyone he knew stole and fought, and so he stole and fought. Like all the fatherless boys, Vince was drawn to the local crews, pegged for boys' jobs—buying smokes, lookout, and delivery. Everyone liked Vince. He wasn't Sicilian, or even Italian, so he could never belong, could never be made, but he also didn't look Irish or Polish or Jewish, or any of the other ethnic shorthands. There was something odd and unapproachable about his curious melancholy and his dead-calm eyes—a quality easily mistaken for fearlessness—and he was that rare kid, at least in his neighborhood, who never had to prove himself.

He was boosting cars before he had a license, but rather than take them directly to the chop shop like the other hoods, Vince drove, windows down, even in winter, wind buffeting his face, out to Brighton Beach for the day, or to Rockaway. More often he just tooled around the city, leaning half out the window like a dog. His first pop came when a foot cop found him double-parked on Reade Street, staring at the Corinthian columns at the base of the massive Municipal Building. "I don't care what people say," Vince told the cop after he was cuffed. "I think it works fine."

It was less a city of neighborhoods and ethnicities than a collection of forms for Vince; he liked the puffed-up, classical area around City Hall, the earnest wrought iron of SoHo, the extravagant stone-mountain bluffs of Central Park West. He used to have dreams of Manhattan without the people, just the buildings guarded by formations of driverless cabs moving in sync down empty streets. Even his early incarcerations had their release in structure: he took strange solace at the thought of an overnight in the classic Tombs, with its turrets and towers and Egyptian pillars. If you were going to be locked up, better to be in a work of art like the Tombs than someplace like the Rock—Rikers Island, which looked a some rural community-college campus, a herd of razor-wire sheep lazily grazing the perimeter.

Back then, Vince would return to Washington Square each time he was released, only to find it thicker with hippies and NYU students, who were shifted to the Village when the Bronx NYU campus closed. On one of these releases, it dawned on Vince that there were two distinct breeds of people in the park now: those who were going somewhere and those who weren't. They were easy to tell apart, the lowlifes—players, pushers, and muggers—

*ambling,* glancing side to side, looking for the next action, and the students—*striding,* walking purposefully across the park, heads down, holding their backpacks like suitcases or babies, their eyes darting around, replaying in their heads the repeated warnings about the park's drug dealers and thieves, panhandlers, runaways, whores, street musicians, and Mafia wannabes, slick men of confidence and vice—men, he hated to admit, like himself.

He was twenty-six, full into his burgeoning credit-card scam—which, for all he knew, he'd *invented*—in jail for the fifth time, when his mother died of a liver infection. When he got out, Vince sat in the square and watched the college kids, trying to figure out what they had that he didn't. He knew he was smart. He probably read more than most of the students with their full book bags. And yet he didn't entirely get what he read. There were entire disciplines and schools of thought that he knew nothing about. Something was missing. Was it simply the sense of opportunity that came from having money and education? Was it a question of patterns of thought; were they conditioned to make better choices? Or was it some personality trait—a drive, an assuredness, some measure of place in the world—some quality that Vince could define only by his lack of it. Perhaps it was something as simple as a lack of ambition. After all, how can you make something of yourself when you've never *dreamed* of anything that wasn't a girl in shorts, a six-pack, a straight flush?

In fact, the only thing that even came close to ambition was an idea Vince first had when he was sixteen, of opening a chain of restaurants called The Picnic Basket, that would serve summer food—sandwiches, fried chicken, potato salads, and pies in a cheaply produced, mass-quantity picnic basket: entire meals to go. The funny thing was—he'd never even been on a picnic, never eaten out of a picnic basket, never been to summer camp. He'd only been out of the city a few times. Maybe that was it: you can only be seduced by what you've never had.

Then, one day before a court hearing, Vince confided his idea to his young lawyer, Benny DeVries, who seemed touched by the idea of a low-level crook opening a picnic restaurant. Benny was a Vietnam vet who'd scrapped his way through law school and represented to Vince all that Vince might've become if he'd known how to aspire. He and Vince developed a friendship that was genuine and served both of them well—Vince occasionally in need of a criminal lawyer, Benny occasionally in need of a criminal. In time Vince stopped charging for the dope and stereo equipment he procured for his friend, and Benny never charged for representing Vince.

Benny was one of those lawyers who got off defending mobbed clients, who liked to talk the talk and lunch in mobbed-up places. He was an aficionado—a little guy who wanted to rub it with the bigs—and at Benny's thirtieth birthday party Vince saw a handful of made guys. That's also where he met Benny's sister, Tina, only twenty at the time, a part-time clerk in Benny's office, small and shy, with big brown eyes. For Vince, this girl became everything: the personification of his ambition and desire. And if Benny never quite came around to his little sister dating a thief and drug dealer, he also never actively tried to convince his sister to stop seeing Vince—at least, not until the trouble came.

The trouble was like any trouble, with all the momentum and hope of a sinking ship. There was a card game and a loan and a shipment and a double cross and a bust, and just like that, Vince was into this crew boss in Queens for fifteen thousand and points, owed another ten in restitution to the court, and was looking at two years upstate. That's when Benny said that the cops had tapes of a threat against Vince's life, and he whispered that he'd gone to law school with the prosecutor. If Vince would testify against Dominic Coletti and his crew, they'd get him into the witness protection program. Vince didn't want to, but Benny said they might go after Tina, and so Vince agreed, and after the trial, when his friend announced what he wanted in lieu of payment, he didn't hesitate. When he went in the program, Vince would leave Tina behind.

He straightens up and looks around Washington Park. He'd allowed himself to think of that as a different life entirely, and that desperate guy—Marty—as someone else, until it all came back around on him. And now . . . he's right back in it. Vince steps around the arch and watches the streams of people, an endless flow. It never dawned on him when he lived here, but now he can't help wondering: Where are they going? Tourists and businessmen and punks and greasers and artists and kids—the NYU students looking even younger, cleaner cut, and somehow more professional—where can all these people possibly be going?

He checks his watch. One. It's possible that Benny doesn't stick to his old Friday routine . . . but as soon as Vince thinks that, here comes the man himself, all five-five of him, looking a bit older, more settled, his blond Afro trimmed to half its size and just starting to gray at the corners, to recede on his long Garfunkel forehead. Benny is in a suit with a blue dress shirt, and a nice wool overcoat. He carries a thick bundle of newspapers under his arm.

Vince ducks behind some park benches, then steps in twenty feet back and follows Benny through the park, up Fifth Avenue to East Eleventh, where the lawyer turns and walks into the Cedar, through the restaurant and straight back to the bar, to a table near the wall. Every Friday during football season, Benny comes here with as many newspapers as he can carry. He orders a pork chop and a beer and reads the sports pages, looking for injuries or disgruntled stars, anything he can use to get an advantage on the weekend games.

Vince watches from across the bar and waits until Benny's pork chop is delivered and heavily salted. Then he walks over and plops down across from his old friend. Holds his duffel bag in his lap. Benny looks up and the left corner of his mouth goes up in a smile.

"Hey," Vince says.

"Son of a bitch," Benny says quietly. He stands up, comes around the table, and hugs Vince so hard and so long that people in the bar begin to stare.

BENNY CHEWS A bite of pork chop and talks out of the left side of his mouth. "His name is Ray Scatieri—Ray Sticks. He used to work for Angelo Bruno in Philly."

"Used to?"

"Last March, Angelo got dead over that shit in Atlantic City. His guys have been shooting each other up ever since. Like dogs on meat over there. This Ray Sticks took the opportunity to get out, came to New York, and has been working here, doing special jobs for the Gambinos while he waits to see what happens in Philly."

Vince swirls J&B scotch in a rocks glass. "What's a special job?"

"Anything the fellas don't want to do themselves. Off-the-record stuff. Maybe they're worried about someone talking, or the contract is a friend, or a cop or a judge—something sensitive. Maybe they don't trust local talent, or they're looking for a guy with a certain specialty."

"Specialty . . ."

Benny blows air. "You know, arsonists. Or those guys who are good at making it look like an accident, or disappearing someone. There's torture guys. Long distance stuff. You know, different specialties."

"So what's this Ray Sticks do? What's his specialty?"

Benny takes a bite of pork chop. "I got this client who knows Ray Sticks, plays cards with him. He says Sticks has the reputation . . . he'll do anyone anytime. No conscience. Guy's a friggin' factory. Full service. Loves his work. But supposedly"—Benny looks around—"he especially gets off doing women."

"Women?" Vince imagines Ray's black eyes again.

"Lot of the old button guys won't take a contract on a kid or a woman. But with the Colombians now, and this cocaine, everything's crazy. All the old rules are gone. Women. Kids. Whole families. Done. And this Ray Sticks, he takes these kinds of jobs, the ones that some of the older guys won't do."

Vince takes a drink.

"Guy's an animal. I'm telling you, Marty, if it is this Ray Sticks they sent after you . . . well, it ain't good. It can't get any worse than that."

"Why me?" Vince finishes his drink and waves the glass at the bartender.

Benny chews on a piece of pork chop and shrugs his narrow shoulders. "I asked enough questions to get myself disbarred and indicted and maybe killed. I got no idea. Maybe someone inherited Coletti's paper on you. Maybe they're clearing the books. Or someone told 'em where you are and they want to send a message to snitches. Who knows why these things happen?"

The bartender brings Vince another drink. He takes a full sip and looks down at the table, trying to put the pieces together. When he looks up, Benny is staring at him.

"What?"

"You look different," Benny says.

A ghost. Vince runs his hand over his stubbly head. "Yeah, this haircut."

"No. Not that. You look . . . I don't know, different." He takes a drink. "So what are you going to do, Marty? You gotta run, right?"

"I don't know," Vince says. "This town where I was . . . if they could find me there, they could find me on the moon."

Vince sighs. "This is gonna sound crazy. But I brought a little money. I was thinking, what if I just repay the money I borrowed? What if I march in and act like it's no big deal. Just go pay it off."

Benny laughs, and then sees that Vince is serious. "How much do you have?"

"How much you think I need?"

Benny shrugs. "Three years' action on fifteen grand, they're gonna want sixty, and they'll probably still waste you on principle."

Vince stares into his bag. "I don't have sixty."

"How much do you have?"

"I brought ten."

"Ten thousand?"

"I got more at home. I'll tell 'em, the only way to get the rest of it is to let me go home and I'll send it to 'em. That'll be my insurance."

Benny stares at Vince, then smiles sadly and takes the last bite of pork chop. "Make sure you hold a couple hundred out for your coffin."

VINCE HAS AN address in Bay Ridge for old Dom Coletti. He walks two blocks and descends the tile steps of the subway station on Broadway, thrilling at the rush of smells and sounds; roasted chestnuts and cigarette smoke and the seizing of train brakes. A couple of kids bump him as he waits for a token and his hand reflexively goes to his wallet as he queues up to the turnstile and then—you're in: fluorescent lights on tile walls, some stoned Latin guy yelling on the dark platform—"*Pacífico!*"—while a woman in a dirty sundress plays the theme to *Rocky* on a hail-pocked clarinet, the case at her feet littered with nickels and dimes from commuters hiding behind tabloid shields; on the platform they shift and step and stare down the tunnel—desperate for the space between them—and you smile at the clacking groan of a train coming, lean out over the tracks down the black tunnel to see the faint

Cyclops light and feel the first breeze—dust and garbage—and then a gust of pure nostalgia as newspapers dance and the B train bursts into the station—*clathup, claathuuup, claaathuuuup*—and squeals and grinds to a stop.

Doors pop and people on the platform drift onto the train, swing around poles into plastic seats, eyeing one another, clinging to purses, backpacks, and shopping bags. The car smells like piss. Vince stands, thrilled to be reading graffiti again, like someone seeing his hometown newspaper for the first time in years. Chulo is still a motherfucker. Jennifer continues to eat big cock. Finally, Vince takes a seat and closes his eyes.

Cross the river, off at Seventy-seventh Street in Brooklyn, Vince walks eight blocks and finds himself in front of Coletti's building, a clean three-story walk-up, almost in the shadow of the Verrazano. He takes a deep breath and starts for the door. Kids on the stoop part for him and he steps into the foyer, reads the name-plate, and rings 3B. After a minute, an old woman's voice comes over the intercom, bursting with static. "Yes?"

"I'm looking for Dominic Coletti."

"Who are you?"

He fights the question's significance. "An old friend."

The door buzzes and Vince goes up a wide staircase, the thick wooden railings carved and tagged with mild graffiti. On the third floor, an old Italian woman waits in a doorway, black wire hair, deep furrows around her eyes and mouth, sprouts of thicker black hair erupting from two big moles on her chin.

"Mrs. Coletti? I'm . . . Vince Camden." Offers his hand.

She ignores it. "You're such a friend to my husband, how come I never heard of you? How come I don't recognize you?"

"I've been out of New York for a few years. My hair was longer."

"And you say you used to work with Dom?"

"Yes."

"At the old place in Queens?"

"Yes."

"You a plumber?"

Vince remembers that Coletti was a plumber by trade, though like all connected tradesmen, he probably never worked a day as a plumber in his life.

"Because you don't look like a gangster. You don't even look Italian."

"No," Vince admits. "I'm not Italian. And I'm not a plumber."

She turns in her housecoat and goes into the apartment. Vince follows her. The apartment opens to a small living room, dusted with age. The simple wallpaper is either faded beige or a white that's gone old and dusty. There are framed pictures of grandchildren on every flat surface in the room—end table, coffee table, TV, sideboard, mantel, and dining-room table. All of the grandchildren, boys and girls, seem to have the same shoulder-length, comb-furrowed, jet-black hair, parted perfectly in the middle.

"What do you want with Dom?"

"I just . . . want to talk to him," Vince says.

"Nobody comes to see Dom anymore." She frowns. "It's a goddamn crime. He made a lot of money for you people. He was always loyal, and when one of you guys went to jail, Dom took care of his family." She leans in close. "And how do you reward him? When he was in did you come to see if I needed anything? Or now? Do you young guys come by? You young guys, making all your money with your drugs, going to the Studio 54. I read the papers; I know about the Studio 54. Do you come over and thank my Dominic? *Grazia, paisan . . . famiglia!* Do you do this, plumber?"

"No," Vince says. "I guess not."

She mimics him: "I guess not." When there is nothing more to add, she turns and goes to a small hallway connecting three doors. Vince follows. She pauses in front of a tabletop shrine— nine votive candles draped with rosary beads and some figurines of Mary and a handful of saints crowded together, looking to

Vince like out-of-work foosball men in robes, yellow hair, red lips, and blue eyes painted just slightly off center.

She crosses herself and opens a door and Vince follows her into a dark room. It smells like decay and shit. In the center of the room is an old hospital bed with a crank at the bottom. Sitting on the bed, naked except for a large plastic diaper, is the last seventy-five pounds of Dominic Cold Blood Coletti. His arms are crooked and his fingers snarled on his bird chest like he's holding on to a branch. His skin is pale bark. One of his legs is draped off the side of the bed, the toenails long and jagged. But it's Coletti's face that gets to Vince. He is in midgrimace, his eyes closed, wrinkled mouth forming over the letter *O*, white scum around his lips. He breathes in rasps and fits.

"He had a stroke," Vince says quietly.

She nods. "The doctors don't even know how many. They say he's having them all the time now. You don't even see them anymore. But he feels them. I can tell." She carefully pushes his leg back onto the bed and pulls a blanket from the floor and drapes it across him, from the stomach down. "Dom. This young man is here to see you."

Coletti's right eye flutters open and he takes Vince in. That eye is noncommittal, but after a moment, knowing.

"Do you want to talk to him, Dom?"

Vince watches the old man's face but sees nothing except a couple of blinks.

"Okay, then," she says. "I'll leave you two alone."

"Can he understand me?"

"Can you understand him?" she asks her husband. He blinks twice rapidly and Mrs. Coletti turns to Vince. "Two blinks means yes. Three means no."

"What does one blink mean?"

She scowls at him. "It means his goddamn eye is dry. If he needs something he'll just blink and blink and blink. Then come and get me."

She leaves and Vince looks around the dark room for a chair. There is a folding chair in the corner and he drags it over, squeaking across the floor. He sits, and leans forward on his knees. He speaks quietly. "Do you know who I am?"

Coletti blinks twice.

"Look, I'm sorry for the way everything turned out."

The eye just stares at him.

"I'm sorry about Crapo and Bailey, too. I didn't know it would be so hard for them. I was in trouble and I didn't have the money and it seemed like the only way—"

The old man blinks three times and then closes his eye. A chalky blue vein runs across the lid. No more excuses.

"Okay," Vince says.

The old man opens his eye again. Waits.

"Look . . . I have to ask you—do you still have paper on me?"

Coletti blinks three times. No. His breath is heavy and stale.

"There isn't some old friend of yours who might still want to take me out?"

Three blinks. The eye stares.

"*Someone* is after me."

The eye just stares.

"It isn't you?"

Three blinks.

"You don't have any idea who it might be?"

Three blinks.

"Okay." In the dark now, he can make out the room. On one wall are pictures of the Verrazano-Narrows Bridge under construction, its ribs exposed. On another wall, photos of thoroughbred horses. He remembers Dom used to love the horses. "Okay," Vince says again. "Thank you." He reaches in his duffel bag and pulls out the envelope of money. He counts out four thousand in fifties—eighty bills—and sets the thick stack on the bed next to Coletti. The old man raises his eye to the top of its lid and then

JESS
WALTER

128

down to his chest. Vince picks up the money and slides it into Coletti's clawed hand—his skin cold and hard. The old man blinks twice, emphatically. Yes.

"It's only four thousand," Vince says. "Less than a third of what I borrowed. I don't know if I can pay off the points, but I'll send the rest of the principal as soon as I get back home. Okay?"

The eye just stares.

"And if you're . . . gone, I'll send it to your wife. Is that okay? Will we be straight if I do that?"

A pause. Two blinks.

"Thank you." Vince pats the old man's chest, and then stands. The eye follows him. "Can I ask you something?" Vince says.

The eye stares.

"Did you always like it, the life?"

The old man just stares.

"What if someone offered to let you start over? New name. New city. Everything. Just walk away. Do you think you could you have done that?"

The eye looks past Vince. Blinks twice.

Then the old man closes his eye. Vince waits for a second and then goes out. The air outside the room is clean and Vince breathes heavily. Mrs. Colleti comes into the hallway, walks past Vince and into the bedroom.

Vince walks through the living room and is at the door when he hears Mrs. Coletti's voice at his back.

"You left that money for Dom?"

He half turns. "Yes."

"Why?"

"I owed it to him."

She stares for a minute and then her eyes narrow. "Marty Hagen." She says his name like a slap. "That's who you are, isn't it?"

He doesn't say anything.

"Goddamn. Do you know that Dom never even blamed you?

Never said a cross word about you. He actually liked you. Do you know he would've eaten that money you owed him. *Eaten it.* That's the kind of man you ruined, you worthless—"

Vince looks at the ground.

"My Dom, he knew Profaci. The Gallo brothers. I fed Joey Colombo right here at this table. In forty years, Dom never crossed the wrong people, never did more than a weekend in jail. He was a pro. Didn't work in his own neighborhood, didn't sell drugs. Raised six kids so they wouldn't have to do what he did, got them into trades and good jobs. Our oldest, Paul, is an accountant. Our youngest, Maria, is a pharmacist in Orange. And then, when his work is done, when my Dominic should be relaxing and playing with his grandchildren, he gets taken down by some stupid thief who can't pay off a debt! For what? A few thousand dollars? Bah!"

Vince looks at his shoes.

"It was like watching a tiger get taken down by a mosquito."

"How much time did he do?"

She waves her hand like it's no big deal. "He pulled a year. They thought they could turn him, get him to wear a wire, but he wouldn't budge. Not Dom. Not for a year, not for eighty. He had character, which you wouldn't know from your ass. But it ruined him. He got out and his hand didn't work right, and then the right side of his face went—" She looks to the old man's door. "Why did you bring that money? What do you want?"

Vince flinches. "I wanted to do the right thing."

She refuses to look away, or to allow him to look away. "Well, you're too late to do it here."

WHEN YOU'RE TAILING someone, it is best to be like a shadow at three o'clock, not *behind* the subject but *parallel* with him—a lane over, or even better, on side streets and alleys, two steps over and one behind. That way the target looks over his shoulder, straight back, and sees nothing. This method requires concentration and anticipation, but it sharpens the senses and eventually you know where he's going before he does. At least that's Alan Dupree's new theory. He walks blindly through the terminal at LaGuardia, feeling more like a tourist than a cop, his first time in New York, looking for a tough guy whose name may or may not be Vince Camden. Needle, I'd like you to meet Haystack. In fact he wonders if that's why Phelps *let* him make the trip when they got it approved, because he realized it was such a long shot. Let the rook waste his time.

Dupree grips the smooth handle of his suitcase and is walking toward the front of the airport when he feels a strong hand clasp his shoulder.

"Hey, slow down, motherfucker. You Officer Dookie?"

Dupree smells booze. He turns to see a big, thick, bald plainclothes in skintight slacks and dress shirt, jacket with shoulder holster, hooded eyelids, and cuffs on his belt. Dupree offers his hand. "I'm Alan Dupree."

The cop ignores the hand and takes Dupree's suitcase. "Fuckin' bosses, eh? Send you 'cross the fuckin' country 'cause some mope gets on a fuckin' plane. I tell you, Dookie—fuckin' bosses. Lazy cunts. Is what they are." An afterthought: "I'm Donnie Charles. Everyone mostly call me Detective Charlie. Or Det-Charlie. But usually just fuckin' Charlie." Every word bursts out of this detective's mouth except *fuckin'*, which Charles stretches out like a gospel refrain, like a whale surfacing. He takes huge strides through the airport, swinging the suitcase. Dupree throws in a running step every few minutes to keep up. "Me, I'm mindin' my own business, my fuckin' lieutenant calls and says he's got some fuckin' needle dick from Seattle needs driving around on some kind-a-homicide whatnot and I think, What the fuck, I need the OT."

Detective Charles rushes through the luggage area and outside, to an unmarked parked at the curb. Covering the backseat of the car is a mound of about twenty shoeboxes. One of the boxes is open to reveal a new pair of Adidas running shoes. A young Hispanic man is leaning on the hood of the car and he straightens up when he sees Charles, who unlocks the car, opens the back door, and hands a pair of shoes to the young man, who nods as he backs away. Then Charles pops the trunk and unceremoniously dumps Dupree's suitcase in. "Fuckin' monkeys. Gotta grease 'em to watch your fuckin' car. You got that in Seattle? Puerto fuckin' Ricans will steal the fuckin' aerial. You got a lot of them PRs in Seattle, Dookie? What are you, about a size ten? Take some shoes."

And they're driving.

Dupree feels the need to swim against the current of Det-Charlie's rant, and to give the illusion that he knows what he's doing. He pulls out the file to brief his liaison, the way he imagines this is done. "We appreciate your help on this." He opens a file. "Our guy's name is Vince Camden. We first contacted him at the scene of a homicide about thirty-six hours ago. He said he didn't know the victim, but later we found his name in the dead guy's Rolodex."

"Uh-huh," Charles says, his head pecking through traffic.

"He came in on his own for questioning and admitted knowing the victim, but he had an alibi, so we let him go."

"Yeah. Uh-huh." Both hurrying and not listening.

"After the initial interview I drove him home and told him not to leave town. Then we found some stolen credit card numbers with his name on them in the victim's belongings, so I went back to ask him a few more questions and saw that he'd run. The house was trashed. Suitcase gone. We got a warrant, searched his house, and found traces of marijuana and more credit-card numbers."

"Uh-huh."

"So I went to the restaurant where this Camden said he was going earlier, and the owner remembered him, said he made some phone calls and took some notes about something. So I went through the garbage—"

For the first time Charles turns, a half smile on his face. "You went through the fuckin' garbage?"

"Yeah," Dupree says tentatively. He holds up a plastic baggie with a crumpled piece of notebook paper inside it. He reads: "'Partner. Bay Ridge. Married. Jerry. Tina McGrath. Long Island.'"

Charles laughs. "Well, that solves it."

But Dupree likes telling the story, even if it's only to himself. "So today I called the airlines and checked their flights to New York and *bang!* Pan Am had this Vince Camden flying from Spokane to Chicago and Chicago into LaGuardia this morning. I'd just missed him. So we booked a flight and called to see if you fellas could help us. And . . . here I am."

Charles seems to have tuned him out. "What's the guy's name?"

"Vince Camden—"

"Camden? Like New Jersey?"

"We think it's an alias."

Detective Charles looks pissed. "Well, what the fuck? Is it his name or ain't it his name? Don't fuck around with me here, Seattle, I'm in no fuckin' mood."

Dupree doesn't know what to say.

Charles hits him in the chest. It hurts. "Aw, I'm just fuckin' with you, man. Don't take nothin' I say serious. That's the thing. You ask any motherfucker, they'll tell you the same thing: don't take nothing ol' Det-Charlie says serious. Unless he gets *this* look on his face." He scrunches up his mouth and nose, looks like a bulldog. Dupree recognizes the glassy eyes: He's stoned. The guy is stoned. "Memorize this face, Dookie. You ever see this face, you crawl under the nearest fuckin' table."

Charles whips his Crown Vic through traffic, in and out, eating up space between cars. "Get out my fuckin' way!" Flies up on drivers' tails and slaps at his siren. "Get off my fuckin' road!"

When he crosses into oncoming traffic to pass a bus, Dupree grabs the dashboard. The car veers back into its lane and Charles flips the siren. "Where these people goin' that's so fuckin' important? Any of you fuckers chasing a murderer? No? Then get off *my fuckin' street!*"

Dupree opens his mouth to remind Charles that as of right now Vince Camden—or whatever his name is—is simply a material witness, but he thinks better of it.

"We gotta reach out to my PBA rep," Charles says, "and then we'll scratch one of my regulars, see if he knows your guy. You like Italian?"

"Actually, there's this girl I thought we could start with." Dupree reaches in his file for the letter that he found in Vince Camden's house. For some reason the name and address were cut off the envelope and the top of the letter, but the woman who sent the letter signed it Tina. It was the reason Phelps agreed to send him: the letter and the sheet of crumpled paper he found in the garbage. "See. A letter from Tina and this name on the paper. Tina McGrath. We think it's the same Tina."

Charles ignores him.

"There was a Jerry and Tina McGrath in Information. And guess where they live?"

Nothing.

"Long Island. I have her address right here. And see. On the paper I found in the garbage: 'Long Island.' See?"

"You want a girl, Dookie? Why didn't you just say so? You come to the big city, you think old Det-Charlie ain't gonna take care of you in that manner? We don't gotta go to Long Island. Fuck that negative shit, Seattle! Think positive."

Dupree opens his mouth to correct Charles, who reaches next to his seat, pulls out a pint of Jack Daniel's and takes a long pull, holds it out for Dupree, then waves it at a car in front of him: "Get off my fuckin' road!"

* * *

TWO HOURS TO kill before he meets Benny. Vince takes the train back to Manhattan. Goes to midtown and walks Fifth Avenue, a river of bobbing heads. It's disconcerting, all those eyes, those faces. He keeps imagining that he sees Ray Sticks in the crowds and between buildings. How long before Ray realizes Vince isn't in Spokane anymore and tracks him back here? He stares at the marquee of a movie theater. One of the three movies is *Altered States,* a novel he started reading a couple of months ago when he was first trying to impress Kelly. It was about a young scientist who puts himself through experiments in a sensory-deprivation tank. Vince remembers the exact point he quit the book, not even thirty pages in, when one of the characters said, "We're born screaming in doubt, we die screaming in doubt, and human life consists of continually convincing ourselves we're alive." But he wouldn't mind seeing how the story ends, so he ducks into the theater.

But the movie is slow and dark and he can't concentrate. He leaves when his popcorn is gone. Walks for a while and then cabs to a little restaurant called Caffe Grigio on Desbrosses Street. Standing next to Benny is a guy in black shirt and white jacket, hands crossed in front of his crotch like a soccer player protecting the goal. The guy is shades of gray—slate eyebrows rising over sunglasses, white hair receding at the temples. His black shirt is parted to reveal a gold chain nestled between the folds of his neck and a bouquet of silver chest hair.

Benny stands between Vince and the other man like a boxing referee. Even with the blond Afro, he's a half foot shorter than either of them. "Hey," he says to Vince. "This is the client I was telling you about. Pete, this is—" Vince can see his old friend reminding himself to use the new name, the way they agreed. "This is Vince Camden."

They shake hands warily and walk into the place, past the cash register and straight to a booth at a window, all set up for them with three place settings and three waters. Pete pulls the chintz curtains and sits nervously tracing his finger on the paper place mat. The place mat says *Beautiful Italy!* Pete traces the shape of Italy on the mat without looking down.

Benny sits on Pete's side. "Okay," he says, "I've filled Pete in on your story. He's agreed to help you out as a favor to me."

"I appreciate that," Vince says.

"But you're never to mention that you spoke to him or that I represent him. If you ask a question and he declines to answer, that's it. Understood?"

Vince nods.

"You are not to repeat any of this information to anyone, not even to me. Pete could get in trouble helping a guy like you."

Vince is surprised at the sting of that.

"So today never happened," Benny continues. "Understood?"

"Sure," Vince says.

"Okay, then," Benny says. "I'm going to sit at the bar because I really shouldn't hear any of this. Wave me over when you're done."

They watch Benny go to the bar and take off his overcoat. The waitress comes over and Pete orders a beer and the veal cannelloni. Vince says he only wants a whiskey sour. When the waitress brings them each a drink and an antipasto plate, Pete takes his sunglasses off to reveal two tired eyes, also gray. He takes a piece of provolone, salami, and an olive. "Benny tells me you're into some shit with Ray Sticks?" His voice is rough and slow, as if he's talking through water.

Vince nods. "I think so. Big stocky guy with black hair and a couple of caterpillar eyebrows. Calls everyone chief—"

Before he can say any more, The Client nods and takes a drink of his beer. "Yeah, that's Ray Sticks. I play cards with that animal."

"So how do I find out who sent him after me?"

"Only one guy could've sent him after you."

"Who?"

Pete picks another olive off the antipasto plate. "Sticks works for this guy Johnny Boy, boss of a Gambino crew out in Queens. Runs everything out of Ozone Park—hijacking, a little shy business, gambling. His brother runs smack. Johnny is like an old-time Cosa guy. A traditionalist. Always talks about returning to the glory of the old days. Shit like that. Real slick. He's squarin' up all the business that fell between the cracks. That's probably where they found you. Between the cracks."

"Do you think he'd let me buy off my debt?"

"Doubtful." Pete frowns, and tilts his head. "John ain't averse to money. But you don't know with that guy. He's high-strung. Watches too many movies. Last March his kid got run over by a car, and he's been buggy ever since. Real unpredictable."

"So how do I find him?"

"Johnny Boy's crew works out of this place, the Bergin Fish and Hunt Club. But I'd stay away from there. Guy like you ain't likely to get a break in a place like that." For the first time he meets Vince's eyes. "No offense."

Vince ignores it. "Where, then?"

"Try to catch him relaxed. He likes to gamble. Gets drunk and throws away ten, twenty dimes a weekend on card games. You play?"

"Yeah. A little."

Pete rips off a piece of the place mat and grabs a pen from a passing waiter. "There's a high-stakes game in an apartment over on Mott Street tonight. I'll vouch for you, get you in the door. You pay my buy-in. Then I'll lose quick and get my ass out of there before you say anything." Pete writes the address on the place mat. "There's always two or three games. I can't guarantee you'll be at Johnny Boy's table, but you flash enough money, look like a mark, maybe even win . . . you might get a shot."

Vince thanks him and the guy shrugs. He looks up to Benny at the bar, and then turns back to Vince. "Look, Benny says you're a good guy, so I'm gonna tell you this one time: Be careful of this guy John. He ain't right. Ever since his kid got killed—" He doesn't finish the thought.

"How old was his kid?"

Pete is picking at the antipasto plate. "Twelve."

"Jesus. And the guy who hit his kid? What happened to him?"

Pete picks an olive from the antipasto plate. Stares at it, shows Vince, then drops it into his water glass. They watch it sink to the bottom of the East River.

THEY FLY THROUGH a tunnel, Detective Charles working the siren, gas pedal, and whiskey bottle in concert. On the other side of the tunnel Dupree sees a sign for the New Jersey Turnpike. He turns back to Charles. "Hey, are we in New Jersey?"

"We ain't in fuckin' Seattle."

Dupree looks down at the file in his hand. "Look, I think we should go talk to this girl, Tina McGrath, before it gets too late—"

"Settle the fuck down, Seattle. I got some business first."

"But—"

"Look, I could've had my fuckin' Friday night off, chased some tail, but when my lieu tells me you poor fucks from Mayberry need some help, I jump! You think it's easy to get an NYPD detective to volunteer to haul your ass around on a Friday night? You might show some consideration for my work 'stead of busting my balls."

"I'm sorry," Dupree says.

They exit the turnpike, drive through close, ratty houses, and after a few minutes, come to a small business area. Charles parks in front of a brick storefront with a dry cleaner in the front and a sign on the side above a screen door that reads NITTI'S.

Charles hops out of the car. "Come on, Seattle. We'll have a bite with my union rep, and then we'll go find your girl."

Dupree sits in the car, unsure what to do.

"Oh, come on! You're like a fuckin' woman." Charles grits his teeth, then leans back in the car and offers a charming smile. "Look, I promise you never tasted food like this. Your guy ain't goin' nowhere in the hour it takes us to eat a bowl of fuckin' noodles. Now come on. Help me out here."

Nitti's is well lit, walls covered with framed pictures of Italian movie stars and snapshots of regular people standing between a small Italian couple, maps of Italy, baskets hung with eggplant and artichoke and strung-up Chianti bottles. The food is set out in pans on a long table in the front of the room—a lasagna, a ziti, spaghetti, meatballs, and sausages, followed by pans of green beans and zucchini. Most of the customers are men, sitting at long picnic tables covered with checked tablecloths, drinking water glasses of Chianti.

The old, hunched Italian man from the pictures calls from a stool behind the cash register. "Two, Charlie?"

"That's right, Guiseppe. This here is Dookie. He's a rook cop out there in California, come to learn how the finest do it."

Dupree opens his mouth to correct Charles, who turns and mutters, "I know you ain't from California, but that old fuckin' guinea wouldn't know from Seattle."

"He a cowboy, then, Charlie? Bang, bang?"

"That's right, Giuseppe. Fuckin' bang bang cowboy."

The old Italian points his finger. "Bang, bang!"

"You're on expense," Charles says. "Pay the man."

Dupree gives him fifteen bucks. Charles grabs a plate and Dupree doesn't know what else to do, so he follows. They fill their plates with food and join a severe man in the corner, thin-faced and wisp-haired, drawing on a cigarette, his cleaned plate pushed to the side, along with a kitchen wineglass. He looks from Charles to Vince and back, sniffs, and takes a drag. "Where the fuck you been, Charlie? It's almost eight."

"I'm on the job tonight, Mike. I told you."

"You didn't tell me shit. Why are you still on the clock?"

"I figured I might need the overtime." He looks at Dupree. "And someone to vouch for my whereabouts."

"Who's the kid?"

Dupree opens his mouth to introduce himself, but Mike hasn't so much as looked at him, so he lets Detective Charles do it.

"This is Officer Dookie. Dookie, this is Mike. My PBA rep. Dookie here is a badge from Seattle. We're helpin' each other on some shit today. We're like partners here—like fuckin' alibis. Right?"

The word *alibis* chills Dupree, but it fades in a bite of the best meatball he's ever had—spiced and meaty, like someone fed a steak to a tomato. "My God, this really is good," he says.

Charles laughs. Mike just stares.

"See, I told you Dookie's okay. He's gonna vouch that I was busy helpin' him out tonight. Ain't that right, Dookie?" Charles pops in his own mouthful of food.

Dupree feels a tightness in his chest. "What are you talking about?"

Mike flicks his cigarette at Detective Charles's plate. "I can't believe you got a appetite after all this. You're a real fuckin' pig, Charlie."

"Fuck you, Mike."

"No! Fuck you, Charlie! You screwed up this time, man!"

Dupree looks back and forth, a bite of meatball still speared on his fork.

"I know." Charles talks through a mouth of baked ziti. "So—"

"So?" Mike stubs his cigarette out. "So I'm tired of saving your ass."

"Come on! Why you gotta treat me like a fuckin' kid? Stop bustin' my balls already and tell me what to do."

Mike sighs. "You're in deep shit, Charlie."

"I know what I'm in."

"It's time you squared up, man." Mike lights a new smoke. "This ain't a free meal you took, Charlie. Or goddamn tennis shoes."

"I know what it *ain't*, Mike. Just tell me what I gotta do."

Dupree looks from one to the other.

"How many times I tell you? You don't mess with this side of the river, Charlie. That girl's father is a Newark councilman. I can't help you over here."

"Did you find out—what's she sayin'?" Charles asks.

"She's sayin'—" Mike looks over at Dupree again. "Are you sure you wanna talk about this in front of . . ."

"I'll go outside." Dupree starts to stand.

Charlie's hand clamps down on Dupree's leg. "No. Dookie stays. No secrets between partners."

Mike shrugs. "She and her girlfriend drove over to Alphabet City to buy a dime bag. You pulled them over, took one of the girls back to your car, forced her to blow you in your car, and then stole their coke."

Dupree has lost his appetite. Pushes his plate away.

"Well." Charles sulks and his bald head is furrowed to the crown. Takes a bite of noodles and points with his fork. "That ain't what happened, Mike."

"Yeah? What happened?" Mike picks a flake of tobacco off his tongue and looks at Dupree's plate, then up at Alan for the first time. His eyes shift back to Charles.

"She practically took off my belt, Mike. I didn't force nobody to do nothing. I was doing her a fuckin' favor."

"Aw, Jesus."

"Come on, Mike. How am I supposed to know she's a councilman's kid? You're fuckin' killin' me here." Detective Charles drains his wine and reaches for Dupree's glass. "There ain't some way we can make this better?"

"Make it better? IA's already got wind of it. How we supposed to make it better, Charlie?" Mike smokes hard.

"Look—" Charles reaches for Mike's arm.

Mike pulls his arm back and points his finger at Charlie's nose. "I know you've had a tough time of it, Charlie. But this shit has got to stop."

"It will. It will. I swear." Charlie seems to smell hope for the first time.

Mike watches the trail of smoke from his own cigarette. "I reached out to the councilman and, as you might guess, he ain't exactly thrilled that his daughter's buyin' coke ten days before election."

Charles points with his fork. "I knew you could help me, Mike."

"Shut the fuck up, Charlie! You're lucky this guy's a sleazeball councilman. If it was my kid, you'd be pissing through a fucking tube!" He takes a breath. "The guy is having trouble with a labor union that's supporting his opponent. He doesn't want to go in-house for this . . . so if you helped him out . . . I don't know." Mike slides a sheet of folded paper across the table.

Charlie grabs the paper and opens it. Dupree sees Mike has written a union-local number and the name Daryl Greene on the page. "What's he want from the guy?" Charlie asks. "Drumstick? Wing?"

"No, no, nothing like that. Just deliver the message."

Charlie beams as if he's won the lottery. "That's it?"

"A *strong* message," Mike says. "After that, I think the councilman will take care of his daughter," Mike says. "But that's only half your only problem."

"What do you mean?"

"Internal affairs has the name of the coke dealer. They think you have a deal with him to pick off buyers from out of town after he sells to them."

"Goddamn it, Mario!" Charles spits. Then he wipes his face

and tries to restore his smile. "I'll take care of that. I'll make that better."

Mike leans forward. "You gotta get this shit under control, Charlie."

"I will, Mike. I will. I promise. After this, I'll take some time . . . get all squared away. Just help me out here." He puts his hands out on the table.

"Yeah. Okay." Mike reaches across and takes Charles's hand, squeezes it.

Dupree has been watching all this with horrified fascination. He clears his throat. "Look, fellas. I want no part of this. Your business is your business. But this has nothing to do with me—"

Both cops turn slowly to Dupree, as if they've forgotten he's there. Mike smiles and pats him on the arm: "How about some more wine, Dookie?"

TWO CARDS DOWN. Three on the flop. Roll one on the turn and then the river— because it can sell you down. There is order and sense to a game of Texas Hold 'Em. Like breathing. Even after three days without sleep. And suddenly it doesn't matter if you're in New York or Washington, if you're Vince or Marty or Jimmy Carter . . . it's just the cards, same cards for everyone, fifty-two in four suits, gently rounded corners, crosshatch designs, the same cards everywhere, and you take to the game as if it could save your life, which of course it can.

Vince starts strong, with a suited king-jack. Decides to buy a pot right off, announce his presence. Bets heavy. Two guys drop. Two more on the flop. Three more on the turn. Vince misses his flush but pulls another king on the river and takes three hundie off a bald guy with thick glasses. The conversation goes on around him: everyone is getting balls busted or is up to his eyes to a shy or has a dickhead for a PO. The patter is familiar and yet Vince can't seem to register the exact details, who says what, whose balls, which shylock, what parole officer. And suddenly it doesn't strike him as that different from the donut-shop talk, or the *normal* ladies on the street: the PTA and the charcoal grill, braces and checking accounts. *Banana apple strawberry.*

Vince folds a hand, rides a low call through the flop, and then folds again. One of the players tries to engage Vince, but he gives minimalist answers. Used to live in the City. Moved to the West Coast. Runs a donut shop in Washington State. Ran into an old friend who said he knew a good game.

He had to buy his way and Pete's into this game, two thousand each, but Pete seems to have taken off without playing and Vince has the feeling he got stuck at the kid's table, with a bunch of no-bodies—bottom of the food chain. So now he's stuck at the first table, fine—nine guys drinking, working cigars, and playing Hold 'Em. If he knows this kind of game—one-time buy-in, 10 percent vig to the house—he guesses there are a couple of other nine-man tables in other rooms in the building, that they'll play until people drop and the tables will come together for a ten- or fifteen-grand buy-in, and if he can just make it through this game, and maybe the next, he'll make his way deeper into the building, to the tables with the deep pockets, and eventually to Johnny Boy's table, where he'll try to buy his freedom.

"You in the army?"

Vince looks up at an old guy with sunken cheeks. "I'm sorry?"

"Your hair. You don't see it short like that anymore."

Vince keeps forgetting about his crew cut. "No. I'm not in the army."

"I was at Normandy myself, Omaha Beach," the old guy confides. "Lost half my platoon in an hour." No one looks up; they've heard this. "Bullets weren't half as bad as the seasickness. It was almost a relief when we landed." The other players ignore the man. "I'll never forget. I watched one guy sink right to the bottom with his pack. Didn't get off a shot. Just jumped out of the boat and sank. Drowned under all that weight."

Vince looks down at his cards. He gets a pair of nines and calls a bluff so transparent it wouldn't win a twenty-dollar pot at the Pit, let alone these stakes. Vince draws a third nine. And for a moment, the idea of squaring with Johnny Boy is less important than the way the cards are falling. The next hand he pulls jack-five off suit, and while he'd normally sit this one out, he doesn't have enough time to play smart and he decides this is as good a time as any to buy a pot. It's a scientific fact: the higher the stakes (and these are about as high as Vince has ever played) the easier it is to bluff, to buy one. It works. The other players fold—lucky because he gets no help. Four folds later, he goes after another pot. Now the other players take notice. They eye him; watch his hands and his face. Two players stay in. The flop: ace, queen, four. Dealer turns a nine and, on the river, a four. Guy across turns his cards: ace-nine. Someone whistles. Vince rolls his cards. Pair of queens. He rakes in another nickel. Two players leave the table, broke after less than an hour. One of them is the old guy from Omaha Beach. He looks at Vince, who can't think of a thing to say. In his mind he sees the old man as a soldier, loaded down, sinking in the black water. "Good playing with you," Vince says. His chips are heaped, not stacked, his original two grand now six. The real players are settling in.

"So when you say you make donuts, do you mean—"

Vince looks over at a guy on his left. "I'm sorry?"

"Donuts." The guy has a rubbery face—deep-set eyes and thick lips, heavy outer-borough accent. "You talkin' maple bars and stuff? Bismarcks?"

"Yeah. Maple bars. Bismarcks. Éclairs. Cake donuts. Everything."

Rubber Face laughs. "See, I thought maybe it was one of them euphemisms. You know . . . make donuts."

The rest of the guys at the table join him in laughter, but one of the players says, seriously, "You make them jellies?"

"Yeah. We make jellies."

The guy smiles. "That sounds good right now. Don't it, Ken? Don't that sound good? A fuckin' jelly donut?"

Across the table, a black-haired boy with ferret eyes shrugs and points to his silk shirt. "I ain't eatin' a fuckin' jelly donut in this shirt. Damn you, Tommy. Grow up. That ain't no donut for an adult."

Vince considers the remaining guys at this table—drivers and second-story guys, talkers, five-to-teners, no talent that he can see; doubtful anyone here is made—and in a moment of the old bluster, he can't imagine any reason why he shouldn't take every cent off these assholes. He bends the corners of his two cards. Pair of tens. Look at that. He expected a lot of things tonight: that he'd be turned away from the poker game; that he'd get in the game but wouldn't find Johnny Boy; that he'd find him, but Johnny Boy would immediately have him hauled away and shot. The last thing that he expected was luck.

With a lead, Vince is ruthless. He bullies and ignores bluffs and his chips rise, tilt, and finally fall against one another like Roman columns. He alternates buying pots and nursing the other players along during his better hands. It is one those rare evenings when the cards themselves barely matter; it could all be in his head. He could play without cards and win half these hands. The other players do exactly what he wants them to do.

When there are three left he goes in: spies his cards (queen-nine) when they come and then lets them sit. Bets light. Lets them raise. Then doubles their raises. They glower, look at their cards, look at Vince, look at their cards, look at Vince's cards (face down, he will not look at them again, and they will wonder, Did he ever look?), look at their cards, look at Vince, and finally call. The flop comes; queen, jack, nine.

Look at that. They can't quit now, not with straights up, and the third player—a quiet guy with jet black hair—is all in. Vince just keeps doubling their bumps until Ken is all in, too. The turn and the river: a six and another queen. Pot's right.

Ken turns a queen-high straight. Jet Black has an ace flush. Great hands. One-in-eighty hands. But Vince has the full boat, queens over nines, and the pot. It's been a long time since he's played in a high-stakes game, let alone won. With a two-grand buy-in and eight other players, Vince has won sixteen thousand dollars in a little more than two hours. Even after paying off Coletti, the vig, and Pete's two-K buy-in, he's up to eighteen. Now all he needs is Johnny.

Vince sits back and finishes his whiskey. The guy with the jet-black hair lights a cigarette and leans back in his chair. "So, you're in donuts."

"That's right," Vince says.

Waves his cigarette over the table. "You play a pretty fuckin' good game of cards for a guy makes donuts for a living."

"Who said I did it for a living?"

The guys laugh.

"You a cardsharp? That what you do?"

"No," Vince says. "I just got lucky. Anyone can get lucky."

"No," Jet Black says. "No. They can't. Anyone can't get lucky. That's the thing about luck. It discriminates like a motherfucker."

Vince just smiles.

Jet Black sticks his hand out. "I'm Carmine. This is my game that you just won."

"Vince." They shake.

"It's early yet. You wanna play a little more, Vince?"

"You saying there's another game, Carmine?"

"Vince . . ." Carmine takes a pull of his cigarette. "There's always another game."

\*   \*   \*

GHOSTS EVERYWHERE. GHOULS, too. Skeletons. Cowboys and princesses and frogs and hobos and costumes that Dupree can't quite make out, weird combinations of masks and capes and fake whiskers. Yoda and Darth Vader each grip a pillowcase. Detective Charles drives slowly down the street, packs of kids drifting in and out of his headlights. They troll a long, straight line of neat, two-story row houses, American flags jutting from half the stoops. "I forgot what day this is," Dupree says. He finds it comforting that they have Halloween even in this upside-down place, where the cops drive around like drunken lunatics, stealing drugs and taking blow jobs. Other than the houses being right next to one another—not a yard in sight—Alan thinks he could be in Spokane; it returns his bearings a little.

Charles parks in front of a small brick building with a plywood sign reading LOCAL 4412. Above the door is another sign, for Jimmy Carter, and in the windows signs for a Newark City Council candidate named James Ray Burke. Charles climbs out of the car. "I'll be right back."

Dupree opens his mouth to protest, but Charles slams the door shut. He walks to the front of the building, tries the door, but it being Saturday, the door is locked. He walks around to the back, and after a moment Dupree hears a window smash. A few minutes later the Burke signs are yanked out of the windows. Charles comes out the front door, smiling, with the two Burke signs and a phone caddie open to a tabbed page. At the car he throws the signs in the backseat and puts the phone caddie in his lap, the tab slid open to the name Daryl Greene.

Dupree doesn't say anything, just stares out the window.

Charles drives along the mowed curbs, reading addresses until he pulls up to a white house with red trim. He turns off the car, looks once more at the phone caddie, then tosses it in the backseat. He turns to Dupree. "Look. I know this ain't exactly what you signed up for. I'm sorry if this seems"—he can't find the word—"bad. But there's more to it than you know. This is a very important investigation." When Dupree doesn't say anything he continues. "Anyway, I'm gonna take care of this little thing that Mike put me on and we'll go find your guy. What's his name?"

"Vince."

"Right. Vince." Detective Charles steps out of the car, then reaches back in and gets his jacket off of the backseat. He also grabs one of the Burke signs and a box of swag tennis shoes. At the curb he looks back once more at Dupree, smiles, then reaches in and—Alan is pretty sure of this—unbuckles the chest holster inside his jacket.

The name D Greene is painted on the mailbox. Two little pirates are on D Greene's porch, having settled on the treat option. An old Scottish terrier sniffs them, then limps back and lies down on a blanket on the porch, emits a big dog sigh. A tall, slender black man leans out the front door, holds the screen with his shoulder, and drops small candy bars into their bags.

Charles looks like a conscientious parent standing in a rock garden just off the porch while the boys get their candy. He looks back at Dupree once. Grins. Something about the trick-or-treating kids sets Alan's mind; he won't let this happen. He'll go along and he won't say anything, but he's not going to let anyone get hurt. This is where he draws the line. Dupree pulls his gun out, holds it between his knees, and turns off the safety without looking down. This is not about the kind of cop he is. This is about what kind of person he is. Tells himself: If Charles goes for his coat, he will get out of the car. Steels himself.

The pirates leave D Greene's porch. Charles rolls up the Burke sign and holds it like a sword, but the boys simply edge past him and he straightens his jacket and walks up the porch steps.

Dupree puts the gun in his left hand, puts his right on the car-door handle.

Charles knocks on D Greene's door, then steps over and pets the dog. The thin black man answers again, and looks down for trick-or-treaters. Charles straightens up from petting the old terrier and walks over, maybe a foot away. D Greene cracks the screen door and listens. Dupree tenses. He's never fired his weapon outside the range. He'll think of this as the range. Put a round paper target right on Charles's back. Squeeze.

It's like watching TV without sound. Charles gestures with the Burke sign and the shoebox. D Greene listens. Charles hands him the Burke sign. He tilts his head left, then right, as if offering two options. He throws his head back and laughs. D Greene doesn't laugh. Charles sweeps his hand around the neighborhood and says something.

D Greene points a shaky finger in Charles's face. Charles shrugs, as if saying: *Hey, slow down. No one is threatening anyone here.* Then he laughs and waves the shoebox in D Greene's face. He puts his arms out to the side, pleading innocence. Then he steps closer and opens the shoebox. D Greene doesn't look inside the box. He says a few words, rubs his temples, backs into the house, nods a few times, closes the door, and turns out the porch light.

Dupree relaxes, lets go of the door handle, and slides his gun back into his jacket. His breathing still feels loud and forced when Charles walks to the car cheerily, opens the back door, and tosses the shoebox in. "Nice guy," he says. "But it turns out he's a size twelve. Guess it's true what they say."

He laughs at his own joke and grabs another shoebox, closes the back car door, and saunters toward the house. He pauses in the rock garden, grabs a rock the size of a softball, and continues up the steps to the porch. He sets the shoebox against the screen door, then walks over to the terrier's blanket, and before Dupree can even form a thought, Charles pins the dog with his foot and swings the big rock into the dog's head. He swings the rock again. And again. The dog doesn't make a sound.

"Ah Jesus," Dupree mutters.

Detective Charles carries the bloody rock to the shoebox,

which he opens with his foot, and drops the rock in. When he gets back to his car, he looks relaxed for the first time since he picked Dupree up. "Always pick *treat*," Charles says. He takes a drink of the whiskey and offers it to Dupree.

"Okay, Seattle. Let's go do *your* thing."

ABOUT JOHNNY BOY: he is just like Benny's client described him—black dress shirt stretched over a barrel, with thick, muscled arms, a big gold chain on one wrist, Rolex on the other. Slick. Good-looking guy, for the type—and he is the type. His hair is threatened back, graying at the sideburns and receding on either side of his head, a thick round tuft of black in the center. His smirk could kick the ass of Vince's smirk.

Vince sits at the open spot—right across from Johnny Boy. He gets ten thousand (more than half his money) in chips—the buy-in for round two of this game. They are in the dining room of an empty apartment, around an oval table, nine guys with varying stacks of chips and full highball glasses. Forests of white stumps smolder in the ashtrays. The guy to Johnny's left holds up a glass and a bottle of Crown Royal. Vince nods, even though he doesn't like to drink when he's winning. In the living room next door, a handful of guys sit and quietly watch TV.

The guy to Johnny's right is fat and friendly, wearing matching tan shirt and tan pants; it's like a jumpsuit, the shirt tucked in at the widest part of the pants. His waistband looks like the equator. "Carmine says you cleaned his table out in two hours. Won every cent. That right?"

Vince shrugs. "I did okay."

"You come here to give us that money?"

Vince smiles. "We'll see."

"I'm Ange."

"Vince."

Ange goes around the table, pointing. "Toddo. Jerry. Huck. Nino. Beans. And you met Carmine."

He doesn't introduce Johnny Boy, who goes last. "John."

"So what's your business, Vince?" asks Ange.

"He makes donuts," Carmine says.

A few guys laugh. A kid comes to the table, whispers in Johnny Boy's ear for almost a minute. He takes in a great deal of information, then turns and gives the kid a one-word reply.

"We're in plumbing," Johnny says when the kid is gone.

No laughter this time.

The stakes are higher here, and the play is better; Vince loses four bills on a suited ace-king. At this table, there is no talk of work or parole or balls being busted. They talk about sports betting, how much they lost on this game or how that lousy spread was. If you didn't know better, you might think this was a roomful of profane football coaches. They like the Packers with points against Pittsburgh ("My dick is smarter than Terry Bradshaw"), Tampa over the hapless Giants ("Fuckin' Giants couldn't score in Times Square"), and the Jets plus nine at New England ("My dick throws a better spiral than Steve Grogan").

Cards go out. Vince pulls an unsuited ace-ten. Opens.

Vince has to admit: it's kind of nice, being back around guys like this. Gives him a charge. The thing that people don't realize about crooks is that they can be pretty funny—except of course when they're not. More football. Seems everyone at the table got killed on the day's college games: UCLA's loss to Arizona State and, especially, Mississippi State's upset of number-one-ranked Alabama.

"Fuckers gave fourteen points and they go out and lose six–three. No fuckin' way that happens, give fourteen and only score three. I don't buy it. It's fishy."

The flop. Vince gets a second ace. Bets big.

"Only an idiot gives fourteen points," Johnny Boy says.

"I'm just sayin', it ain't out of the question that somebody got to that fuckin' quarterback," says Carmine.

"Oh bullshit."

"I'm just sayin' it ain't out of the question."

"No. No." Johnny Boy drains his drink and turns on the guy. "It is totally out of the question. It is completely out of the fucking question. It is fifty fuckin' miles out of the question."

"Look, John. All I'm sayin'—"

"All you're saying is that you're totally ignorant, Carmine. Who is gonna do this thing you're proposing—the fuckin' CIA?"

Carmine's voice is losing steam. "I'm just sayin' it's possible."

"No. No. It ain't *possible*. Do you think Bear Bryant is gonna let some kid piss away a national championship? Has Alabama ever thrown enough forward passes for a quarterback to lose a game? What the fuck's the matter with you?"

Turn. River. No more help for Vince. He has a pair of aces. Hopefully it's enough. Bets large. Ange and Johnny Boy stay with him.

"I'm just sayin' it's possible, that's all. You can fix anything."

"You stupid motherfucker." Johnny Boy is pissed. Waves his drink and it's immediately refilled. "You could've dropped this, but you're too fuckin' stupid. Okay. You wanna know why it ain't possible? You want me to tell you?"

"Yeah."

"Because I didn't know about it."

"Because you didn't know about it?"

Johnny drains another drink and it's refilled again. "That's right."

Everyone at the table is laughing except Vince, who is concentrating on the twelve hundred bucks in the center of the poker table.

Pot's right. Vince shows aces.

Carmine is intent on pushing this. "So you're saying that if you don't know about something happening, then . . . then it didn't happen?"

"Now you're getting it." Johnny flips his cards: two eights. With the common cards he's got three of a kind. Winner.

"So if some guy in China invents a flying car but you never hear about it—"

"Did not fucking happen."

"What do you think, Johnny, you're God or somethin'?" Carmine asks.

"No." He sweeps in the chips. "Not yet."

**THE FIRST THING** Dupree notices about Tina DeVries McGrath is that she is curvy for a short girl, with wild, reddish brown hair and unimpressed, show-me-something eyes that make Dupree want to talk faster than he probably needs to. She wears a long nightshirt and stands in the doorway holding the screen open at the same short angle that D Greene held the door for Detective Charles.

"I told you. I don't know anybody named Vince Camden. Now, if you don't mind. It's late and my husband has to work tomorrow."

Dupree hands over the letter in his hands. "Did you write this?"

She looks at the letter and Dupree sees a shudder in her lower lip. She covers her mouth and pretends to cough. "I don't know what you're talking about."

"Do you know why the name was cut off the envelope?"

She looks at Dupree, then down at the letter in her hand. "I'm sorry. I don't know anything about it."

"You didn't write this letter?"

She stares.

Dupree takes the letter back. "At least tell me if you've had contact with him."

Nothing.

"Look, I can talk to a prosecutor and compel you to cooperate, Mrs. McGrath."

She considers this like a chess player staring at a midgame move. "I told you. I don't know what you're talking about."

Vince looks back at Detective Charles in the car. He wanted to come to the door and help Dupree, but Alan was afraid of the kind of help that Charles would give; he wonders if there's some language here that he doesn't speak, some trick to getting New Yorkers to talk. Maybe she has a dog he can kill.

Behind Tina, a broad-shouldered man in Jockey shorts and short curly hair comes down a hall and into the small living room. "Tina? Who's at the door?"

She says over her shoulder, "It's nothing, Jerry. I'll take care of it."

Dupree remembers the date on the letter—a little more than a year ago—and sees his opening. . . ."Why don't I talk to your husband about this letter. Maybe he knows something—"

Her head snaps forward. "No. Please."

Jerry McGrath is at the front door. "Who is it, baby?"

Dupree looks at Tina, who opens her mouth but clearly doesn't know what to say. So Alan offers his badge and guesses right that Jerry won't realize it's not an NYPD shield. "Hi, Mr. McGrath. We're looking for a robbery suspect we thought might be in your neighborhood. Have you seen anything out of the ordinary tonight?"

"I haven't," he says.

Tina smiles and pats her husband's chest. "I'll take care of this, Jerry. You go on back to bed. It's late."

He smiles, a sweet-looking guy. "Thanks, baby." He looks down and maybe realizes for the first time that he's in his underwear. He shrugs. "I work at four."

"It's fine," Dupree says. "I'm sorry to disturb you this late."

Jerry trudges back to the bedroom and Tina steps out on the porch, closes the door behind her. She takes the letter and reads the envelope. "Look, I don't know any Vince Camden. I wrote this to my old boyfriend. Marty Hagen. But I haven't seen him in three years." She turns the letter over in her hands. "He didn't answer it."

Dupree writes the name Marty Hagen on his notebook. "About six feet tall? Brown hair? Has kind of has a . . ." Dupree tries to replicate Vince Camden's smirk.

"Yeah, that's Marty."

"And you never heard him use the name Vince Camden?"

She shakes her head.

Dupree writes this in his notebook. "Does he have any friends or relatives here?"

"His parents are dead. He doesn't have brothers or sisters. I don't know about extended family. He never mentioned any." She looks back in the house to make sure her husband isn't listening. "You could try my brother. Benny. They were friends. Benny was his lawyer." She gives him Benny DeVries's phone number and address.

Dupree pulls out a business card and writes the name of his hotel on it—then looks over his shoulder at Detective Charles, staring at him from behind the wheel of his car. Almost midnight. "Look," Dupree says, "if you see Vince—I mean, Marty—if you hear from him, please call and leave a message for me at this hotel."

She nods, takes the card. "So what makes you think he's coming to see me?"

"He wrote your married name on a piece of paper the day he left. And this letter was on his nightstand."

She looks surprised, maybe flattered, and then pulls her features tight again. "What did he do?"

"He was stealing credit cards."

She rolls her eyes as if that information was obvious. "You came to New York for stolen credit cards?"

"We also think he may have information about a homicide."

"You don't think he—"

"Maybe. We don't know. Look, Mrs. McGrath, if you see him—"

She nods and looks down at the card.

"One more thing. Do you have any idea how he ended up in Spokane?"

She cocks her head. "What do you mean?"

"Why he moved from New York to Spokane?"

"Well . . . I assume you put him there."

"*We* put him there?" Dupree feels the last tinge of his jet lag.

"After he testified. I assume that's where you guys moved him."

And then everything makes sense—the lack of a record or a driver's license, the phony name, the letter with the name torn off. "Jesus. He's in witness protection?"

"Yeah. You didn't know that?"

Dupree laughs and rubs the bridge of his nose. A shadow. A ghost. "No," he says, "No, I didn't know that."

JOHNNY BOY THRUSTS a big index finger in Vince's face. It looks like a sausage with a manicure. From Vince's vantage it is centered between the big man's bleary eyes.

"One mistake," Johnny says. "One fuckin' mistake."

Vince doesn't breathe. This is my fault, he thinks. Some things you just don't bring up with drunk people.

It's late. There are only five players left at the table—Vince, Johnny, Carmine, Beans, and Ange. The money has moved around, mostly between Carmine and Ange. They're each up about thirty-five thousand. Beans is more or less even, playing with his original ten. Johnny lost his ten thousand an hour ago, but his face went crimson and his upper lip disappeared and the other guys quickly loaned him another stake and he promptly lost eight thousand of that. Johnny is stone drunk, down to his last two grand, and forgetting to look at his cards before he bets. Vince, meanwhile, has lost whatever luck he brought to the first table and only conservative play and a nicely timed flush have kept him from being wiped out. He's down to his last fifteen hundred.

He tries to ignore the meaty finger in his face, wishing he hadn't brought up the subject.

Johnny looks around the table. "How about you ignorant assholes? Any of you dickheads know what Jimmy Carter's mistake was?"

Carmine: "Not bombing the fuckin' Iranians the minute they took the hostages."

Johnny finally puts his finger down and Vince relaxes. "Nope."

"Letting those OPEC fuckers raise gas prices."

"Nope."

"Not having Billy whacked the minute he got elected."

They all laugh except Johnny, who shakes his head. "His one mistake was this." He looks around the table, and then satisfied, sits back in his chair. "He forgot not to be a pussy."

The guys howl, laugh, raise their glasses, and yell *salut.*

"I'm dead fuckin' serious. People will follow a drunk. Even a retard. They'll follow a stone criminal. Psychopaths and lunatics and queer bullies. But if they think you ain't got balls—even for a second—you're fuckin' done."

"So you think Reagan's going to win?"

"Hell yes, Reagan's going to win. This is a whole new thing comin' here. It's gonna be fuckin' flags and parades and armies and virgins and 19-fuckin'-50 all over again. A pussy can get elected once, but not twice. We can't go eight years without kicking a little ass. We like to kick ass. We pretend we don't. But we do." He waves around the table. "The people out there . . .

they're no different than us. It's no different than when we got stuck with Big Paul as boss instead of Neil. I wish we could have Reagan run our shop."

The guys at the table look around nervously.

"You watch. We'll have our own Reagan one day . . . rise up . . . a real boss, somebody with some fuckin' charisma, somebody people respect, come in and restore a little pride to the operation . . . glory. Kick the asses that ain't been kicked the last three years. Startin' with that fat fuck pussy Big Paul!"

Ange reaches over gently and puts a hand on Johnny's big forearm. "John. Come on. Don't talk about that here."

"I ain't sayin' nothin'." Johnny pulls his arm away, licks his thin lips. "I'm just sayin' . . . I'm just sayin' that's the one thing people won't forgive. If you can't be a man . . . fuck you. Get out of the way and let someone else be boss. That's all I'm sayin', Ange. That's all I'm sayin'."

The guys raise their glasses to punctuate and hopefully end this line of talk, but Johnny ignores them and keeps rambling. "It's like fuckin' Reagan! That guy could be our boss! I'd follow him. He knows! He knows to be a man and people follow. He knows you gotta earn for your friends and you gotta be a man and gotta protect your family. You gotta stand up, no matter what. You know why? Huh?" He looks around the table, then waves at the wall. "Because the people . . . out there . . . they're all different, the spics and fags and Upper East Side dickheads and little old Chinese ladies ... but they all got one thing in common. All of 'em." John finishes his drink.

"They're afraid. Scared to death. That's all they want in a boss. You know? Someone who ain't scared. That's all. Like when you were a kid, the way you looked up to your old man." The guys make eye contact, grow quiet, as if they know what's coming, as if he's crossed this drunken threshold before. "That's all." Johnny's face reddens and his eyes bulge wet. "So when some *motherfucker* drives his fuckin' *car* into your fuckin' *kid!* And when he drives that fuckin' car around the neighborhood with no respect for the grief of a mother! And when that woman has to look at the dent where her fuckin' boy spent the last breath of his life! I don't care if you have to go to jail the rest of your life, you stand up and you do something!"

The guys mutter: "That's right, Johnny." "That's right." "It's okay, John."

Johnny falls back. "You fuckin' do something."

The guys shift in their chairs, desperate to change the subject.

"So . . ." Ange wants to say something but can't come up with anything.

It is Beans who steps in, to the relief of the others. "You think we'll ever elect an Italian president, John?"

He doesn't seem to hear. He stares at the poker table.

Beans continues, "I mean, if the Irish can get a guy in there, why can't we?"

Carmine looks at his cards and bets. "What about D'Amato? If he beats Javits and that bitch with the glasses, I could see him makin' president someday. That guy's fuckin' hilarious."

Johnny sighs and looks around; it's as if he's returned to their table older and disoriented. He sits back in his chair and closes one eye to see his cards. Strokes his hair. "D'Amato could never be president. He's goin' bald. That's the second thing people want. Hair. You can't be a pussy and you can't be bald. Who wants a bald pussy president?"

"What about Ford?" Carmine says. "He was bald and he was a pussy."

Johnny slaps him. "First off, he wasn't elected, you stupid fuckin' ignorant cockbite! He was fucking handpicked after that fucker Agnew got his dick in the wringer. And he played fucking football at Michigan. You think a pussy plays football at the University of fucking Michigan? He was a lineman, for fuck's sake! Jesus!" The other guys stare at their cards and hope to ride this out.

Vince forces himself to look down at his hand. A pair of tens. Okay. The storm seems to have passed. Now or never. He bets five hundred. Ange and Johnny—still sulking—call. The others fold. On the flop Vince gets another ten. Bets his last five hundred. They call him all in. He gets no help with the turn or with the river. Ends with three tens. It's a good hand. Johnny's got nothing. But Ange has three queens.

"Sorry, Donuts." Ange rakes his money in. Vince stares at the chips being raked into Ange's pile. He looks over at Johnny, who is also watching those chips. Vince can't believe it. He lost. The money he was going to use to pay off his debt. Just like that. He's still got about six grand in his bag, but it won't be enough. Not even close. It's over.

Johnny stands up and lurches against the table. "I gotta piss." A fibrous strand of spit connects his lips. Vince just sits there, staring at his cards.

So that's it. You have to run. What about Canada? Sure. Open a restaurant, maybe the picnic-basket place in Canada. What's the French name for picnic?

Vince backs away from the table, thanks the guys, and starts to leave. But he surprises himself and turns, follows Johnny Boy to the bathroom. He tries to look like he's just waiting for the head. Stands outside in the narrow hallway listening to the stream. What are you doing? Run! If you run now, you'll never stop running. Maybe this is as good a place as any to make a stand.

He can feel his heart in his ears. There is a small end table in this hallway with magazines stacked on top, *Reader's Digest* and *Saturday Evening Post.* Seems so odd to have these magazines here. He opens the *Reader's Digest* and turns to his favorite part, the Real Life Drama, amazing tales of escape and endurance. This one is about a guy whose car went over the bank into a river and the guy spent two days with the water up to his neck before he was found. Vince reads to the first quote. *"I knew I was going to die."* They always say that in Real Life Dramas. People always knew they were going to die.

Vince closes the magazine. This is the third time this week he's known he was going to die. But then . . . he's always known, hasn't he? People always know. What else is going to happen? And yet people always seem so surprised. Vince imagines that if he makes it out of this he'll write and submit a Real Life Drama to *Reader's Digest:* I played poker across from the very man who wanted to kill me. *And then I followed him to the bathroom. As I stood there looking at magazines . . . I knew I was going to die.*

Johnny is in there a long time. When the flow is finished he stays in the bathroom, clearing his throat. Then it sounds as if he's talking to himself. Vince has decided again that he should just forget it, walk away—*O, Canada!*—when the door opens and Johnny steps out, comes face-to-face with Vince.

He's a heel shorter than Vince, who is surprised at the man's thickness—sitting across from him, you don't get a real sense for his gravity, the density of those arms and that chest; it's as if he's about to burst. His eyes are half lidded and he seems exhausted. Vince has the sense that the guy making jokes at the poker table all night has been a character, a blustery act—and it strikes him that we all have to be alone sometime; we all look in the mirror and see whoever is really there. Even monsters go to bed.

His own voice is deafening in his head: Say "Excuse me," and edge into the bathroom. Canada! They got their own football league in Canada. *Just trying to get to the bathroom.* It's cold in Canada.

Johnny stares at him, expectant and then angry, and Vince has the strongest urge to ask: *How many dead people do* you *know?*

And you can't help wondering which the great man would count first—the boy hit by the car or the man who drove it. Which comes first: grief or revenge? Which face does he see when he goes to bed at night, when he wakes up disoriented and afraid? Which face haunts *his* sleep? But that's not what Vince has come to ask, and so he steels himself, does his best to hold this man's flat, cold eyes. And before he speaks, the last voice he hears is, ironically, Johnny's: *Stand up and do something.*

Vince takes a deep breath: "Mr. Gotti," he says, "I owe you some money." When Johnny doesn't react, Vince continues. "I'm the guy you sent the guy to kill."

New York, New York

1980 / November 1 / Saturday / 1:38 A.M.

# chapter 卌

Still no answer at Benny DeVries's apartment. Dupree hangs up the pay phone and walks back to Charles's car. He climbs in. "Nothing," Dupree says. "Look, you can go home. No sense both of us sitting out here."

Charles, chewing on a toothpick and staring into space, shakes his head. "I'm good." They are parked outside Benny's apartment, which seems nice to Dupree, but which Charles claims is in a dicey neighborhood. The lawyer hasn't been home all night. Dupree knows it would be too much to assume he's with Vince Camden/Marty Hagen, but it's worth waiting just in case. He's tried a couple of times to get Charles to go home, but Charles always waves him off and says he doesn't want to get in trouble when Dupree gets himself killed.

Still, Dupree is relieved to see the big cop sobering up, glad to see him coming down from whatever he was on when he picked Dupree up at the airport—frantic and edgy, with those wet, flat eyes. Now he's staring, unblinking, out the window. "I never minded stakeouts," Charles says. "It's nice. Quiet."

The streets are slick with the steam rising up from the sewer.

There is a surprising amount of traffic. Cabs tear past; couples stagger down sidewalks.

"First thing in the morning I'll get our file on Hagen for you," Charles says. "Weekends are tough, but I'll get it."

"Thanks." Dupree settles back into the seat of Charles's Crown Vic. This does feel okay, sitting in front of a suspect's apartment, waiting—it's as reorienting as the trick-or-treaters. He even finds himself thinking of Charles with the kind of concern he'd get for any partner. "So you're in some trouble."

Charles looks over, and then at the front window again. "Yeah." He rolls his thick neck. "Not that it matters, but what Mike and I were talking about . . . didn't happen like that. I didn't force that girl to do anything. We were laughing, joking. She wanted to come back to my car. It was her idea. She was all over me, practically begged me. I swear on my mother's eyes I was giving that girl a break. Keeping her out of jail. It's a goddamned blow job. Who gets hurt?"

Dupree looks out the window, at Benny DeVries's building.

"Let me show you something." Charles opens his wallet and pulls out a piece of paper with a number on it. "Look. I even got her number. I thought she liked me. I was gonna fuckin' call her. I thought we hit it off." Charles shrugs dismissively at his own explanation. "Turned out it was a phony number." Even so, Dupree notices that he puts the number back in his wallet.

They both stare out the window. Quiet. After a moment, a cab pulls up to DeVries's building. Two men step out. One of them has curly blond hair; the other is older, thicker, a big guy with gray hair and a stolid, heavy-browed look that even Dupree recognizes: the guy is mobbed up. They stand in front of the building, talking and glancing around. The cab waits.

"Curly Hair." Charles sits up in his seat. "Is that your guy?"

"That's not Camden, no. Might be Benny."

"'Cause I know the other guy. Pete Giardano. He's a shy, does

some book." Charles seems genuinely intrigued by this development, and Dupree wonders how long it's been since Charles did
real police work. The two men are on the street, only a few feet
apart, talking and nodding. Finally, they shake hands and Pete Giardano climbs back into the cab. The curly-haired guy leans down
and says something into the back window, then watches the cab
drive off. As soon as Dupree sees that the guy is walking toward the
building, he opens his car door and calls out: "Benny?"

Benny DeVries turns, first curious about who is calling his
name, then alarmed. He pretends to wave as he moves quickly toward the door of his building.

Dupree angles across the street, holding up his badge. "Slow
down, Benny. I'm a cop. I just have a couple of questions."

DeVries looks unsure, but he waits as Dupree steps onto the
curb and shows his badge. "I'm Alan Dupree. From Spokane,
Washington. I'm looking for a friend of yours. Vi—" He catches
himself. "Marty Hagen."

"Marty?" DeVries smiles. "God, I haven't seen Marty Hagen
in . . ." He blows air out his mouth and looks up in the sky. "Jesus,
I don't remember exactly when. He's not in any trouble, is he?"

"Maybe," Dupree says. "I understand you represented him?"

"Yeah. Theft. A couple counts of fraud."

"He went into witness protection a few years ago?"

"Yeah. Marty got in trouble, owed some money to some people."

Dupree hopes he remembered the name right. "To Pete Giardano?"

DeVries laughs and looks in the direction the cab just went.
"Pete? No. I'm Pete's lawyer. We were having a meeting that
turned into a bunch of drinks." He laughs. "Look, I don't know
what happened to Marty after the feds took him away. He disappeared. You know they don't even let those guys talk to their
lawyers?"

"I didn't know that," Dupree says.

"Yeah. They're just . . . gone." He shrugs. "Look, if there's nothing else . . . I'm exhausted."

"I talked to your sister." Dupree sees the first bit of worry on the attorney's face.

"Has she heard from him?"

"No," Dupree says.

Benny is relieved.

"So what can you tell me about his case?"

"Not a lot," Benny says.

"Maybe you can just tell me what I'll find in the file Monday morning. Who he testified against." Dupree smiles. "Where the bodies are buried."

"There aren't any bodies. Nothing like that. Marty got busted on a credit-card scam. That's all. He had to borrow some money from a made guy up in Queens to get out and the guy's family wanted a bigger taste of the business. He took some risks trying to pay them off, got busted again, and it just got worse from there."

"He couldn't repay the loan?" Dupree asks.

Benny nods. "And the fellas were afraid he'd talk. The FBI heard some guys say they were gonna make him dead for it. So we took the deal—put him in witness protection if he'd testify. Old story. Happens all the time."

"They put him in witness protection over a credit-card scam?"

"They were targeting this crew, hoping to get the guy above him to turn. And the guy above *him*. You know. Like dominoes," Benny says. "It all fizzled out, ended with some plea bargains."

"And he had no history of violence?"

"Marty? No. Marty's a thief. He's not a violent guy. Marty is —" Benny looks up at the streetlights smearing the night sky "—funny. He's a bright guy. If he'd been born in some other neighborhood, with money, and opportunities . . . I don't know . . ."

"So, if he came back to New York, where would he go?"

Benny stares off. "Marty? I don't think he'd come back. But if he did, he could be anywhere—wandering around staring at the buildings, hanging out in bookstores . . . sitting on a pier with his feet in the water. Hell if I know."

"He have any other friends?"

"I'm the only one. No others I know of."

"Girlfriends?"

"Only one I knew was my sister."

They talk for a minute more and then Dupree thanks Benny DeVries and exacts the same worthless promise he got from Benny's sister: "If you hear from Vince, you'll call me, right?"

"Sure," Benny says, and takes the cop's card without looking at it. Dupree starts back for the car, trying to add this up. Almost two in the morning.

In the car, Charles is leaning on the wheel. "So?"

"He's seen him."

"He tell you that?"

"No." Dupree shrugs. "But he talked about him in present tense. Isn't that weird? If you hadn't seen someone in three years, would you talk about them in present tense?"

"Right, right," Charles says. He looks at DeVries's building, and then back. "What the fuck is present tense?"

**WHEN DOES THE** day turn? Clocks and calendars say midnight, but the man who lives his life by a clock is no better than a robot. Daylight? Letting the sun determine is only slightly less arbitrary. So what? Consciousness? Does the day begin when you rise out of bed into it? Is there a fixed moment when you pass from one to the other? Even awake, Vince has felt the turn from one day to the next; no rule says when it happens, you just know it when it does. If he had to peg it, he'd say closing—when the bars shut down. That's generally when the day ends for Vince. Two o'clock in Spokane, three here in New York. That's when Vince has most often felt himself moving from one day into the next, when the world changes and he feels delivered.

Vince sits at the poker table, beneath a low ceiling of cigar and cigarette smoke, highball glasses sticking to the felt table. Ange, Carmine, and Beans look up from their cards, enthralled, waiting to hear more. Johnny seems uninterested, although it was he who dragged Vince back to the table after hearing the whole story—showing no reaction as Vince explained his debt, the witness protection program, and barely escaping from Ray Sticks. Now he listens patiently, like a jury, as the guys pepper Vince with questions.

"So, then what?" Ange asks.

"Well. The marshals sit you down at a table. And you talk about the places where you've lived or worked or traveled. Anyplace you might have friends or family. They cross out those cities and states and the states bordering those states. Then they take the places that are left and they look for a city big enough for you to blend into, big enough to have a federal office but not so big that you'll fall in with whatever action might already be there."

Beans shakes his head. "So you don't get any say in it?"

"Not at first," Vince says. "At first, you just wake up in this town and everything is different. Not just the buildings and the people, but everything: the language, the smells . . . The sky in this town where I live now—it's huge. And it's closer than it is here. Right here." He reaches up, as if he could touch it. "Big and blue and white at the edges. No smoke or traffic. And trees! When you're driving through, you got no idea it's even a city because the houses are all built in the trees."

"No shit." Carmine leans forward on the table, smiling. "Like it's invisible?"

"Sort of. And the people are funny . . . they live in this perfect place, but it's all they know, so they all assume it's gotta be better somewhere else."

"I heard there's places in Montana where you catch fish out your front door." The guys all look at Beans.

"Well, there's a river running through Spokane. It's mostly filled with bottom-feeders. Suckers. Nobody bothers fishing in the river because it's fast and has waterfalls and rapids, and anyway, you can't throw a rock without hitting a lake up there. These cold mountain lakes are twenty, thirty miles long and so deep they still haven't found the bottom in some of them."

"No shit."

"The water comes from glaciers. There's one in British Columbia, couple hours north, where you can see the ice at the top of the lake. There are rivers to the south where you can catch a hundred-year-old sturgeon, twenty feet long."

The guys shake their heads.

"What about the women? There a lot of broads?"

"Not a lot, but the ones there are . . ." Vince begins to describe Kelly and is surprised that it's Beth who appears in his mind. "Nice," he says quietly.

Ange asks, "The government give you a lot of money?"

"At first you get a little. But they retrain you and expect you to go out and earn it yourself straight. So I took baking courses."

Beans, Ange, and Carmine nod intently. Johnny works his drink and stares at Vince, noncommittal and flat.

"I'd always wanted to open a restaurant," Vince says. "So I got this job making donuts and figured I'd try something on my own later."

"Italian place? They got good Italian out there?"

"No," Vince says. "Macaroni and ketchup joints. But I don't cook Italian anyway."

Ange shrugs. "I could give you some recipes."

Beans looks for room in his own overflowing ashtray for a butt, then flicks it into Carmine's. "What else could you do? Could you be . . . I don't know . . . a doctor?"

Vince shrugs. "I doubt you could be a doctor, but maybe. I mean . . . theoretically, I guess, you could be anything that any other person could be. You get to start over."

"Hey." Carmine lets out a sort of giggle. "You know what I'd be? Marine biologist. You ever see them guys swim alongside dolphins? That's what I'd be. I'd move to Hawaii and swim alongside them dolphins all day." He turns to Gotti. "They can communicate with each other, John." He makes sharp clicking sounds.

The other guys sip their drinks and seem to be imagining their new careers. Except John, who just stares. Not at Vince, just out into space.

"You get to pick your own name?" Ange asks.

"Sort of. They help you with that, too. They try to give you something you'll remember. Like with me, Vince was my dad's name."

"No shit." Ange turns to John. "That's nice, huh, John? He picked his fuckin' father's name. Ain't that nice?"

John drinks his whiskey.

"You know what I'd pick?" asks Beans—short and bald, with a long scar from his eye to his lip. "Reginald Worthington Edenfield, the Third."

"It's kind of overwhelming sometimes," Vince says. "You get to start from scratch. No record. No debts. It's like . . . being born." He reaches in his wallet and, in a moment of shared excitement, produces his voter registration card. "I just got this."

Ange looks at the card and passes it to Carmine, who turns it over as if it's written in French, then hands it to Beans, who passes it along to Johnny.

John turns it over in his hand, wads it up, and flicks it off the table. "Big deal," he says. "You and a hundred million other morons."

The guys are quiet.

"So," Vince says finally, "how did you find me?"

The other guys look over at Gotti, who shrugs. "What makes you think you were lost?"

Smoke. Quiet.

"Come on." Johnny Boy drains his whiskey and it's like his head is on a cracked swivel, lolling right and left and then back. "Deal the fuckin' cards."

Carmine deals to himself, Beans, Ange, and John. "And this is the first time you been back, Vince?"

"Yeah." Vince is glad they're calling him by that name, hopeful that they'll make the distinction between Vince the repentant baker and Marty the snitch. He watches the cards go out to the other players and wishes he were still in the game; he doesn't like watching the cards go around and past him. Doesn't like the symbolism of being *out*. "When I recognized Ray Sticks I knew I had to get out of town. I thought about running—even a few minutes ago, I thought about running. But I decided it was more important to face up to what I'd done. Pay my bills."

Beans shakes his head in wonder. "I been wondering where Sticks went. You had him on a job this whole time, boss?"

John looks up but doesn't answer.

Beans turns back to Vince. "Boy, you must've shit your pants."

"A little."

"Still, it takes balls to come back here," Ange says hopefully, glancing over at John, who doesn't seem to hear. "Don't it takes balls, John?"

Vince has the feeling that Ange is serving as his default attorney in this, arguing his case in front of John.

Vince looks from John to Ange and back. "Yesterday I went to see old Dom Coletti and made good with him."

Beans smiles. "No shit. Old Cold Blood? How's he doin'? I heard he had an attack or something. Moved into a little apartment in Bay Ridge."

"Yeah," Vince says. "A stroke. He doesn't look good. I paid him what I could and made arrangements to pick up the rest. So at least I'm square with him." He cuts a glance to Johnny, who doesn't reveal anything. "I was hoping I could do that with you, Mr. Gotti. I was hoping I could square my debt."

Johnny takes a drink of his whiskey and looks up at Vince with eyes that register nothing but their own opaqueness.

DETECTIVE CHARLES PULLS up to Dupree's hotel, puts the car in park, and turns the key off. He says he'll get Dupree the file on Marty Hagen in the morning and they can start going through the names. Charles yawns. "So, are you married, Seattle?"

Dupree spins the ring on his finger. "Yeah. Couple of years."

"Kids?"

"Not yet. My wife is getting her degree. After that we want to have a baby."

"Yeah? What's she gonna be?"

"A speech therapist."

"No shit." Charles lifts his head, eyelids heavy. "So she'll do . . . what . . . what is that?"

"Speech therapy—therapy for people who have speech problems."

"That makes sense."

Dupree reaches for his door handle. "So you can help me get Hagen's file tomorrow? 'Cause I don't want to screw with the marshals service. It might take weeks."

"Oh yeah, fuckin' feds. I'll get you the file."

"I'll take care of it from there. You don't need to waste your Sunday with me."

"Aw, we come this far. I wanna see it to the end."

"It's not necessary," Dupree says.

"I need the overtime."

"Put in for it. I'll tell your lieutenant you were with me all weekend."

"Nah, I'll save you a lot of time looking for the places you gotta go. And I might even know some of the guys, like Pete Giardano." Charles reaches up to turn the key. "Besides, I leave you alone and you get killed, it'll be my ass. So I'll pick you up about noon. Okay?"

"No," Dupree says, as firmly as he can. "Thank you."

"What?" Charles looks over at him. He laughs. "Are you fuckin' kidding me?" Then his face reddens and drains. "You don't want my help?"

"No."

Charles stares for a long time. Dupree wants to pull away, but he feels challenged, and he stares right back.

"You know what I love about guys like you?" Charles asks finally. "You think you know all about the world. You think the job is a certain thing and your life is a certain thing and you can just go along, fuck-all blind. Well, you know what? One day, ten years from now, you're gonna realize . . . it ain't about who's a nice fuckin' guy or who deserves trouble. It's about how there's us—" He back-hands the city. "And them.

"And one night, when you're walking down a dark shit-smellin' hallway with junkies all around and you hear the click of a forty-five next to your fuckin' ear, it'll all be clear to you and you'll realize that having those guys behind you is the only thing worthwhile in this world. That's why they put us in the same uniform, why they give us the same shield. Because that comes first, Seattle! We're brothers. Just like your real brothers. If your fuckin' brother needed help, if he was sick, what would you do?"

"Call my mom and ask why she didn't tell me I had a brother."

"Fuck you, Seattle," Charles says.

Dupree opens his mouth to say something, but decides not to press his luck. He steps onto the hotel sidewalk in front of a line of cabs, their drivers leaning back and sleeping. Dupree thinks hard about what the big cop said (*if your brother was sick*) as he watches the unmarked police car pull away from the curb. He looks back at the cabs.

* * *

**JOHNNY LOOKS UP** from his cards, as if he's decided something. "Lift your shirt."

Vince lifts his shirt to his neck and spins.

"Pants."

Vince waits a moment, then unbuckles his pants, and drops them to his ankles. The guys at the table make a point of not looking up—all except Johnny.

Satisfied that Vince isn't wired, Johnny asks: "So what will you do?"

Vince is fixing his clothes. "I'm sorry?"

"If . . ." He dips his chin forward and catches a belch just before it leaves his mouth. "If I cancel this contract, what will you do?"

"I don't know." Vince is amazed that he hasn't even thought that far, that he hasn't considered what would happen beyond this point. He can tell by the look on Johnny's face that the answer is important. As soon as Vince poses the question to himself, he knows the answer . . . and hopes it's the right one. "I guess I'd go back to Spokane. I'd mail you the rest of the money and . . . I'd just live."

John stares, so Vince continues.

"I rent a little house there. Got a job I like. And friends." Again, he finds himself thinking of Beth. "I wouldn't mind trying to make a go of it. You know, legitimate."

Johnny finishes his drink. He looks at his cards, then at Ange on his right. "What's the bet?"

"Five to you, John."

John looks down at his chips. He has exactly five hundred. He looks up at Vince again. His eyes are slits. His head moves in tiny figure eights. His tongue takes a full second to wet his lips. "How much money you got?"

"Well, I gave four to Coletti today and—"

John waves his hand. "How much fuckin' money you got?"

"On me? I have another six thousand, but it's all the money I have. Like I said, I've been saving to open a restaurant, but when I get back I figured—"

John holds his hand out.

"I was hoping I could pay you when—"

Gotti's hand remains out, bobbing like a boat on rough water.

Vince looks around the table, then reaches in his pocket, pulls out the thick roll, and drops it in Johnny's hand.

Johnny Boy drops it in the pot. "I see your five hundred, bump you . . . how much did you say?"

"Six thousand."

Carmine and Beans stare at each other, then at Ange.

"Call me!" John spits. "Call my fucking raise, Ange."

They just stare. Finally John leans across the table and grabs a handful of Ange's chips and throws them in the middle. "Call my fucking raise!" He reaches over to Beans and Carmine, too, rakes chips with his arms, until Vince's roll of cash is surrounded by mounds of chips.

"There!" John yells. "Pot's right!"

The guys don't know what else to do, so one by one they show their hands. Beans has queens. Carmine has a queen-high straight. Ange has two pair. They stare at Gotti, who looks past his cards at the twenty-five thousand in the center of the table. Then he looks up at Vince.

"Be on a fuckin' plane tomorrow," Johnny says.

Vince looks at the pot—where his money sits.

John looks at the money, too. "I don't care if you have to hijack the thing, be on a goddamned plane by noon."

"I will," Vince says.

"You got two weeks to send the rest of my money."

"Okay."

The other guys stare at John's cards, still curled in his big hands.

"And if you ever come back here, I'll do you myself, you rat fuck son of a bitch."

Vince nods.

They are all quiet for a moment, staring at John's cards—even Vince, who has been handed back his life.

Finally, Ange clears his throat. "Uh, John?"

The big man sighs and drops his cards on the table. A six and a two. He's got nothing. Not even a pair. The guys don't know what to do. John stands up and walks to the window, stares out. Vince takes the opportunity to back away from the table and edge toward the door. He looks back briefly and sees the guys at the table, still staring at the pot, and Gotti at the window, his round shoulders pulled in on his chest like an old man. Just as he closes the door behind him, Vince sees Johnny turn back toward the table, as if he's just gotten an idea—or had a change of heart.

DETECTIVE CHARLES DRIVES down Sixth, turns on B, and tools along the curb for a block. He sidles next to a hooker carrying her heels in her hand and she smiles, bends down, and jaws with him. "Hiya, Charlie. Buyin' or sellin'?"

"Neither." He offers her a drink from the bottle at his side. "You seen Mario?"

"He was down with the fellas earlier," she says, and points down the block. She straightens up and Charles drives away, goes two more blocks, and parks in front of an old apartment building, soot brown with a rusty exoskeleton of fire escapes. He takes a long drink from the whiskey bottle, screws the cap, and climbs out of his car. He reaches in the backseat and pulls out two shoeboxes. Two Dominican men are sitting on the stoop, drinking from beer bottles. "Guys," Charles says, "how'd you make out tonight?"

The men say they did okay and one of them soul-shakes Charles's hand.

"Seen Mario?"

The guy jerks his head toward the building. "He upstairs wif' some patch he pick up downtown. You want me drag his ass down here, Charlie?"

"Yeah," Charlie says. "But don't tell him it's me. Tell him there's someone down here wants to buy weight from him." Charles hands each man a shoebox. They take out the shoes and smile at them. "Did I get your sizes right?"

"Yeah, you did good, Charlie." When one of the guys has his new shoes laced, he climbs off the stoop and starts upstairs. His feet glow in the new shoes. While he's gone, Charles walks back to his car, opens his trunk, and pulls out a tire iron. Closes the trunk.

The first Dominican comes down the stairs with another guy—smaller, with black-rimmed glasses and a ponytail. The little guy is smiling at first, until he sees Charles. He holds his hands out in front of him, then breaks out in a full run. But the big cop has the angle and is on him before he makes it five steps.

"I din't do nothin', Charlie! I promise I din't tell nobody nothin'!"

Charles doesn't listen, just holds him by the ponytail and swings the tire iron; it thuds against the smaller man's arms and head. His glasses go skidding across the sidewalk and clatter against a parking meter. "I told you not to fuck with me, Mario."

Mario pulls away and scrambles against the stoop of the apartment. One of the guys there kicks him back toward Charles. Mario feints left and darts right and Charles drops the wrench to chase him. He catches Mario around the legs and they crash into the brick building, their long shadows grappling alongside them between the spaced streetlights. It takes Charles only a second to overpower the smaller man.

"I promise, Charlie! I din't say shit to no one! Please, Charlie!"

Bent at the waist, Charles drags Mario by the hair back toward the stoop. He reaches behind himself to grab the tire iron where he dropped it. But it's not there. He feels around, then straightens up and looks over his shoulder to the guys on the stoop.

"What the fuck?" But the guys on the stoop are empty-handed, too, staring past the big cop.

Charles turns and punches Mario as hard as he can, in the side and the face. "Where is my fuckin' tire iron?" But Mario's hands are empty, covering his head, and he's sobbing, and it's not until Charles turns his head a few more degrees that he sees Dupree step out of the shadows with his tire iron.

"Dookie?"

"You can't do this."

"Do what? I'm questioning a fuckin' suspect here." He lets go of Mario, smiles, and suddenly lunges toward Dupree, getting a firm grip on Alan's shirt before the tire iron cracks against his skull.

Charles is knocked back a few feet and lets go of Dupree's shirt, but amazingly, the big cop doesn't fall. The men on the stoop scramble back into the building. Charles watches them, then turns to look over his shoulder at the open back door of a cab. "You tailed me in a fuckin' cab?" He laughs, then reaches up and feels the bolt rising above his temple. "Gimme the wrench." He takes a step toward Dupree, who hefts the tire iron again and steps back.

"Mario!" Dupree yells. The kid looks up at him. "You got relatives somewhere?"

Mario hesitates. Charles looks from Dupree to Mario and back. "Mario," Charles growls. "Don't you fuckin' move, Mario!"

"Mario!" Dupree yells again. "Go!" Finally Mario scrambles up, picks up his glasses, and sprints away. Dupree and Charles watch him go.

Charles smiles, even and cool. "What the fuck do you think you're doing?"

"You were right," Dupree says. "You do need my help."

Charles laughs at him, and rubs the lump on his head. "You just let a major drug dealer go, Seattle. You are so fucked." There's a slight rattle to his voice. "Now gimme that tire iron." He laughs again and Dupree is amazed at his tolerance for pain. "Come on. I'll drive you back." He rubs his head, turns to go back to his car, and . . . with speed that belies his size—reaches into his jacket and has the gun unholstered and aimed in the same amount of time it takes Dupree to step forward and swing the tire iron again, catching Charles flush in the mouth.

Teeth crack, blood mists, and Charles's face jerks to the right like it's been yanked by wires. The gun clatters to the sidewalk and Charles lurches down the block, fighting to keep his balance, his body just ahead of his pigeon toes. "Waith," he says, "waith." He sprays blood as he speaks. Amazed that the man could still be standing, Dupree admires him just a bit as Charles tries to get his feet under him, listing down the sidewalk, until he finally topples: face, chest, and arms all hitting the sidewalk in a heap like a fallen tree.

**VINCE'S FEET HIT** the sidewalk; he breathes deeply the damp air. So that's it. You're free. You can fly wherever you want, be anything. And yet . . . haven't you always been free to some extent? The question is whether you could do those things you had the freedom to do . . . the lake and the crows.

No, it's not over. Vince watches a produce truck back up to the basement door of a restaurant, the owner using his hands to indicate two feet, then one foot. It's as if the owner is signaling Vince— his proximity to danger.

The whole thing reminds Vince of the way he wakes up just before his alarm goes off—the knowing burst of anxiety he feels just before a hand lands on his shoulder. He turns around and sees the smiling round face of Ange, in his tan jumpsuit. "Hey, Donuts! Good news. John axed me to drive you to the airport."

"Drive me?" Vince asks. *Going for a ride?* "You . . . uh . . . you know what, Ange? That's really okay. I can make it."

"Aw, I have to insist." Ange sticks out his bottom lip. "John wants to make sure you get there safe. And he wants me to have a little talk with you. Okay?"

"Sure." Vince's mouth goes dry. Of course. They can't just let you go. You can't snitch and then go. The whole system breaks down if they just let some rat waltz in and apologize for breaking the only rule these assholes have.

Ange holds up a roll of bills. "John axed me to buy your airplane ticket, too. Since he took all your money."

"That's really not necessary," Vince says. "I can borrow the money."

Ange waves him off. "John insists. Look, he's really not a bad guy." Then he leans toward Vince. "But you do have to get out of town. Between you and me, Donuts, I don't think John likes having you around."

Vince nods. Of course John doesn't want him around. And yet Vince is somewhat glad that it's Ange; of all the guys at the poker game, he's the one Vince liked the best, the one who seemed to understand the appeal of getting to be someone else for a while, of getting to be Vince Camden. No, if someone is going to push the button . . . Ange will at least make it quick. Painless. And maybe Vince can even talk him out of it.

"Come on, Donuts. Let's go."

They walk to Ange's car, a red Dodge Diplomat. Vince could try to run, but even if he got away from Ange . . . if they could find him in Spokane, Washington, they could find him anywhere. His mind is racing, trying to think of a way out, when something else occurs to him. "You think we could make one stop first?"

Angelo considers. "The boss wants you gone."

"There's this girl . . . I'd like to see her once before. . ."

Ange looks back over his shoulder and then nods. "Yeah. Okay."

"And then it'll go quick—right, Ange?"

"Don't worry about it, Donuts. You'll be home in no time."

DUPREE SITS IN the hospital waiting room, eating a donut and drinking a cup of black water. He's staring at an empty nurses' station, when Mike, Charlie's union rep, edges down the hall, unsure what awaits him. Dupree stands up and forces a smile. "Hey, Mike!" he says, as if they've been friends for years. "Thanks for coming down. It'll mean a lot to Charlie."

The PBA rep—thin, gray hair, drawn face—comes on him expectantly, as if thinking, This had better be good. An announcement goes over the hospital PA for a doctor and Mike looks over his shoulder for just a moment.

"He's fine," Dupree says. "Don't worry. I guess they're gonna have to operate on his jaw, though. It's gonna be wired shut for a while. He's not gonna be able to talk. Which might not be such a bad thing, huh?"

"The nurse said he got jumped?" Mike says.

"He was helping me on my case. We were interviewing some people in—what is it, Alphabet City? And someone just stepped out of the shadows, jumped him, and hit him with a tire iron. Twice . . . I think."

"Someone . . ." Mike says.

"Yeah," says Dupree. "Someone."

They stare at each other for a long time, and then Dupree shrugs, smiles, and looks away. "I'm sorry I couldn't help him. I'm no good in situations like that."

"That right? You don't like to fight?"

"No. Not much." Dupree checks his watch. "Look, I gotta take off. But I thought it'd be a good idea to have someone with him when he comes out of surgery. He's gonna be pretty confused. Be good to have someone calm him down, tell him to lay low."

"Lay low?"

"Yeah." He looks carefully at Mike. "Tell him I appreciate his help. Tell him as far as I'm concerned, we're done."

Mike gives a quick nod; he can't promise anything, but he seems to understand the terms of the truce. "Look, I don't know how much you know about Charlie . . . what happened to him . . ."

"More than I want to know."

Mike shrugs. "He was a good cop . . ."

Dupree just stares.

Mike can see that it doesn't matter and he shrugs. "Okay. I'll see what I can do. You need anything else?"

"As a matter of fact . . ." Dupree pulls out a pad and writes down the name Martin Hagen. "He was supposed to get me a file on this guy. Can you help me with that?"

Mike says he'll try.

Dupree starts to leave, but Mike calls after him. "How long are you here?"

"As long as it takes to find this guy."

"Well," Mike says, "if I was you, I'd hurry."


IT'S LIKE A vision there in front of you—a memory you haven't actually had but could describe completely. Eight o'clock Saturday morning, cool and overcast, and right there, across the street, Tina comes out on her small porch to get the paper. Barefoot, wearing a short terry-cloth robe that stops right in the middle of her muscled thigh. Her dark hair pulled back into a ponytail. A glimpse of white silk inside the robe. Everything Vince once believed he could ever want in life is contained in this picture: a woman, a house, the morning paper. And for a moment he feels some bitterness about the smallness of his dreams—it's not as if he wants to be president, and yet he couldn't be further away from even this simple life, this thing that other people fall into without even trying, that other men rebel against, abandon on their way to bus depots and train stations and taverns. Vince stands across the street, against the hood of Ange's car. Inside the car, Ange is leaning on the wheel, pointing and smiling, and his thick lips mouth the words: *Is that her?*

She stands stock-still, reading the paper, flipping the pages, and he wants to go over, he really does, wants to stand next to her, to feel her breath on his chest, to feel the tiny blond hairs on her thigh, just below the robe's edge.

A car drives by between them and Vince is shaken from his thoughts. But Tina doesn't look up from the paper. Inside his car, Ange holds up his hands and raises his eyebrows. His thick face shows alarm and he mouths again, *Talk to her!* But before Vince can decide, Tina turns with the paper toward the house. She opens the screen door and steps back inside. The door closes behind her. And Vince stands there, across the street, leaning on the car.

Ange climbs out and leans on his doorframe. "Hey, wasn't that her, Donuts?"

"Yeah. It was her."

"Then what the fuck? You make me drive all the way out here and you ain't gonna talk to her? I thought you was gonna talk to her."

"I don't think I can," Vince says. "I don't know what to say."

Ange looks at the house and then back at Vince. "She's pretty."

"Thanks, Ange."

Vince considers the house—narrow and clapboard, just like the two houses wedged on either side, painted white and yellow, with window flower boxes and an American flag. It's just the kind of life Vince would've wanted to give her, and what she insisted she didn't need—at least when they were together, back when Vince was incapable of this kind of life.

Ange stays leaning on the car door. Scratches his black hair. "So you're telling me we drove all this way and you ain't even gonna fuckin' talk to her?"

"I guess I just wanted to see her."

"How long has it been?"

"Three years," Vince says.

"You never called her? Or wrote her a letter?"

"No."

"How come?"

Vince watches the windows, for any sign of her. "I promised her brother I'd leave her alone. He didn't want her to get hurt."

"Huh." Ange nods. "That's kind of . . . Jesus, that's sad."

Vince shrugs. He starts back for the car, opens his door, starts to climb in, and then stops. "Look. I know what's goin' on."

Ange's eyes narrow. "Yeah?"

Vince nods. "John would never just let me go, would he?"

"Donuts . . ." Ange shrugs. "Look, it's complicated. You gotta understand about John. He's got a lot of responsibility. There are rules. It's a whole system of precedents and ways of doing things. Everything has value. Everything costs. You can't just let someone walk away. Not without getting some"—Ange searches for the right words—"compensation. This thing is bigger than you or me. Or even John. This thing goes back generations. This thing is bigger than all the people involved. That's why it works."

"But we don't have to go along. You and I . . . we can just step outside of it."

Ange smiles. "What would I be, I step outside this life? I'm gonna make donuts? Come on." Shrugs his big round shoulders. "Get in the car."

Vince looks once more at the windows of Tina McGrath's house, but they're as cold and flat as Johnny Boy's eyes. He climbs in the car.

"Cheer up, Donuts. You done the right thing. From here on out, it's the easy part." Ange starts the car. "You ready?"

Vince leans back in his seat and closes his eyes.

*   *   *

**MARTIN HAGEN'S POLICE** file is thick but shockingly light: nine arrests, at least four convictions, but not one violent crime. No assaults or armed robberies—nothing more serious than theft and fraud. It's certainly not the file of a killer. Dupree jots down the name of Hagen's probation officer and a couple of addresses to check out, but there is precious little in this file of the person Martin Hagen that might lead Dupree to finding Vince Camden. Dupree reads about stolen credit cards and stolen cars and stolen property and stolen checkbooks, but there's something missing.

The last entry in the file is a brief investigator's report (. . . *based on his environment and his seeming lack of remorse, Hagen is a likely threat to re-offend . . .* ) prepared for the prosecutor in the case. Clipped to it is a four-page excerpt from an FBI wiretap in which two unidentified suspects were overheard saying they had to find someone to "take care" of that "Irish rat Hagen" and that he should "dig himself a hole" somewhere. The page is notarized and signed by two FBI agents.

Also written on the report is a phone number for the DA investigator who worked the case—a woman named Janet Kelly.

Even though it's Saturday, he calls, and apologizes when it turns out to be her home number. She's pissed, at first, to be called so early on a Saturday. She's no longer even with the DA's office. She quit a year ago to take a management job in the corrections department. Dupree apologizes again, this time for calling so early, and asks if she remembers the Martin Hagen case.

At first it doesn't register, but Dupree reads her report back to her. "Oh yeah," she says. "A credit-card guy. Charming son of a bitch, if I remember. He'd steal bank cards and buy TVs, washing machines, stereos—then sell the stuff to these two guys who worked for some old Mafia captain. He was into them for some money, so they were milking him a little. It looked like a big case at first, but it crapped out on us."

"How?" Dupree asks.

"He had this slick lawyer, went to law school with the deputy prosecutor on the case. Convinced the guy that this Hagen was sitting on a goddamn gold mine of information, that this credit-card case was just the goddamn tip of the iceberg."

"And?"

"More like the tip of an ice *cube*."

"Do you think he was holding back on you?"

"No," she says. "I honestly don't think he knew anything except his own credit-card deal. I don't think he was connected at all, just your garden-variety thief. But by the time we realized it, we'd already given the guy full immunity."

"And put him in witness protection for a credit-card scam?"

"Well, there was also the FBI wiretap. It looked like the guy was gonna get clipped if we didn't get him in the program."

Dupree pulls it from the file. "Yeah, I saw that report. But if you're right and the guy didn't know anything, why would there be a contract out on him?"

"You're asking the wrong person. You gotta talk to the FBI about that."

Dupree stares at the FBI report. Something is off. "You said you remember Marty Hagen. Do you remember what he looked like then?"

"Yeah, sure. Good-looking guy. Looked like trouble."

"Did he look Irish to you?"

"I don't know."

"Hagen's a German name."

"I don't see what——"

"On the wiretap, these guys say they're gonna take care of 'that *Irish* rat Hagen.'" Dupree holds the sheet close to his face and turns it sideways to look down the line of type.

On the other end of the phone, Janet Kelly laughs. "I don't

know what to tell you. These aren't the kind of guys to lose sleep over some guy's ethnicity. Now, if there's nothing else . . ."

Dupree just keeps staring at the page. "Yeah, no. That's it. I'm sorry." He hangs up the phone and stares at the file. He won't be able to talk to the FBI until Monday morning. Which means he's got two days to watch the door and wonder when Detective Charles is going to climb out of his hospital bed, walk to his car, and—

Dupree looks around his hotel room: notes spread on one of the beds, the other disheveled from a few hours of rough sleep. Suddenly he feels so small. Who is *he* to find this guy in New York, to figure out mob politics and the intricacies of New York law enforcement, to make an enemy like Donnie Charles? Amazing that a person could be so alone in a city of seven million people. He stands. There is barely space between the two beds for his legs; he has to turn sideways to wedge his way around the furniture in the room. He can hear sirens outside, and the first morning traffic. He opens his curtains and looks down Seventh Avenue toward Times Square. It's overcast. He watches the traffic, and wonders what the density and speed of a place like this does to the people over time, wonders if he'd be any different from Charles if he lived here; or maybe place doesn't have anything to do with it. Eighteen years Charles has been a cop. Maybe eighteen would do that to anyone. Dupree is struck for a moment with something like panic and he wishes he could write a letter to himself and mail it, to be opened in the year 1998. *Dear Alan, Be careful. Don't be a prick.* He picks up the phone and dials. The ring is harsh.

"Hello?" She sounds worried.

"Debbie."

"Hey there." Her relief washes over him.

"I'm sorry to be calling so early. It's just . . ."

"I'm glad you called. I miss you, too. When are you coming home?"

"I don't know. Monday maybe."

"How's New York? Is it beautiful?"

"Yeah," he says. He could touch all four walls of this hotel room without taking more than a couple of steps. "It's . . . something." He wishes he could just curl up next to her on the couch, on their couch, in that place he knows so well. Mostly, he wishes this case were over, and that he'd never seen Donnie Charles at the airport yesterday. He can picture the big detective—jaw wired shut—driving across the city, bottle by his side, his black eyes staring ahead.

"Maybe we could go there together someday, Alan? No work. Just do the tourist stuff. See the Empire State Building. Take a carriage ride in Central Park."

He leans back on the bed and closes his eyes. "Sure."

LAST THOUGHTS: THERE hasn't been a really funny television show since *Get Smart*; patty sausage is better than links; how long does the phone company keep sending bills after you're gone; the passing game is killing professional football; Italian food is vastly overrated; it would've been cool to own a dog.

Vince stares out the window, watching the buildings pass. He can't keep up with his own brain, and he tries to concentrate on the things he's seeing—to limit himself to visual stimuli. He wonders how long you get to carry memories—wonders if they go out with the lights. What about all these things you've seen: the sunrises and straight flushes. What happens to all of that when you're gone? Greedily, he wants a few more images . . . nothing profound, just some beauty to look at. He wishes he could ask Ange to drive south—most of his favorite buildings are in lower Manhattan: City Hall and the old Standard Oil Building, the marble and cast iron faces of Chambers Street—but they're heading north. Vince racks his brain to come up with the buildings he'd like to see north. The Met . . . The old Carnegie Mansion. The Ansonia and the Arthorp on Broadway.

Twice Vince puts his hand on the door to jump out in traffic, but both times he loses his nerve. They take the exit toward La-Guardia, and Vince wonders why Ange is keeping up the illusion that he's going to get on a plane. Maybe the airport is where Ange does this kind of business. Maybe Vince's corpse will be packed into a crate and shipped to Sicily.

There's a kid on a bike staring from an overpass and Vince makes eye contact with him and wants to cry for the flash of future he feels from that kid's eyes. He wishes he could just follow that kid and spend the rest of his life on a bike, zipping in and out of traffic, the freedom of it, closing your eyes and taking your hands off the handlebars . . . the only thing moving in a static world—a kid is invincible from the seat of his bike, or so he thinks. Invincibility: that's what Vince misses. He closes his eyes and can see the parked cars bleeding past, the people on their stoops, can almost feel the wind on his face and in his hair.

Jesus, it'd be nice if there were someplace to dump all those things that you've felt and seen, like taking the film out of a camera. That's why people write books and stories, no doubt, to leave some impression behind, to share a sense of the beauty and pain. This is what I saw! Or graffiti: I was here! Goddamn it, I was here! Why the fuck didn't you ever write anything down; why didn't you record your time here? How hard could that be?

And then, strangely, the car turns into the airport and Ange lays on the horn and serpentines through the cabs and pulls into the turn-around in front of ticketing—men hauling hard Samsonite to the curb, women smoking with one hand, carrying travel bags with the other, the taxis swarming like summer mosquitoes. Ange puts the car in park and turns to Vince. "Here we are, Donuts."

Vince doesn't know what to say. "You're . . . you're just gonna let me go home?"

Ange tilts his head. "Yeah. John told you that you could go home. Why? What'd you think we were doing?"

"I thought . . . but . . . you said it wasn't that easy."

"Yeah, John wants a favor from you. You didn't get that?"

"No," Vince says. "I thought you were going to—"

"Going to what?"

"You know . . ."

Ange grins. "You thought I—"

"Yeah." He frowns and mocks the big man's voice. *"This thing is bigger than us, Donuts."*

Ange stares at him and then explodes in laughter. His hands go to his big gut, and his dark eyes squeeze into slits. "You thought . . . Oh, Jesus! I never said I was gonna . . . I just said John had plans for you. That's all."

"Well, of course you didn't *say* you were gonna do that. Who tells someone they're going to shoot him?"

Ange can barely talk through the laughter. "That's fuckin' hilarious, Donuts. You thought I was going to—and you just sat there! Oh, fuck! You cool son of a bitch!"

Ange laughs so loudly that a couple walking by with matching suitcases stops and looks into the car. "I . . . I can't believe you just sat there, thinking I was going to—"

"Well, you could've been a little more explicit. What'd you say—I couldn't go without . . . compensation?"

Ange is crying. He hisses laughter, reaches over, and puts his hand on Vince's shoulder. "You thought . . . Oh Jesus . . . Jesus, Jesus, Jesus. That's fuckin' hilarious!"

Now Vince is laughing, too, and the two of them are doubled over, struggling to catch their breath, slapping the dashboard.

Finally, Ange wipes his eyes and shakes his head. "God, I like you, Donuts. I wish you could stay around. You'd really liven things up. And just so you know, if I was gonna do that, we always send two guys for that." He wrinkles his face as if he's eaten something sour. "It's really hard to do by yourself."

Vince wipes his own eyes with the back of his sleeve. "Then what's the favor? what's the . . . *compensation?*"

That word breaks Ange up again and he looks like he's going to have a heart attack, slaps at his chest and makes a gun with his finger, points it at Vince, who falls—head to his knees, crying with laughter.

"Oh-my-God," Ange says when he can talk again. He hums a last laugh and reaches into his pocket, produces a roll of bills, and presses them into Vince's hand. "Okay." Catches his breath. "Here's what John wants you to do: take this money, fly back to that little pissant town where the FBI apparently sends all the rats, buy a gun, and shoot that snitch Ray Sticks between his lyin' fuckin' eyes."

Chicago, Illinois / Columbus, Ohio

1980 / November 2 / Sunday / 4:13 A.M.

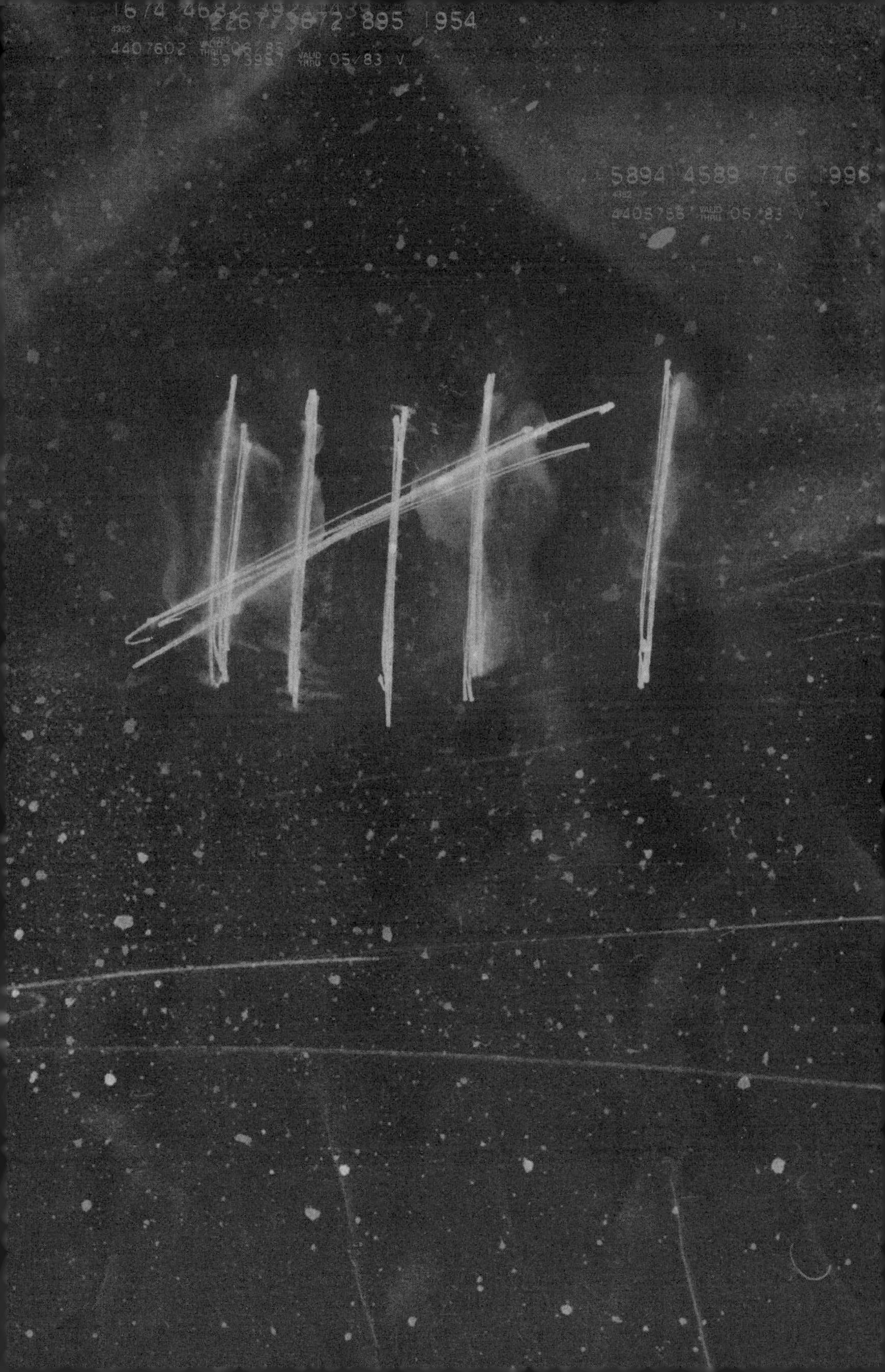

# chapter ~~||||~~ |

*He sneaks off to the bathroom to be alone, as he often does now, slips out of his shoes, and just stands in front of the mirror, staring at the strange, wan face that opposes him: sandy hair gone gray and an overall quality of melting—the '76 smile long since faded, eyes drifting at the corners. He turns on the hot water. Out there, the room will have dissolved into pacing and hushed voices . . . the meeting of worried eyes. He knows that when he leaves the room there is only one topic of discussion: how to handle him, how to direct him away from his flawed instincts. Their deference aside, he knows how they feel. Shoot, he feels the same way. Long ago, they convinced him that he was not tough enough, not decisive enough, too religious. Long ago, they convinced him that they couldn't afford his genial naïveté—this stubborn belief that if he does his best, the best will happen. Long ago, they convinced him that the opposite is in fact true. He is his own worst enemy.*

*Now he believes what they believe—that it is their job to protect him from himself. Their common enemy stares back in the mirror. Steam rises from the hot water. He sets down his briefing papers and puts his hands beneath the tap, holds them there as long as he possibly can, happy for any physical sensation that gets him out of his own head.*

*"Ow!" He shakes his red hands and waits to see if anyone heard. But it's quiet. It gives him a perverse thrill, to be so by himself like this. He is never by himself anymore. And yet he is always alone . . . and the more people in a room, the more alone he is. He runs his warm, wet hands over his face. Afterward . . . if it goes badly . . . what then? Golf? Go on TV? Go back home? What does a person do when this is over? When you've reached this place and been sent back down—wanting. He forgets sometimes that this is also about him . . . about his life, that there is a person at the core of this enterprise. Cad-dell will get a new batch of numbers and say, matter-of-factly, that they're still facing the basic problem: people simply don't like him. Not his administration or his policies; him. And the others in the room will nod and take notes, as if they're talking about a dish soap or a TV show, and he will try to do the same, but inside is a voice, weak-ened, but still: Wait! This is* me*! They don't like* me*! It's really an amazing thing—the polls show that they believe he is a better man than his opponent, that he is more intelligent, more compassionate, and less likely to lead them into a catastrophic war . . . and still they want the other guy.*

*He wonders sometimes, Who are these people? Who are these people who can believe that a man is good and smart and honest and charitable . . . and still not like him? What kind of a people are these? He still hears the pollster speaking directly at him for one of the few times:* Look, the problem is this: You remind them of their weaknesses.

*Sometimes, he feels as though he's sitting on the other side, with the men in the room, looking at the buffoon behind that desk like a puzzle that can be solved, like a product that can be sold better, and that's usually when he excuses himself to go to the bathroom . . . to look for his own face in the mirror, to see if he's still there.*

*He turns off the water and takes the briefing file off the counter. Opens it again, as if there might be something he's missed in State's report on the conditions for release: noninterference; return of the Shah's wealth; the unfreezing of assets; and the cancellation of lawsuits. And even then, the hostages will be released a few at a time, trickled out over months.*

*Three months ago, this would have been good news. Three months ago, just having a coherent adult negotiating on the other side would have been a tremendous development. But now, two days before the election . . . this is simply what it is. It is not progress and it is not news and it is nothing but what it is. Bad weather. For weeks, he has listened to coercive voices suggesting that Iran's war with Iraq is the only answer: trade arms for people. He resisted this, but now he sees why it kept coming back. It was his only chance of winning.*

*Instead, he clung to the genuine hope that an agreement could be reached, that the Iranian parliament would come back with reasonable conditions. And now . . . What's the quote Jody is always repeating, from a masked student on the embassy steps in those first days:* We have brought America to her knees.

*His knees.*

*Who are these people who believe he is to blame, who mistake bluster for bravery? What sane man would want to lead these people?*

*He looks at his watch. Too early to call Ros. Sunday. Chicago. Sunday in Chicago. He pictures his schedule—meeting with black ministers. This was to be a key day of campaigning, last big push, shoring up the base for the stretch. He was going to turn the tide today and he's been moving to this point for weeks: twenty hours a day, dawn on the East Coast, night on the West: rallying labor unions and teachers and ethnic ministers.*

*They don't like him.*

*Sunday. Chicago. Sometimes at home, when he couldn't sleep on Sunday mornings, he'd rise early, careful not to disrupt Ros, reach to the nightstand for his Bible, and run his fingers along the gilt-edged pages, thinking about that day's Sunday-school lesson. He'd lay the ribbon aside and simply allow the book to fall open. That's what he'd like to do now, but he knows what the guys in the room would do: stare at their shoes, roll their eyes. There's a Bible back on* Air Force One. *There has to be one in this hotel room; no doubt there's a bed somewhere and, next to the bed, a Bible. Or have they stopped doing that, putting Bibles in hotel rooms?*

*Sunday. Chicago.*

*He closes his eyes and tries to picture the ribbon and the soft gold-edged pages cracking and the book falling open, and he sees, in his mind, the Psalms of David, both willful and desperate, the plea of a strong man, the cry of a king:* Judge me, O Lord; for I have walked in mine integrity.

*He opens his eyes, reaches out and touches the face in the mirror, the cool glass.*

We can go a couple of ways on this, *Jody was saying just before he left the room, and then the two sides made their cases, the two ways they could use these conditions to political advantage. The hawks said that he needed to shake a fist and say,* No! These terms are not acceptable! *Flags and fists; look presidential.* After a year, we refuse to bend to Iran's terms. We will not be held hostage. *He thinks of this way as the sword.* Out-Reagan Reagan, *one of them said. The second way is to claim victory. Imply that the terms are close and that the actual release of the hostages is a mere formality:* Only a matter of time. We have been delivered. *Contrast his statesmanship with the belligerence of his opponent. He thinks of this path as the shepherd. The sword and the shepherd. These are his choices. And the implication:* There is still time to make good of this.

*Raised voices argued these two points, fingers pointed, men in suit coats and open collars paced around:* Last chance for . . . It is imperative that . . . *And then Jody raised his hands and they all stopped and looked, not at Jody, but at him. His decision. The future depended . . . Waiting. Did they hate him with every bit of themselves, hate his shortcomings and his weakness, his lack of both gravity and humor? Did they hate him as much as he hated himself?*

*They waited. How long is a moment? He looked from face to face and then at the briefing papers in his lap. Someone cleared his throat.*

*In this job you always disappoint half the room.*

*And that's when he left, excused himself, and now here he is, alone, staring at this face in the mirror, trying to remember when he was simply himself, before he was a collection of disappointing polling numbers and failed ideas, of weaknesses.*

*There is a third way, too.*

*Sunday. Chicago.*

*The briefing papers fall open to the most recent photos of some of the Fifty-two.*

*I have walked in mine integrity.*

*At that moment he decides.*

*He will walk back out to the room, and announce that they are flying back to Washington. Canceling today's campaign appearances. He will not raise the sword and he will not claim victory. He will tell the truth: we are simply not there yet.*

*And in all likelihood he will lose.*

*Sunday. Chicago. The face in the mirror stares back.*

*Maybe after . . . life will begin again. Maybe his face will return to him. Maybe he'll wake up in a bed and know where he is and judge himself by who he is instead of by what he is not. The men back in the room will stare. They will try to talk him out of this. But, no, he'll say. I'm sorry. We're going home. No politics today, fellas. Today . . . today, we walk in our integrity.*

*Sunday. Chicago. Who are these people? He takes a breath, looks once more at his own face—hopeful and frightened—opens the door, and walks out into the room.*

**THE FELLAS ARE** *cocky and assured, ties off, all triumph and strategy, when one by one they notice the big man in the doorway, his black* *hair perfectly combed and parted—it's a running joke among them that he must sleep standing up, like one of the horses from his movies. That Nancy takes him out to the stable, puts blinders and a bucket of oats on his head, and out he goes.*

*They snap to attention, almost as if . . . as if he's already won. "What are you doing up, Governor? You have a big day tomorrow."*

*He holds his hands on the doorframe and leans forward so that his upper half is in the room while his legs remain out. It's the Duke's old entrance; he uses it sometimes when he wants to command a room without actually having to enter it. The fellas see it as his gift: a kind of opaque showmanship—detached control.*

*"Well . . ." He smiles and the polls jump two points; his eyes are friendly slits. "Well, maybe I couldn't sleep."*

*The fellas laugh; this is not a problem he has.*

*"Whatcha got there?"*

*"The terms, sir. The Iranian parliament's terms for releasing the hostages." Everyone in the room is bent over the five-page briefing report that the president's people sent over as a courtesy.*

*He saunters to the window and looks out. The sun is just coming up, bruising the clouds to the east. There is a stunted skyline, but nothing else to tell him . . .*

*"Columbus, Governor."*

*He continues to stare.*

*"Ohio."*

*He speaks to the cold window: "When I was making* Dark Victory *with Bogart, the director was this horrible little Jewish fellow named Edmund Goulding and he was always trying to get us to do it bigger and with more emphasis. He used to say, 'We gotta make it play in Ohio, too. Make sure they get it in Ohio.' For the longest time I hated Ohio."*

*He turns and betrays no sense of emotion, and as they often do, the fellas wonder if he understood his own point. "How about we don't put that in my speech today?"*

*More laughter.*

*A copy of the report is offered, but he waves it off. He likes things like this on notecards and, besides, he doesn't have his glasses. He hates his glasses; in fact, he chooses to wear one contact lens instead when he has to deliver speeches, and he reads with that one eye, just so he won't have to admit he wears reading glasses. As if vitality were elective. "Tell me," he says.*

*The fellas look from one to another: "Basically . . . it's untenable. They're asking for the kitchen sink."*

*"Unfreeze assets. Give back the Shah's money."*

*"Naked pictures of Suzanne Somers."*

*"Oh," he says. "Let's get ourselves a set of those."*

*The room breaks up.*

*"So . . . what does it mean?"*

*The fellas struggle to contain themselves. "Well, sir . . . it means that he is not going to be standing on a tarmac today or tomorrow with the navy band playing behind him while those fifty-two people get off an airplane and kiss the ground."*

*"That's going to be you on that tarmac, sir."*

*Laughter. Someone claps.*

*"No, no. Come on." He hates this kind of thing, is superstitious about celebrating too early. In '64, he refused to admit he'd been elected governor of California even after Pat Brown conceded.*

*His face is cautious, almost angry. "We'll use the army band instead."*

*Applause around the room.*

*He holds his hands up. "How are they playing it?"*

*"Apparently, they're flying back to Washington. I'd guess he claims victory and hopes that no one notices that the actual hostages are still in Iran. Either that or he rattles the saber. That's what I'd do. Have him shake his fist and say, 'We will not bend. We will not be pushed around by these extremists.'"*

*"What else could he do?"*

*"He could ask Amy what she thinks."*

*Half the room breaks up.*

*"Or admit he has lusted for the Ayatollah in his heart."*

*The other half.*

*"And how do we play it?"*

*"That's the beauty. It plays itself. We look like we're taking the high road—"*

*"Right, like . . ."*

*"Like we're above it."*

*"Ooh, I like that, being above it. I want to stay above it. Can we do that? Can we be above it?"*

*Heads nod. "We don't comment directly on the crisis. We preach caution . . ."*

*"It is our deepest hope that blah blah blah."*

*"The prayers of a nation . . ."*

*"This is not about politics . . ."*

*"Get back to the business of blah blah blah."*

*He looks back out the window, where the sun is up and the clouds have faded back to gray and white. On the other side of those clouds is Washington. Two days. He has the sense of being a general in the final days before riding upon a great city. Like they've ridden all the way from Sacramento to Washington. Be a good movie. He returns to the doorway, likes this vantage best. "Numbers? Do we have numbers yet?"*

*The fellas turn to one another and smile. "They're still preliminary . . ."*

*"But we have them?"*

*"Wirthlin wants to present them himself."*

*"But we have numbers?"*

*"Yes. We have numbers."*

*He waits.*

*The fellas can barely contain. "Eleven."*

*His arms fall to his sides. My God. This is going to happen. "Eleven?" He stands dumbly in the doorway, the Duke cum Gomer Pyle.*

*"I mean, there's a margin of error and it doesn't factor in . . ."*

*"Eleven?" With two days?*

*"Yes, sir. It's ours to lose."*

*The others shoot a glance—Ours to lose?—bad form, especially given the late summer fuckups on the KKK and Taiwan and the way he said trees cause most of the pollution and that they shouldn't waste money investing in intellectual curiosity, the way he can veer dangerously off point and talk out of his ass, the way he lost eight points in a week. The fellas cannot allow him to drift again. But he doesn't seem to notice their concern. He is blessed with a short memory. He is blessed with deep stores of confidence. He is blessed, most of all, with an 11 percent cushion. Two days before. "What was that you said before? About us having deep hope?"*

*"It is our deepest hope . . ."*

*"No. Wait." He smiles; his whole face smiles, the pure joy of a seventy-year-old kid. "It is MY deepest hope."*

*They all look. This is it, then. This is what it feels like.*

*"It's about me now. It's MY deepest hope."*

*He stands in the doorway a minute longer, watching them do their jobs. He wanders back down the hall to his room, turns off the light, and lies on his back in bed, in the dark, listening to his own breathing and wondering which tie they've picked out for him today.*

Spokane, Washington / New York, New York

1980 / November 3 / Monday / 7:20 A.M.

chapter 卌 ||

David Best struggles to extricate himself from the driver's seat of a champagne-colored Mercury Bobcat, his belly carved like a plump roast by the edge of the steering wheel. When he's finally out he looks back at the car contemptuously, pushes the door closed, turns in the parking lot, and finds himself face to face with Vince Camden.

David jumps back and covers his chest. "Vince. Jesus. You scared me to death."

"I can't believe you brought Ray Scatieri here."

David still looks scared; takes a step back. "What? What are you talking about?"

"Ray Scatieri. You put him in the witness protection program and brought him to Spokane. Jesus, David. Do you have any idea who this guy is? He's an animal."

David's big cheeks flush red and he looks all around, then clenches his lips. "Goddamn it, Vince. You are not to have contact with anyone else in the program—"

"Oh, we're having contact all right," Vince says.

David looks grim. He glances over his shoulders, both ways. "Come with me."

Vince follows David into the building. It's early and the lobby is empty. The steel doors slide open on the elevator and they ride in silence to the sixth floor, David refusing to make eye contact. Vince fights a yawn. Hasn't slept more than a few hours in a week.

The marshals' oak lobby is empty. They go into David's office and he sits at his desk, puts his hands out to the side—a gesture of surrender, or of endless possibility, or there is no difference: "Okay," David says. "Where now?"

"What?"

"When witnesses come in contact with each other we move one. So . . . where? Your pick. Where do you want to go?"

"I don't—" Vince looks out the small window: an overcast morning. He hadn't thought of that. Sure. Why not just let them move you somewhere else? Get away from Sticks and Lenny and from this thing that Gotti wants you to do and just . . . disappear. Start over. Fresh. Just fly away.

David reaches in a drawer and pulls out a map, unfolds it on the desk between them. "You told me once you wanted to start a restaurant? Okay. We'll help. You pick a city and we'll find a building for you."

The map shows the entire country, veined with highways and rivers, mottled with mountains, the states eyelined in black, separated by different colors, capitals marked with stars. There is solace in these familiar shapes; you run your fingers over the borders and remember a grade school puzzle—and it's like that, like it's your pick: each state a puzzle piece, the smooth, parallel edges of Tennessee, all those rectangles in the center, the jagged surfaces of the river-border states. When you were a kid, you used to take the little wooden Florida and Idaho from the puzzle and pretend they were guns—the panhandle barrels. You used to shoot the other kids with Florida, for God's sake.

"Hawaii?" David suggests, as if he's offering a drink. "California?"

Vince's eyes drift up from the map to the photo of President Carter—even four years ago, you could see the burdens of choice and fear on his face—and Vince knows.

A single moment can sometimes connect you to your time. President Carter stares in solemn agreement. It's like this: You're out there living your own life, and then, every four years, they give you a say—a tiny say in how this moment should proceed, and it is both real and abstract, like the black borders around the states, a creation of the very thing it is—a small say in which incremental direction we will go, and sure, it's a cynical process: reactive, reductive, misguided—but goddamn it, if every four years it does nothing more than make you stop and realize that you're part of something bigger, then maybe every time it's a tiny fucking miracle.

Vince touches his own head with his fingertips and says, quietly: "Why did you bring Ray Sticks here, David?"

David pushes away from the map. "Vince. I can't talk to you about this."

"David, the guy is bad—"

"That *guy* is potentially the most valuable witness in the country, Vince."

"But here? Did you have to bring him here?"

David raises his big shoulders in a full shrug. "What do we do, Vince? Three thousand people in this program, a good number of them wise guys, and we can't put 'em in New York. Or Detroit. Or Cleveland. Or anywhere the mob operates. Okay, so take out the twenty biggest cities and their suburbs. Take out Vegas. And Atlantic City. What's left? Lexington? Des Moines? Phoenix? Spokane? You tell me. Where are we supposed to put the dump, Vince? Whose neighborhood gets the garbage? Where are we supposed to put a guy like that? Where are we supposed to put a guy like you?"

Vince deserves the sting. "Are there others?"

"Here?" David considers before answering, then shrugs. "Sure. Any given time, there might be four or five. This is actually a good city for us. Italian community. Affordable. Isolated. Lots of service jobs. Federal offices. Big enough that you guys can blend in, but not so big that you can get into a lot of trouble."

Vince wonders if he knows any of them, and immediately begins thinking of the type: that dishwasher at Geno's, the short limping guy who used to play cards at Sam's. He remembers the word Officer Dupree used: *Ghosts.* "You just can't put someone like Ray Scatieri in a place like this, David. He's a criminal."

"Oh yeah?" David sighs. "What's he do? Gamble? Steal credit cards? Sell dope?"

Vince looks away, at the picture of Jimmy Carter.

"How about you, Vince? You live pretty well making donuts?" David's face betrays no emotion. "Look. We know it's a challenge to go straight. When you're in the fox business, sometimes you lose a hen."

"And sometimes you gotta move a fox twice." David leans forward and pushes the map in front of Vince. "Come on, Vince. Pick a new town. Pick a new name. Leave all this paranoia and your little scuffling operation behind."

Of course he's right. It's the only way to escape both Ray Sticks and Johnny Boy. And maybe himself. After a moment, Vince picks up the map. Start over. Really do it this time. Evaporate. Vince looks down at the map.

"Good." David smiles. "I'll start the paperwork." He walks into the outer office. Closes the door behind him.

Vince stares at the southeastern point of New York State, where the island of Manhattan looks like the tip of a sliver . . . a tiny, harmless speck of a place. The world. Benny is on that speck, and Tina. Just a day ago he was on that island, in a car with Ange, talking about how to kill Ray Sticks. That's the problem with a map like this—it can only show the surface of things, not the truth beneath. How does David know about the dope and credit cards—his *scuffling operation?*

Vince stands, looks around the office, and when he opens the door to the lobby David's thick back is to him and he's on the phone, whispering: "I'll keep him here until—" David straightens up and aware that he's being watched, turns, and sees Vince standing in the doorway. David mumbles something about having to go and hangs up. He looks up at Vince as if seeing him for the first time. "You cut your hair."

"That the police?" Vince asks.

David stares, as if trying to decide whether he can get away with lying. Finally, he shrugs. "They sent a cop to New York. He figured out you were in the program. This Detective Phelps called me last night, said they wanted to talk to you. They're on their way, Vince."

"What did he say?"

"Phelps? Said you were involved in some stuff—stealing credit cards. Selling dope. And they want to question you about a homicide."

"I already talked to them about it."

"Well, they want to talk to you again."

"I didn't kill anyone, David."

"When he gets here, we'll tell him that."

"I already told him."

"We'll tell him again."

"Are you detaining me, David?"

"I'm asking you to stay here and cooperate with the police."

Vince looks around the office. "And what are my chances of making it to the lobby and out the door before they get here? Before you call security?"

"Come on, Vince." David laughs.

"One in five? One in ten?"

David doesn't blink.

"My move, David?" Vince backs out of the office and walks casually to the elevator. He expects David to pull a gun or tackle him, or at least call building security, but the big man simply tags behind like a younger brother.

"Aw, come on, Vince," he says. "Wait and talk to the police. We'll straighten this out and then we'll get you relocated again. Come on. Just talk to them."

"I'll turn myself in tomorrow." Vince steps onto the elevator. "There's something I have to do first."

"Vince. Think! Don't be stupid."

Funny. Those were the exact words Ange used at the airport after he laid it all out: The FBI had Ray Sticks over some shit in Philadelphia and he'd been wearing a wire for the last few months while he supposedly cooled it in New York. And then, one day, he was just gone. Sticks potentially knew enough to put Gotti and his crew away for years, so Johnny Boy's deal for Vince was simple: fly back to Spokane, kill Sticks, and the rest of his debt would be cleared off the books. You'd be doing the world a favor, Ange said, and Vince knew that was true enough. And if he didn't kill Sticks? Well, they'd come collect on both of Vince's debts. It was when Vince said that he wasn't sure he could do it that Ange smiled: *Don't be stupid.*

The elevator doors close on David's worried face and Vince pushes the button for the second floor. He gets off and walks casually down the hall to the stairwell, goes inside, and climbs down the stairs, past the first floor, to the basement. The door opens on a concrete-floored hallway. Vince walks until he reaches a custodial closet, opens it, and finds a pair of coveralls. He slips into them and keeps walking through a door to the loading dock in back of the building, grabs a huge box of toilet paper, and holds it on his shoulder, above his face. He emerges on a ramp in the back of the building, climbs it to the street level, and is about to cross the street with the box when an unmarked police car squeals around the corner. As it passes, Vince sees the big mustached detective, Phelps, and another cop in the front seat. They roll past and Vince walks casually across the street, angles into Riverfront Park, sets the toilet paper on a park bench, unzips his coveralls, steps out of them, and walks calmly through the park.

IN HIS SMALL office, beneath a diploma from Fordham and a handful of framed photos of himself with acquitted gangsters, Benny DeVries seems more relaxed and cocky than he was the night Dupree questioned him on the street. Dupree takes the chair across from Benny's desk and thanks the lawyer for seeing him again.

"This shouldn't take long. I just have a couple of follow-up questions."

Benny looks impatiently at his watch. "I told you everything I know."

Dupree shakes his head. "Well, no. You didn't."

"What are you talking about?"

"That night you said you hadn't seen him—"

Benny leans back, smiling, entertained. "Yes."

"—I asked you to call me if you saw Vince?"

"And I said I would. Look—"

"It just hit me this morning. I said *Vince*, not *Marty*. I never told you that his new name was Vince. You said you hadn't heard from him since the trial and yet you knew his name in the program was Vince."

Benny DeVries stares at him for a moment, and then breaks into a broad smile. "Yeah. That's funny. I mean . . . it's worthless: I could have inferred that you were talking about Marty, or maybe you used the name Vince earlier in the conversation. But yeah . . . that's pretty good."

Dupree leans forward and makes his pitch. "Look, Benny, the

last thing I want to do is drop out of the sky and cause you a bunch of trouble."

"Trouble," Benny repeats, the smile still on his face.

"I just thought we should talk once more *before* this gets to the prosecutor or the bar association—"

The smile grows. "The bar association!"

"See, I might be able to help you out if you tell me where Vince is, but you gotta do it now, before the shit starts to rain down."

Benny laughs, then lights a cigarette, still smiling. "You really need to get yourself a *bad cop*." He draws on the cigarette. "Now . . . what's your name again?"

"Dupree."

"Okay, Detective Dupree. First, let's assume that I had seen our friend and I lied to you about it. My dick will climb out of my pants, grow wings, and fly across this room before you find a prosecutor in New York to wade into the issues of privilege and charge me on something as small as this. Number one. Two, the prosecutors wherever the fuck you're from—assuming they walk upright—don't have jurisdiction. And three, as far as the bar association, I can give you the phone number for the head of the disciplinary committee, if you want, because I was the best man at his fucking wedding!

"And even if you *could* charge me, it would be your word against mine, and in the end, it doesn't even matter. Do you want to know why?"

Dupree is quiet.

"Because you didn't ask if I'd seen *Vince Camden*. You asked if I'd seen Marty Hagen. Well, there is no Marty Hagen anymore. You guys took care of that. So either way . . . I told you the truth. I haven't seen Martin Hagen since his trial. Have I seen Vince Camden? You didn't ask me that. Now get out of my office and don't come back without a warrant, you piece of shit!"

"I don't think you understand what I'm telling you—"

"Oh, I understand someone trying to put the screws to me!" Benny is worked up, red-faced, and doesn't quite want this to end yet. "How long you been a cop?"

Dupree looks down at him. "Five years."

"How old are you?"

"Twenty-seven."

"How long have you been a detective?"

Dupree considers lying, but doesn't want to give the guy the satisfaction. "Three weeks. I'm temporarily assigned."

"You're a rookie." Benny leans forward on his desk and smiles. "How do you like my city so far, rook?"

Dupree smiles. "It was a long weekend."

Benny laughs, and leans back in his chair. "You want some advice, you stupid simple bastard?"

"I don't think I can afford you."

"Pro bono."

Dupree waits.

"My advice is this: Go home. This place isn't like where you're from. There's more corruption and backstabbing and bribery in the opening of a restaurant in New York City than in every crime ever committed in your little town."

Dupree considers him. "We got sleazy lawyers with bad haircuts in Spokane, too."

Dupree pulls on his coat, then reaches in his satchel and pulls out a single sheet of paper from Martin Hagen's file. "Let me give you some advice. Next time you decide the only way to keep some guy from marrying your sister is to get him into the witness protection program, I wouldn't doctor up an FBI report."

He slides the page down in front of Benny, who doesn't look at it.

"So is that perjury? Or obstruction?"

Finally, Benny looks down at the page.

"The FBI agent who got the warrant for this tap said it came from another case, some guy named Breen." Dupree points to the page. "Somebody went through it and substituted Hagen's name for Breen's. I happened to tell this FBI agent how you went to school with the prosecutor in the case, and it turned out to be the same guy who prosecuted Jerry Breen. You believe that coincidence?"

Benny's hand goes to his temple. On the street outside a driver lays on the horn.

"So where is he?"

"I don't know," Benny whispers. "I saw him two days ago."

"You'll call me if you hear from him?"

Benny nods.

Dupree straightens up to leave, then, at the last moment, bends at the waist across the lawyer's desk. "So how was that, Benny? Bad enough for you?"


TIC WALKS INTO the kitchen and breaks into a huge grin. "Mr. Vince! You came back!" Tic is wearing the baker's apron, dusted with flour and sugar. "How was the funeral, man? All sad and shit?"

"It hasn't happened yet," Vince says.

"People been coming in here nonstop asking about you. Cops. And a couple of other guys. The old man is freaked out. Oh!" Tic jumps with a realization. "Here, man. This is yours." He unties the apron and holds it out for Vince.

"No." Vince shakes his head. "It's yours now."

"I'm not the baker," Tic says. "You're the baker."

"No, I'm not staying, Tic. I just came back to do a few things. This is yours. You're the baker now."

Tic stares at the apron. "It's like you're Obi-Wan and I'm Luke. This gives me chills, no lie." He takes the apron and bows.

Vince pats him on the shoulder. He steps past Tic to the closet, goes in, and turns over the bucket. Climbs on it, feels around in the ceiling tiles for his key. He takes the key to the trapdoor and descends down to the basement with his backpack. Yanks on the chain to turn on the light, glances up the stairs, then moves the empty bags, pulls out his lockbox, and opens it. It's all there: twenty thousand and change.

Vince looks around before picking up an empty flour bag from the floor and stuffing the money into it. Then he shoves the bag in his backpack. Back up the stairs, Tic is wearing the apron, holding out a folded sheet of notebook paper. "Oh, you know that hot girl who always gets a dozen on Wednesdays? Farrah? She came in first thing this morning and left this for you."

Vince holds the note in front of his eyes:

*Vince: Please call me. I need to talk to you about something important. Kelly.*

Vince uses the kitchen telephone. Kelly is relieved to hear from him and wants to know if he has time to talk. She agrees to pick him up two blocks from the donut shop, in the alley. When he hangs up, Vince goes to the doorway of the kitchen and looks back over his shoulder into the donut shop. Tic is standing in Vince's usual spot behind the display cases, his foot on a milk crate, talking to one of the old guys about Sunday's NFL games, whether or not the Steelers' win over the Packers means they're finally on track. Nancy is walking around filling up coffee cups. Wisps of cigarette smoke are strung above the Formica tables like smoke from campfires.

What if you could you take mental snapshots—fix the world in time and place? Then you could go through your memories like an album: the last time you saw your parents together, the sky from the driver's seat of the first convertible you ever stole, the morning you left Tina in bed and turned yourself over to the FBI. It strikes him that this place was as close as he ever came.

Vince takes one last draw of the rich smells—donuts and coffee and cigarettes. He backs out of the doorway, hoists his backpack on his shoulder, and walks through the kitchen and out the back door.

DUPREE SLUMPS ON the bed in his hotel room. "He's there?"

"Yep," Phelps says on the other end of the phone. "I called the deputy marshal on his case last night and told him what you'd found out about Camden. He said he'd cooperate. Then this morning he called and said Camden came by his office."

"When did he fly back?"

"Apparently while you were sightseeing at the Statue of Liberty."

"Did he say anything?"

"He told the guy he didn't kill Doug and that he had something to do but that he'd turn himself in tomorrow. And then he ran off. We got surveillance on his house, but so far . . . nothing."

"What about the girl?" Dupree asks. "His alibi. You got someone over there?"

"We're a little shorthanded right now," Phelps says. "County found a guy shot in the head and stuffed in his own car trunk last night. I'm tellin' you, rook: it feels like one of those days. We'll talk when you get back."

After he hangs up Dupree goes to the bathroom, retrieves his shaving kit, and stuffs it in his suitcase. He was going to see Dominic Coletti today, and check back in with Benny, but now there's no need. He calls a travel agent, who puts him on hold, comes back, and says there is a United Airlines flight from

Kennedy to Denver in ninety minutes. If he makes a short connection he can be back in Spokane by ten P.M.

He calls Debbie to tell her, but there's no answer. He unloads his gun, puts the shells in his shaving kit and packs the gun next to the shoulder holster in his suitcase, grabs his jacket, and races out the door into the hotel hallway. He runs to the elevator bay, turns the corner, and finds himself staring at the broad back of Donnie Charles, who is looking down the hall to see which way the room numbers run. His big head swivels back and he faces Dupree head-on.

About Donnie Charles: the right side of his jaw is crimson and yellow, swollen as if he were chewing a plug of tobacco. His mouth is wired shut, inside and out; the wires are strapped around the back of his thick, terraced neck, run beneath his jaw, and disappear finally between lips the color and shape of nightcrawlers. The welt above his eye is flat and oxblood red. His right eye socket is a slit, deep purple.

They face each other for a moment and Dupree can't help himself; he edges a step backward. "I don't suppose you're here to take me to the airport?"

Charles reaches in his pocket and comes up with a small spiral notebook and a pen. He scrawls on the notebook and turns it to face Dupree.

*what time*
*flight*

"Hour and a half."

Charles nods. Then he moves forward so quickly that Dupree barely has time to react to the knee that lifts him off the ground, and deposits him on the patterned carpet with a thud. He sits up and Charles kicks him in the face, sending him rolling across the floor. When he can focus again, Dupree sees Charles towering over him, curled around the pen and notebook. Finally, he bends down and turns the notebook to face Dupree, who has to block out his own rasping breath to concentrate on the words:

*not going to*
*make flight*

**KELLY DOWNSHIFTS AND** parks her Mustang II across from Aaron Grebbe's house. "Vince. Can I ask you? Did something happen the night you went out with Aaron?" Her blond hair is pulled back into a ponytail and Vince wonders how she gets her hair so tight on the sides of her head; it's a flat, grooved surface, shiny and perfect—a hundred different colors of gold. She shifts in the open palm of a blue bucket seat; it's all he can do not to trace the long line of her blue-jeaned leg.

"No. Nothing unusual," Vince lies.

"It's just  . . ." She nods at Grebbe's split level house. "He didn't come to work this morning. He hasn't campaigned. He missed a candidates' forum last night. He won't even take my calls. I just . . . I don't know what to do, Vince."

Vince looks around. "Where's his truck?"

"His wife must've taken it. He's alone in there." She glances over to Vince, as if he might be wondering how she knows. "I sat here this morning and watched the house. He just walks from room to room. I think he's drinking." She covers her mouth—those long, elegant fingers—and Vince is aware that he looks at her the way he looks at architecture, admiringly, even longingly—but always from a distance.

"I didn't know who else to call. I thought you might know what to do."

"It's okay. I'll talk to him." Vince pats her shoulder. He grabs his backpack and opens the car door.

"Vince?"

Looks back.

"Will you tell him . . . that I'm sorry? That I didn't—" She doesn't finish.

Vince nods, climbs out of the car and into the street. Across the street he climbs the steps, rings the doorbell, and hears shuffling inside. The peephole goes dark. A second later the door opens.

Aaron Grebbe is unshaven, wearing sweatpants and no shirt. He is broad-shouldered and solid. He is also drunk. "Hey. It's my one supporter."

Grebbe turns and goes into his house. "Come in. Pour yourself a drink. I was just watching *Match Game*. You like *Match Game*? I like *Match Game*."

He follows Grebbe into a sunken, carpeted living room, where a stand of bottles is spread across the blond-wood hi-fi. Grebbe plops down on the couch with a tall glass of brown liquor and a couple of melting cubes. Vince goes to the forest of bottles and finds most of them empty. There is a bottle of dark rum half full, however, and he pours himself a small glass and plops down on a brown leather recliner. Grebbe reaches into an overflowing ashtray, fingering the butts until he finds a cigarette worth smoking.

The sound is turned all the way down on the big console TV. Gene Rayburn is grinning wildly; he says something to one of the contestants.

"So, are you okay?" Vince finally asks.

Grebbe looks from the TV to Vince. "Excellent."

"Kelly called me. She's worried."

Grebbe takes a swig of the drink in his hand. "I can't talk to Kelly right now."

"Your wife found out?"

Grebbe looks as if he might cry. "I love Paula. I really do. If I had thought for one second . . ."

"What happened?"

"The night of the . . . thing . . . after I dropped you off I came home and she was up. And you know the funny thing? I haven't told that woman the truth in two years. Except that night. 'I met this guy,' I tell her, 'this gambler. And we went to an after-hours poker club and I talked to some voters and then some guys tried to strong-arm this guy and I saved his life. I actually saved someone's life.'

"She just stared at me. And then she said, 'You're having an affair.'" He laughs. "I could've lied. I could've told her anything, that I was making campaign signs, that Reagan's son took me out for breakfast. But no. I had to tell the one thing she'd never be-lieve: the truth."

"I'm sorry," Vince says.

He shrugs Vince's apology off. "I still could've passed it off, or at least not told her about Kelly. I'm good at lying, you know? I'm excellent, really. But I started thinking about what I'd seen. The people at that poker game. The guy in the car . . . I could've shot that guy, Vince. I mean—I *wanted* to! What does that say about me? I mean, what separates me from someone like him? There must be something . . . there must be something that separates someone like me from someone like—" He looks down at the glass in his hands. "I want to be a better man."

He shrugs. "So I told Paula that I was sorry. That I didn't mean for it to happen. It just did. She asked who it was. I said it didn't matter. She said, 'Of course it does.'

"So I told her." He's quiet, and after a moment Vince leans forward.

Grebbe looks up, and seems surprised that Vince is still here. His head dips from side to side. "She took it pretty well. She nod-ded, like she knew that's who it was. And then she went to her room, packed a bag, got the kids, and . . . just left."

"Do you know where she is?"

"Paula? At her sister's."

"You gotta get cleaned up. Go over there."

"She won't talk to me."

"Don't call her. Go over. Be a man. Tell her you'll never do it again."

Grebbe suppresses a little belch, and then looks around wildly, as if he's going to be sick. He stands and goes to the bathroom, but Vince can't hear anything over the running tap water.

Vince sits for a moment, then looks at the drink in his hand, walks across the shag living room, and grabs Grebbe's drink. He takes it to the hi-fi, takes the bottles in his arms, and marches them all to the kitchen, where he dumps the ones that still have booze in them down the sink. He puts the empties on the back porch. Back in the living room, Gene Rayburn is congratulating a woman in huge glasses as the number "$15,000!" flashes on the screen below her face. The water is still running in the bathroom.

After a minute, Vince walks down a narrow hall—lined with school pictures of the handsome Grebbe children in front of dappled backgrounds—to a closed bathroom door. He knocks lightly. Nothing. "Hey! You okay?"

Finally, Grebbe opens the door and comes out. Squeezes past Vince. The bathroom behind him smells like stomach acid and booze. "Sorry," he says.

In the living room, he seems more upset by the fact that *Match Game* is over than about getting sick and having his drink poured out.

"So what are you gonna do now?" Vince asks.

"I think *$20,000 Pyramid* is on."

"The election tomorrow—"

"That doesn't matter anymore."

Vince watches the TV for a minute, then stands up and starts for the door. But he stops. "Look, do what you want. I don't care."

He scratches his head, trying to figure out what he means to say. "But what about all that stuff you were saying the other day?

When you said you couldn't wait to get up and get to work every day. *A better zoo is a better zoo.* Because, for what it's worth, that was the best thing I've ever heard from a politician. Maybe from anyone."

Grebbe is considering the coffee table, his head in his hands.

Vince stares at the TV and then shrugs. He grabs his backpack, walks to the door, and opens it. But he spots the newspaper on a table next to the door, slides the rubber band off, and flips through it until he comes to the classified ads. Then he steps out into the cool afternoon air and opens the newspaper on the porch. He runs his finger along the real estate section until he finds it. Looks up. Across the street, Kelly is leaning back in her car seat, staring at the ceiling of the Mustang. Vince waits on the porch until he hears Grebbe turn on the shower in the house behind him. Then he walks across the street and climbs in the car. "He's gonna be fine. He's getting cleaned up."

"Did his wife——"

"Yeah."

"Oh God."

Finally, Vince turns to her. "Look, you gotta stay away from him now. You know that, right, Kelly?"

She looks down and her shoulders crumple as she cries. The thing about architecture is that some buildings are just better from a distance. Vince waits patiently, until she wipes her eyes and takes a deep breath. When he's sure she's done Vince holds out the folded newspaper. "Do you think you could drop me off at this address?"

DUPREE SHIFTS HIS weight and tries to find a comfortable place in his lower back for his handcuffed wrists. His ribs ache when he breathes deeply. The two on the bottom left side might be broken.

The bruise on his cheek feels like a shortcut to his brain. He leans forward in the backseat of Charles's unmarked car. He hasn't been in handcuffs since the academy. They're uncomfortable. Charles flips around a corner and Alan falls against the pile of shoeboxes. Winces from the pain in his chest. Rights himself.

"I told my lieutenant all about you," he lies. "They're gonna come straight to you if anything happens to me."

Charles simply drives, doesn't look back. Dupree stares at the horizontal lines in the back of the man's bald neck and head, divided by the strap from his jaw brace. Dupree is glad for the strap; otherwise, he couldn't tell where neck ends and head begins.

"The people in the lobby of the hotel heard me yelling. They saw the whole thing," Dupree says. In fact, they stared at Dupree as if he were some kind of bank robber, or pervert, his hands cuffed behind his back, dragged by an arm through the lobby by the big detective, who held his shield in front of him. Dupree made a lame attempt to get away at the curb and Charles simply bounced his head off the top of the car once—a slick move that, once his head cleared, and assuming he somehow gets out of this alive, Dupree filed away to use sometime himself.

He tries to catch Charles's eyes in the rearview. "All it's gonna take is one call to the hotel and my lieutenant is going to know what happened. With that wired jaw, you're pretty easy to identify."

Nothing.

Dupree falls back into the backseat. They drive north along Central Park and Dupree finds himself staring out the window, shocked that a city of this speed and size and density would have at its core a place so beautiful and serene. Joggers, skaters, people on bikes, old ladies with sweatered dogs. Dupree looks up at Charles, one hand on the wheel, other on the window frame. Then he looks down at his suitcase, on the floor at his feet. He pinches it between his ankles, glances up at Charles's back. If he could somehow get the bag onto the seat behind him, open it, take out the gun, find the shells, load it, and then spin around and shoot Charles—all of this while facing backward, with his hands cuffed behind his back.

Plan B: "Hey, don't I get one phone call?"

Charles drives up Amsterdam, past Columbia University, into Morningside Heights. Harlem. Alongside the car, the neon fades and the brick storefronts are pocked with graffiti and caged with bars. Charles drives. The blocks become a blur of faces and brick buildings, and Dupree falls back into his seat and closes his eyes. Finally, the car slows and Dupree opens his eyes. The sign reads 153RD STREET and they are driving along an ivied, rock wall that opens into a wrought iron gate that Dupree reads backward through the back window.

TRINITY CEMETERY. That doesn't sound good. Charles drives slowly along what looks for the world like a country road, cresting low grassy hills thick with the leaves of shedding elms and oaks, toward a cloister leading to a country church. Dupree can't believe this place exists in the city, at the top of Manhattan. He looks around. There are a handful of cars and people along these winding roads, bowing in front of graves, placing flowers, making their way to mausoleums.

Finally, Charles stops the car, climbs out, and opens the back door. He grabs Dupree by the arm, yanks him out of the unmarked, and drags him along the road, up one of the grassy hills, to a headstone ringed by flowers and stuffed animals. At the grave, he pushes Dupree down among the plastic flowers and vases. Dupree's face is pressed against the cool slate. He pulls himself back up to his knees and reads the flat headstone: I SOUGHT THE LORD, AND HE HEARD ME, AND DELIVERED ME FROM ALL MY FEARS. MOLLY ANNE CHARLES, MARCH 9, 1978—NOVEMBER 11, 1978.

Dupree looks up. "Your daughter."

Charles purses his lips and writes furiously on the pad.

*heart defect*
*valve stuck*

"I'm sorry," Dupree says. He looks at the dates again. Almost two years to the day. "She was born with it?"

He writes:

*four surgeries*
*expensive*

Dupree can imagine where something like this leads, can picture Charles working through the problem in his mind of how to make the extra money to pay for the rising medical costs—the fear and anger and helplessness.

*she was*
*always crying*

He could try moonlighting, but that won't even come close. Meantime, he's at work every day seeing the money drug dealers throw around. It makes him sick: thugs driving BMWs, rich kids driving their parents' cars into the city to buy coke. And the first time, it must have been so easy: nothing, a drink of water from a river.

*fought with*
*my wife got*

Charles concentrates on the pad, his face twisted. He seems to be searching for a word. Finally, he turns the pad.

*lost*
*I was*

Dupree nods. Who can say what he would do in that situation? How far he'd go? He catches the eyes of a woman walking by; he imagines how odd this must look: him on his knees in front of this small gravestone, his hands cuffed behind his back while the big detective with the mashed face looms above him with a pen and pad.

*at work*
*the night*

Dupree looks back to the grave. There are faded cards and plastic flowers and a stuffed elephant with big floppy ears. Charles turns the page.

*she died*
*it's like*

He concentrates on the notebook, turns the page again.

*I never*
*knew her*

Finally, Charles seems to have finished. He lets the pad fall to his side. Dupree shifts his weight to his right knee and manages to pull a foot underneath himself. Pain shoots through his ribs and the knob on his cheek. But he manages to stand. Charles doesn't do anything to stop him. Dupree straightens, looks Charles in the eyes, and says, quietly, "I'm sorry." Then he takes a deep breath and prepares to be hit. "But it doesn't matter. You know that, right? It doesn't change anything."

Charles stares at him, his eyes flat and cold.

Dupree gets even closer, even quieter: "In some ways . . . it makes it worse."

And finally the tears come, arcing over the sides of Charles's cheeks. He shoves Dupree and the young cop flies to the ground, skids against the headstone, knocking the toys and flowers over. Charles lurks above him. He throws his head back, but he can't get his wired jaws apart and the sound that comes is the moan of a dreaming child—a low shivering hum over the grassy hills.

**CHOCOLATE CHIP COOKIES.** Vince smells them as soon as he climbs the porch of the small stucco house. The screen door sticks, and he smacks himself in the forehead yanking on it. The door, however, is smaller than its opening and he can see horizons of light along the edges before he opens it.

Beth looks tiny sitting alone at the dining-room table, behind two stacks of "Open House" informational flyers on either side of a plate of cookies. She is wearing a tan suit, the sleeve rolled up on her left arm to make room for her cast, which rests on the open page of a magazine. "Vince?" She catches herself smiling and quickly looks down at the table. "What are you doing here?"

"House hunting."

She ignores this. "People have been asking about you."

"The police?"

"Yeah. And this guy, Ray."

Vince doesn't like the way she said his name, the familiarity in her voice; she's slept with him. He feels a shiver along his spine. "You gotta stay away from that guy, Beth. I don't care how much he pays you. Stay away from him."

"He's been coming down to Sam's the last couple of nights. Playing cards. He says you guys are old friends. He reminds me of you."

"Beth—"

She stands up and gives him an awkward hug, pulling away the whole time. "Thanks for coming, Vince. You didn't have to."

He grabs her shoulders. "Promise me you won't see this guy, Beth."

She recoils and returns to her chair. "So, are you back for good, Vince?"

"No," he says.

She nods, her face betraying nothing.

"Beth, I mean it. You have to stay away from this guy."

She just stares at him.

"I just want to know you're safe."

"Well." She tries a smile. "You don't get to know that."

Vince takes one of the flyers. "How's the open house going?" The house looks worse, if possible, in the picture, tiny windows set at random in a mound of pink stucco. Two bedrooms. One bath. Oil heat. Tar roof. Asking price: $32,500.

"I had some people over the weekend, but you're the first one today . . . it almost feels like Larry gave me a house that he knew would never sell. I don't know—to teach me something. Keep me in my place." She picks up one of the cookies, turns it over in her hand, and sets it back on the plate.

"Nah. The weather's just bad for house hunting," Vince says. "But you look good sitting there. Like you belong." Vince wishes there were something else he could say. "Aren't you going to show me the place?"

"You don't have to do that, Vince."

He looks around: metal cabinets in the kitchen, dripping faucet, water damage on the living-room ceiling. "How will I know if I want to buy it unless you show it to me?"

"Vince. Don't do this." She offers him the plate of cookies.

He takes one and eats it in two bites. "Did you make these?"

"Vince."

"I'm serious. These are really good. This is my business, Beth. I'm a baker, remember? This is a great goddamn cookie. I mean it. Perfect ratio of dough to chip, cooked just enough to hold together, but not too brown."

Vince takes another cookie, and then sets his backpack on the table. "Listen. I might need to hide some money for a while. So tell me." He unzips the bag, takes out the flour bag, and slides it across the table. "What will they take for this shithole?"

IT'S A FAIRLY simple transaction: with Vince at her side, Beth deposits Vince's $20,000 into her bank account (raising the balance to $20,428.52) and then the bank draws up the home-sale papers. Since she's putting more than two thirds down, they agree to loan her the rest with the house as collateral, although the 20 percent interest rate raises her payment to nearly $160 a month—as much as she pays now for her apartment. Over the course of the thirty-year loan, Beth will pay almost $50,000 in interest. It's an amazing racket, Vince thinks; he got better points when he borrowed from the mob.

Still, Beth was ecstatic when she offered $28,500 and the seller jumped. Of course Larry refused to waive his commission, and so the percentage he promised Beth—under the table, of course—is going to him. She declines the inspection and the appraisal, and says she'll take care of insurance herself. She nods quickly as the loan officer goes over the rest.

Throughout, Vince is aware that he's never felt this good. He has to cover his mouth with his hand to hide his smile. Every few minutes Beth looks over her shoulder at him, and he doubts her hand would be big enough to cover her own smile.

She's been smiling like this since he opened the flour bag and showed her the cash and said, "I want you and Kenyon to live here."

She had flushed and caught his eyes. "Are you—" But then she hadn't finished the sentence, as if afraid to ask for anything more.

"Not yet," he said. "I have to do something and I might have to go away for a while." He took a breath. "But when I come back, yeah, I'd like us to try." He found himself believing it.

She argued with him, at first: "I can't do this, Vince. I can't take your money. You told me you were saving to open a restaurant."

"I can do that later," he said. "Please, Beth. Take it." And suddenly he pictured Beth and Kenyon sitting on the porch, waiting for him to come home from the donut shop—only it's not him, it's his father—and that's when Vince realized: *That is your dream.*

When she finally agreed, it felt great to see the look on Beth's face. Except for the movies, he'd never seen someone so happy that they actually started crying.

The bank loan officer slides the papers toward her. "This has to go to the sellers. So it will take a few days, but since you don't have a house to sell and since you're waiving the inspection and appraisal, I could see it closing as early as two weeks. If the sellers agree, you could move into your house in a month."

Beth grabs Vince's hand and squeezes it. She leans over and whispers in his ear. "Hurry back."

CLAY IS WAITING at the normal time, at the normal spot, at a picnic table at Dicks Drive-in. Vince walks up, sets his backpack on the bench, and plops down. "You can't believe the week I've had," he says.

Clay doesn't even look up.

"You're not still mad about the car. It's an ugly car, Clay."

"I take all the risk and get none of the rewards."

"You should buy American."

"If I get caught, it's my career. My life."

"You're right, Clay."

Clay looks up, surprised.

"That's why we have to call it off," Vince says.

"What do you mean?"

"I mean we're done."

"What do you mean, done?"

"Done. It's too hot, Clay. The guy who used to make the cards got killed the other night. You understand? Dead. The cops are all over me. And there's a guy in town, a dangerous guy—a connected guy. Do you hear what I'm saying?"

Clay doesn't say anything.

"This guy wants me to turn you over to him, Clay. He wants your name."

"So give it to him." Clay pushes his glasses up on the bridge of his nose. "Tell him I want to meet him. I want to do business with him."

"You don't *do business* with a guy like this, Clay. You give him your money and he shoots you in the face."

"I want to meet him."

"No."

"Look, Vince, you can quit if you want, but I want to keep going. I can do more. I can take twice as many cards, make twice as much money."

Vince bends down and speaks in a low voice. "I've told you a hundred times. You can't take more cards. You'll get caught."

Clay shakes his head. "I didn't ask you to protect me. Give me his goddamned name. If you're too scared to keep going, then at least get out of my way."

"Clay."

He fumbles around in his pocket and uses two hands to hold something beneath the table.

Vince smiles.

"Look under the table, Vince."

"Goddamn it, Clay."

Clay flashes it quickly—dull gray—and then puts it back under the table.

"Are you gonna shoot me? Here? At Dicks? 'Cause there might be a place with even more witnesses. Although I can't imagine it, offhand."

Clay looks around at a handful of people sitting at the tables or in their cars. "We'll go for a drive," he says.

"Where are we gonna drive, Clay?"

"I don't know. The woods."

"What woods?"

"I don't know. There's woods everywhere."

"Who holds the gun while you drive?"

"I do."

"How can you do that? Sitting right next to me? The minute you look down at the road, I'll just take it from you."

"I'll make you drive."

"I'm not driving to the woods so you can shoot me."

Clay looks down at the table, trying to figure it out. "Goddamn it, Vince! If you won't give me more money, at least give me this guy's name!"

"Listen to me, Clay. This guy will suck you dry, get you to steal all the cards you can, and then dump your body in the river. You understand?"

"I mean it, Vince. This is your last warning."

Vince sits back. "It's been a bad week, Clay." He takes a french fry. "I haven't slept more than a few hours in . . . I don't know, five days? Every time I turn around someone's threatening me. This is the first time someone has actually pointed a gun at me, but I gotta tell you—it's the first time I haven't been even a little bit scared."

Clay stares at him, his lips twitching, until finally he sets the gun on the table between them. "Damn it, Vince. It's not fair."

"No." Vince takes the air pistol by the barrel, opens a small hatch, and shakes a single BB into his open palm. "It's not fair."

THERE IS A moment when all the work that can be done is done. Plays have all been made, strategies and mistakes. The various people are in position and there's nothing more than the wait— no more running or politicking, compromising or pleading. It's going to be what it's going to be, and all that's left is for the thing to play itself out. And at that moment, time is measured in sighs, regrets and ironies; these are the seconds, minutes and hours of the night before.

Vince walks with his head up, staring at the tops of the buildings—a quick architectural survey to record it all—the profiles of converted brick tenements, the handful of decent office buildings, and his vote for the best structure in Spokane, the nineteen-story, terraced Deco mass of the Paulson Building. There are a few other decent ones, sure—the County Courthouse is impressive and the Davenport Hotel is nice, though the locals' affection for a fading old hotel is a little bit over-the-top. Vince guesses there must be a hotel just like it in every city in America—every city with its own tiny Plaza. He steps into P.M. Jacoy, the corner newsstand, and buys a good cigar for later. Checks his watch: quarter to six. First thing to kill is time.

Vince angles down Sprague Avenue and the best line of bars in the city. A person clings to the late sun of August and September, but when the fall turns, this early darkness is a nice surprise. Heels click on the cold, shimmering sidewalk. Vince walks past a couple of good candidates before turning into a hotel lounge with a small crowd and a color TV above the bar. He grabs a stool—

amazing how the feet fall naturally against a bar railing—and catches the bartender's attention. "Beam and Coke."

When the guy delivers, Vince makes his pitch: "You think we could watch the news?"

The bartender looks from Vince to the TV, on a shelf above a rack of cashews and chips, jars of pickled eggs and sausage. "You kidding? It's Monday night. I touch that TV and I'll lose my arm." On the TV, Cleveland's quarterback Brian Sipe is warming up; Cosell is suggesting he has a chance to break the Browns' career passing record tonight.

"The election's tomorrow," Vince says. "Come on. Ten minutes of news. Then we can turn it back to the game. What do you say?"

There are eight other men in the place, six of them saddled at the bar like Vince. One of them, a guy in a spackled sweatshirt and worn painter's pants, leans forward and catches Vince's eye. "We don't come down here to watch the news. We could watch the news at home."

The bartender is amused by the exchange. He stretches his hands out on his considerable gut and says to Vince, "Tell you what, friend. You find me one other guy in here wants to watch the news and I'll turn the TV for ten minutes."

Vince looks down the bar. He's met with six blank stares. "Come on, fellas. What do you say? What if the Iranians let the hostages go today?" The men at the bar turn back to the TV. Vince looks around the lounge. The only other people in the place are two suits hunched over a table, deep in a conversation about something. Vince hops off his bar stool, slides past the worn pool table, and hovers above their table.

The suits are draped over two vaguely Irish-looking men, easy in their professional appearances, like second- or third-generation lawyers. One of them is big and bearish and just starting to gray at the edges, the other small and precise with black furrowed hair. They're both in gray suits with the ties loosened, bent over a table half their size, eating steaks and drinking from highballs. One of the guys is familiar. Vince catches the tail end of their conversation, the smaller guy checking his watch—"We have to be upstairs in twenty minutes . . ."—before they turn together to take in Vince.

"I'm sorry. But I need one more vote to turn the TV from the ball game to the news. What do you guys say? Ten minutes of news?"

The smaller guy tries to wave him off. "We're only gonna be here a few minutes."

But the big guy is curious. "Why do you want to watch the news?"

"Well. The election's tomorrow."

"You don't say? Tomorrow?" Something about this is greatly amusing to the two men, and Vince feels a bit off balance, and then remembers where he's seen the familiar guy. He's a congressman. Starts with an *F*. But Vince can't come up with the name. "I had no idea," the guy says. He's probably in his forties, aging like a farm kid or a boozy lawyer, managing to be at the same time boyish and jowly. His voice is authoritative and friendly, but the edges are soft, like he's talking with a hunk of steak in his mouth. "It doesn't look like they want to watch the news." He gestures to the guys at the bar, their heads lined and tilted up at the TV like they're feeding from a high trough.

"It'd be good for 'em," Vince says.

"You think so?" asks the big congressman. He laughs. "Okay. You got a deal." He stands, raises a draft beer, and covers his heart. "Esteemed colleagues, the representative from Table Six in the great state of Washington—"

The other guy laughs.

"—home of glorious wheat fields and aluminum plants, cool, clear rivers and snow-capped mountains, and the finest bar patrons in this great country, proudly casts his vote in favor of ten minutes of misery and heartache courtesy of the national news."

The guys at the bar raise their glasses in confused reverie as the bartender reaches up to turn the channel.

"Thank you," Vince says.

The two guys at the table raise their drinks to Vince, who makes his way back to his stool. On TV, Jimmy Carter is somber, his brow creased. He does not look like a man running for reelection. Apparently he has cut short his campaigning and left Chicago to announce that the Iranians' demands for release of the hostages are still unreasonable: *I know that all Americans will want their return to be on a proper basis which is worthy of the suffering and sacrifice which the hostages have endured.* The news cuts to Carter and Mondale walking across the White House lawn, their arms around each other, as if supporting one another, then cuts to the Ayatollah waving to throngs of wild supporters and then to the Iranian parliament, ties and turbans and sunglasses, long beards and thick mustaches—as Dan Rather outlines the conditions for the hostages' release: *return of the late Shah's billions of dollars, unfreezing of Iran's assets . . .*

Then to Ronald Reagan, shaking hands and waving to a throng that rivals the Ayatollah's for size and zeal: *Obviously all of us want this tragic situation resolved. That's my deepest hope, and I know it's yours.*

The news jets back and forth between Iran and the United States: the family of one of the hostages, Iranian students dancing on a burning American flag, Edmund Muskie, Warren Christopher, an Iranian oil rig, a line at a gas pump, a line of unemployed—the rush of images crashing together into a flow that might be history or might just be noise, disconnected and selective like memory, and loosed of all context—children on cots in a homeless shelter, unsold cars on lots, missiles emerging from underground silos, and a commercial for spaghetti sauce that prompts the bartender to reach up and turn the TV back to the football game.

And that's it. There is what you *believe* and there is what you *want* and these things are fine. But they're just ideas, in the end. History, like any single life, is made up of actions. At some point, the thinking and believing and deciding fall away and all that's left is the doing. The bartender steps away from the TV and smiles at Vince. "Sorry," he says. "But your time's up."

Spokane, Washington

1980 / November 4 / Tuesday / 12:03 A.M.

# chapter ~~IIII~~ III

Vince stands in the street-lit shadows outside Sam's Pit, his hands deep in his pockets. It's early yet, but he can see Sam moving inside. Vince takes the piece of gum he was chewing and tosses it in a field. Rolls his neck from side to side. Cold. In front of him, the Pit glows like a country hearth. He supposes he's as ready as he's going to be.

Walks up the steps. The door sticks and then gives way to the warm foyer and a smiling Eddie, who is holding a rack of battered chicken.

"Hey, Sam."

"Goddamn it, Vince Camden! Where you been?"

"Traveling a little."

"People been asking on you. The police even come by the other night."

"Yeah. I talked to them. We got it sorted out."

"I says, 'Who you askin' on? Vince Camden? Hell, turn back 'round and go on outta here, 'cause Vince Camden is the most law-abiding character ever come through that door.'" Eddie winks. "That smart-ass cop, know what he says to me? 'Sorry, Sam, but that ain't sayin' a great deal.'" Eddie throws his head back and laughs. "Son of a bitch had a point, too." He looks down at the tray of chickens. "You're early for cards."

"Yeah, I know," Vince says. He follows Eddie into the dining room, and sits at the counter while the chicken is seized by the grease-filled frying pans. No one is in the dark dining room behind him and the only light is in the kitchen, making it seem like Eddie is cooking on a stage.

"That new fella Ray been askin' on you, too," Eddie says. He pours Vince a whiskey neat from a bottle under the table.

"Does he come in a lot?" Vince puts a five on the table. In a single motion Eddie swipes the five and leaves three bucks.

"Ray? Last couple nights he been comin' in regular, right around two o'clock, hittin' up the whores and whatnot. Ain't much of a cardplayer but he does pretty good with the females, I guess."

Wait for the guy to come to you. Easy enough.

"So where'd you go?" Eddie asks.

"Home for a few days."

Eddie looks up from his chicken. "No kiddin'. Where's that?"

"New York."

"That's what I heard. So you got people back there?"

"No." Vince is almost surprised to hear himself admit this. He doesn't have people there. His people are here now. When does a place cease to be home?

"Me neither," Eddie says. "I got a kid over to Seattle won't talk to me, and a sister in Indiana got kids, but I don't look in on them. Beyond that . . . my people are long gone."

Vince swirls the booze in his glass, takes in the smell of the chicken and the warmth of the stove. "You ever count?"

Eddie looks up. "Count?"

"Yeah. How many dead people you know. I did that the other day."

"No shit. How high you get?"

"I was at sixty-three when I stopped counting."

Eddie stares at him as if waiting for a translation, then waves him off with a breaded thigh. "Hell, I lose sixty-three a year. I go right past the front page, sports, funnies, go straight to the obituaries. Make sure I ain't in there." He talks while he uses tongs to turn splattering drumsticks and thighs in black pans on all four burners. "No, I don't need to count, Vince. When your time is up . . . you know." He looks up and meets Vince's eyes. "You're a young man, yet. Probably get invited to a wedding for every funeral you go to. Me, I can't remember the last wedding I went to. But I get a note for a funeral ever-goddamn month." Eddie carries a pan to the sink. "I'm so tired of funerals I'll probably skip my own."

Vince opens his mouth to say something clever, but superstition or simple fear kicks in and he thinks better of it, raises his glass, toasts the old man's back, and drains his whiskey.

THE CARDPLAYERS TRICKLE in one at a time and each time the door opens Vince tenses, but instead of Ray he gets smiles and handshakes, pats on the back. "What, you need more of our money?" Jacks practically hugs him and the whiskeys go down easy, and before Vince knows it he's back at his usual spot at his usual table, watching the cards, which blend like liquid between his fingers, and he's amazed at the way the cards always come together, amazed how they never crash edges and break the shuffle. He can do this a hundred times and never fuck it up; a hundred times and each time they'll mix as cleanly as two pitchers of water being poured together. And, at that moment, how can you fear a blunt object like Ray Sticks, so earthbound and simple, when you are capable of such magic, when you're capable of flight? He slings the cards around the table and they glide across the smooth surface and stop right where he dreamed and would it be so hard for this night to never end, for this card game to go on forever?

Jacks gathers in his cards. "The night my wife finally leaves me, we stay up all night trying to fix things. 'Come on, baby,' I say. And I ask her, 'What's the problem?' She says, 'You're not smart enough or sensitive enough and all you care about is food and football and you don't listen or make enough money and you're mean to my family.' Christ-Take-Me-Home, the woman got a list goes on four hours. And then she leaves. Packs some clothes and walks right out the door."

Vince looks at his cards.

"That night, I sleep alone for the first time in twelve years," Jack says. "And I sleep like shit, too, keep looking over to her side, the pillow tucked under the bedspread, the way she's made it for twelve years, only now it might just stay that way forever. Finally I wake up for good at four in the morning, in them sweats make you stick to the covers, only you're cold, not hot. You ever get those?"

Jacks tosses in two dollars to open.

"Now, I never remember my dreams. Never. But this night, for some reason . . . four in the morning, my dream comes back to me clear as I'm sittin' here. Clear as if it really happened. In this dream, I'm at a football game, best seats I've ever had. It's the Raiders and the Dolphins. And the Raiders are killing 'em. Shula's in fuckin' tears."

Vince takes a bite of chicken—hot and perfect and greasy—drinks his whiskey, and calls the bet.

"Now, I love football. But I've never had a dream about it. Next morning, I pick up the paper and the TV game is the goddamn Raiders playing the goddamn Dolphins, just like my dream. Now, maybe I knew they were playing and it was in my—what do you call it?—subconscious, but I swear to God I had no idea those two teams were playing. So I'm thinkin' it's a sign, right?"

Jacks takes a pull from the champagne magnum he keeps between his tree-trunk thighs. "So an hour before kickoff, I call around, find out that the Raiders are six-point underdogs and I think this all must be happening for some reason, so I take Oakland and the points like it's Muhammad Ali fighting Barry Fuckin' Manilow. Two Gs. Credit. All the money I don't got in the world."

The guys whistle and, one by one, bet or fold without looking away from Jacks.

"Soon as I do it, I feel like an asshole. All day I got this terrible feeling, like I made a big mistake. Christ, I got no job and I'm gonna bet two grand on a lousy dream?

"Terrible game. The Raiders can't move the ball for shit. With a minute left, Dolphins are up thirteen–zip and my six points are as worthless as dimes in a casino."

The guys smile, lean forward.

"So I'm sittin' there, gonna lose two grand that I don't have, and suddenly my life makes sense to me: Peggy leaving, the bankruptcy, this string of bad decisions, a whole life of fuckups, really, and as soon as I admit that to myself, it's like a fuckin' miracle: Stabler hangs one up and fuckin' Freddie Belitnikof of all people gets behind the safety and hauls it in, and bang, forty seconds to go and goddamn Oakland pulls to thirteen–six. All they gotta do is hit the extra point and I push the bet. A tie. I don't win . . . but at least I don't lose either. And that's the hell of it. I mean: I want to win, sure. Who doesn't? But come on. In the end, what more can a guy like me ask for . . . than to not lose?"

Smiles and nods around the table.

"So they line up the point after, and for the first time in years, I start praying, right? The kind of praying that's more like making a deal, the kind you do when your wife finds the other woman's bra or the jury's considering the evidence?"

Knowing laughter.

"*I swear I'll go to church. Stop drinking. Be nice to children and old fuckers.* I'm praying and the Miami players wander up to the line and by this time I've run out of prayers so I'm offering to do anything if they'll make this point: *I'll eat shit off a sidewalk. I'll suck off a dog.*"

Heads roll back. Tears are wiped.

"Anything to make this point. And come on! It's a goddamned

extra point; they make these in their sleep. It's gonna be okay, I realize, and as soon as I think that, I'll be goddamned if the snap doesn't go high and of course God would never let me push this game. He and I both know I don't deserve a push. The ball sails high over the holder's head, and I fall forward off my chair and wish I were dead . . . and I will be goddamned if that son-of-a-bitch backup quarterback doesn't do the most amazing thing I've ever seen. He jumps up and he somehow snatches that football out of the air—"

Jacks holds his hands high above his head, the guys grinning.

"And right there, on my knees in front of our nineteen-inch TV, I start crying. Like a goddamn baby. I whimper as that holder somehow gets that ball down just as the kicker is running toward it and I think, you know what, you son of a bitch, sometimes even a guy like me catches a break."

Guys cover their mouths.

"And right, then, that kicker runs up to the ball, his footwork perfect, the line holding, and I'll be goddamned if that goddamned kicker doesn't do the goddamnedest thing I've ever seen in a football game. All that worthless dog-fucker has to do is kick the damn ball and I don't lose two grand. Kick the ball and I break even. Instead, that cockbite son of a bitch takes his three steps and he falls on that thing like it's a fuckin' hand grenade. Apparently, he can't get that high snap out of his mind and he just falls on it, lays there on that ball like it's a goddamned cheerleader. Game over. I lose two grand."

Howls of laughter. Guys slap the table.

"Couple days later, Peggy called. Said why don't we give it one more try?" Jacks shrugs and mutters. "Bitch."

THE LAUGHTER HAS faded to drunken hums, and Vince has nearly forgotten why he's there as he rakes his cards in—a pair of sixes—

and it's not until he bets and hears the door open that Vince realizes this game can't last forever and by then it's almost a relief to look up and see the pocked cheeks, sharp sideburns, and aviator sunglasses of Lenny Huggins. Lenny looks around the room, settles on Vince, shakes his head, and starts walking over. He walks differently than he did before; Vince recognizes that walk, the confidence. He looks for the outline in Lenny's jacket.

Just him and Jacks left. The cards are flopped and two more sixes hit the table. Vince smiles to himself. Four of a kind. You've got to be kidding. Lenny approaches warily. "I'm out," Vince says, and pushes the money in front of him over to Jacks.

"What are you doing?" Jacks asks.

"I gotta go," Vince says.

"Vince." Lenny Huggins has reached the table. "I can't believe you're here. I heard you came back, but I really thought you was smarter than that."

"No," Vince says, "I'm not."

The guys at the table follow the conversation like a tennis match.

"You ready?"

"Where's your buddy?"

"He's waiting for us."

"I hope you know what you're getting into, Lenny."

"Is that some kind a warning?"

"Yeah," Vince says. "Some kind." He pushes his chair back and Lenny jerks away from the table, his hand going to his waist. Okay, Vince thinks, now you know where the gun is. If it goes badly, that might be a good thing to know. Vince stands and reaches for his backpack.

"I'll carry that for you," Lenny says.

Vince hesitates, and then tosses it to him. He still has his cards in his hand. He flips them up on the table and the guys stare uncomprehendingly at his four sixes, all except Petey, who is smiling up at him.

"See you tomorrow, Vince?" Petey asks.

It's funny, the casual way people toss something like that off. That's sort of a basic unit of happiness, a minimum daily requirement . . . tomorrow. How many times does someone ask that and you just say yes without thinking, when in fact there are any number of reasons it might not happen? Vince looks at Lenny, then back at the table. "Sure," he says. "Tomorrow." And he starts for the door.

**LENNY THROWS VINCE'S** backpack in the trunk. Then he has Vince open his coat and lift his shirt and his pant legs. Satisfied, he motions to the front seat of the Cadillac. "You drive," he says to Vince.

"I've had a lot to drink."

"Go slow."

"I don't know where we're going."

"I'll tell you."

"How about if you drive and I tell *you* where to go."

"Get in," Lenny says.

He has Vince drive west through downtown. It's dark and cold; they swing from streetlight to streetlight on the dew-slicked streets, the buildings distorted by their own shadows, tilting toward them—a city of parallelograms, a city of sharp angles. "You must get terrible mileage," Vince says.

Lenny watches him closely. "What?"

"An eight-year-old Cadillac. What do you get? Ten? Twelve?"

"I get fifteen," Lenny says.

Vince laughs. "No way you get more than twelve."

"Highway, I get fifteen."

"Nope. There's no way, Lenny."

"Shut the fuck up, Vince!"

"Okay." Vince drives. "But there's no way."

They drive in silence for a few minutes and then Lenny snaps.

"You're such an asshole, Vince! Why do you gotta know everything all the time?"

"Twelve?"

"Yes," Lenny spits. "I get twelve."

He has Vince drive to a motel at the base of the Sunset Hill, at the west edge of downtown, etched into a basalt, pine-covered hill that guards the city like a wall; it is bisected by the old four-lane highway leading into town, which lost the traffic when the interstate was built parallel to it. But the highway still has the old fifties and sixties motor hotels that used to herald the beginning of the city, with their hopeful modernist signs—faded Technicolor horseshoes and curling, lighted arrows. ABOVE-GROUND POOLS! HOURLY RATES! COLOR TV!

They park at the far end, in the dark dark, outside a one-story row of motel doors—as the headlights roll across the face of the building, Vince can see the doors are marked with odd numbers between one and nine. There are no other cars in the gravel lot.

"Nine," Lenny says. He nods toward the end of the building. "Knock once and then put your hands on your head. I'll open the door and then you go in."

"No password? You ought to have a password."

"Shut up, Vince."

They climb out of the car. Vince closes the door behind him and walks across the parking lot, the gravel crunching beneath his feet. He goes over it in his mind: the first part is going to be the toughest. Make it through the night and you're home. Vince stands in front of the door, calms his jangly nerves, and knocks once. Then puts his hands on his head. From behind, Lenny reaches around him and opens the door. It swings into a dark room, lit only by a lamp on an end table. He pushes Vince inside.

They step into a narrow motel living room—a couch, a chair, a TV, and an end table—connected to an even smaller kitchenette, a Formica table, and one kitchen chair half on the living room carpet. There are two closed doors off the living room, most likely leading to a bedroom and a bathroom.

"Sit," Lenny says. Vince sits in the chair. Above the couch is a strangely calming painting of a mountain landscape, with a line of black trees in the foreground. It's one of those paintings you can't quite get your arms around because the perspective is all fucked up—the foreground trees less focused than the mountains they shield. Still, he likes the trees. You could hide forever in a forest of fuzzy trees.

The bedroom door opens then and out comes Ray Sticks, wearing his dark slacks and a dress shirt open to a V-neck T-shirt. No shoes. He slicks back his black hair. "Hiya, chief." Ray leaves the door open behind him and it takes a second for Vince's eyes to adjust before he sees, in the windowless bedroom, on the bed, huddled against the headboard . . . Beth. Her cast is gone and she's holding that red arm tenderly against her side. Her left eye is bruised.

"He broke my arm!" she says, and starts crying.

Vince's head falls forward to his chest—his *plan* suddenly seeming naive and reckless. Goddamn it.

Ray looks into the bedroom and back. "Technically, I rebroke her arm."

Vince forces himself to open his eyes. He looks past Ray into the bedroom. "Are you okay?" he asks.

She nods once. Pats her hair down and sets her face in anger toward Ray.

Vince says, "Look, I'm not giving you anything until I see her walk out that door."

"That door?" asks Ray. He stands above Vince, smiling.

But it is Lenny who begins pacing around the room and speaking: "Look, Vince, I told you from the beginning this could go easy or it could go hard—"

Ray looks back at Lenny, then smiles at Vince, goes to the kitchen, and opens the refrigerator.

"And you chose the hard way," Lenny says. "I didn't want—"

"You don't need her," Vince says to Ray's back. "Let her go."

Lenny slaps him. Vince's face barely moves. "Hey! Up here! I'm talking to you, motherfucker!" Lenny says.

But Vince continues to address Ray. "I mean it. I won't tell you anything until she's gone."

Ray turns and smiles over his shoulder. "Sure. Whatever you say, chief." He grabs two apples, a paring knife, and a dish towel, and returns to the living room.

Lenny looks from Vince to Ray and back. "What the hell's going on here? Why are you two talking to each other? Talk to me."

Ray ignores him. He spreads the dish towel out on the coffee table, sets the apples and the knife down on it. He sits down on the couch.

Vince can't take his eyes off the knife. "Let her go and you can have the mailman. He wants to talk to you. He wants to steal more cards."

"So call him," Ray says. He picks up one of the apples and the knife. "Invite him over."

"I can't tonight. It's too late. He unhooks his phone. I'll call him in the morning. We meet at this restaurant. I'll take you there."

Ray begins slicing the peel off one of the apples. "I don't know. Morning's a long time away, chief."

Vince leans forward. "I got some money."

Ray laughs. "Yeah, your girlfriend was saying something about that. Said you two were gonna buy her a house."

Vince tries not to show his deep disappointment.

Ray wipes the knife blade on the towel. "We decided we'd go down tomorrow and withdraw the money. Have a little party." He winks.

Lenny stares at Ray. "What the hell's going on here? What's everyone talking about? This is my deal now."

Ray stands, reaches in his pocket, and comes out with a twenty-dollar bill. "Go get us something to drink."

Lenny looks from Ray to Vince to Beth and back. "It's three-thirty in the morning. Where am I supposed to find something to drink?"

Ray just stares at him, until finally Lenny grabs the twenty and starts to turn for the door. Ray grabs Len's shoulder, reaches into his coat to his waistband, pulls out the gun he was packing, a black semiautomatic, and puts it in the back of his own waistband. "I don't want you to shoot your balls off," he says.

Lenny looks briefly at Vince—a shudder of understanding, maybe—but he goes out for booze anyway.

"That guy's a fuckin' idiot," Ray says when Lenny's gone. "How could you work with such morons?"

"You take what you get."

"I guess." Ray walks to the bedroom door, the knife still in his hands. Beth shrinks beneath his eyes. "Honey, your boyfriend and I are gonna talk awhile. You get some rest." Then he closes the bedroom door and sits on the back of the couch, his feet on the cushions, so that he's still above Vince. They stare at each other.

"She's nice," Ray says.

Vince looks back at the painting behind Ray, those black trees inscrutable.

"You know who I am?" Ray points to his own chin with the knife.

"Yeah," Vince says. "I know who you are."

"Say it."

"Ray Sticks."

Ray smiles at the sound of his name, like a thirsty man getting a drink. "So you *are* from back there."

"Yeah."

"That's what Lenny said, but I just thought he was full of shit. So who were you? Would I know you?"

"No," Vince says.

"You a mechanic? Work in somebody's crew back there?"

"I stole credit cards. Same as here. I wasn't connected."

"Oh." Ray is disappointed. "That's too bad." He sits back on the couch and considers Vince. "So you're nobody, but then you come here—and you know a few things . . . how to play cards. All of a sudden you're the man, right? King of the gangsters." He laughs. "Shit."

Vince is quiet. He watches Ray shave the peel off the apple, just taking the thinnest layer of rind, so that the white apple underneath is still tinted red. Ray looks up, his thick eyebrows arching. "I hate peels. I don't like crust on my sandwiches either."

He finishes one apple, then sets it down—raw and exposed—and starts on the other one. "So what do you think about this place?" Ray asks.

"Spokane?" Vince shrugs. "I like it."

"No, you don't. You can't."

"I like it a lot."

"No shit?"

"Yeah."

"You wanna know what I hate most about this place?" Ray asks.

"What?"

"The pizza. You can't eat it. It's a fuckin' crime. I mean, come on. Where the fuck do you go for a slice around here?"

"You get used to it," Vince says. "I've kind of developed a taste for deep-dish."

"No! Come on! How can you eat that shit? It's pepperoni on French toast. You can't get used to a thing like that. What kind of place is it, you can't get a fuckin' slice of pizza? Or a sandwich? You ask for a fuckin' cheesesteak in this town, they look at you like you're askin' 'em to grill a fuckin' baby."

Vince smiles in spite of himself. "You ever try to catch a cab?"

Ray's hands go to the top of his head. "I been in both of 'em."

They laugh.

"And the fuckin' drivers!" Ray is incredulous.

Vince nods. "I know. I know. It's like a whole town of old people. Even the young people drive like old people."

"I never seen anything like it. So polite, it makes you wanna puke. I'm here a week, I pull up to one of them . . . *four-way stops*. What the fuck is that?"

Vince laughs. "I know. I know."

"Four assholes sittin' there, each with their own fuckin' stop sign, everyone staring at everyone else like it's a damn tea party. Sit there ten minutes mouthin' to each other, 'You go. No, you go. No, I insist. No, really.' I tell you, chief, one of these days I'm gonna drive up to one of them four-way stops, pull out my gun, and shoot every one of them motherfuckers in the head."

Vince is smiling, nodding. Glances at the bedroom door.

"And what about——"

Vince is up and across the room before Ray can finish the sentence, and while he's quickly disappointed, he's also duly impressed by how quickly the big man uncoils and comes off the back of the couch with a glint of stainless, and the sharpness of the point of that paring knife in his cheek, just below his eye, and it's that pain and the force of Ray's big hand on his throat, squeezing, that convinces Vince to let go of Ray's shoulders and allow himself to be pushed back into his chair.

Vince coughs and feels his tender throat, then runs his hand over the slash in his cheek. It's small, little more than a nasty shaving cut. And yet he remembers the tip of the knife against his cheekbone, just below his eye socket, and the sound of his own bone being scraped makes him shiver.

Ray stands above him, holding the knife, a look of sheer boredom on his face. "Let's see."

Vince pulls his hand away and shows the big man the cut.

"I missed your eye. You're lucky."

Ray stands there a minute more, looking around the room. "Okay," he says, as if he's glad they're through with that silliness.

He wipes the spot of red off the point of the knife, and then sits on the back of the couch again. He halves, then quarters, then eighths the apple, tosses a piece to Vince, who catches it. Ray looks like he forgot something for a moment. "Where were we?

"Oh." Ray smiles and claps his hands. "What about the broads? Have you ever seen such ugly broads? I don't know whether I'm supposed to bang 'em or have 'em chase sticks."

LENNY COMES BACK with a three-quarters-full bottle of Kahlúa.

"What the fuck is that?" Ray asks.

"Kahlúa. It's a coffee liqueur."

"You brought me chocolate fuckin' milk?"

"You can make White Russians. Or . . . them mudslides."

"Mudslides."

"Yeah."

"Mudslides." He looks at Vince. "We're gonna fuckin' make mudslides."

Lenny looks from Vince to Ray. "I couldn't find any open stores. It's four in the morning, Ray."

"So where'd you get this?"

"I drove to my house."

Ray looks to Vince and shakes his head. *You believe the shit I have to put up with?* He opens the Kahlúa and sniffs it. Takes a drink. "Mudslides?"

"Okay, Vince, here's how it's gonna go down," Lenny starts. "You're gonna set up a meeting with the mailman. Introduce us."

But neither Ray nor Vince even bothers to look at him.

"So did they give you that name?" Ray asks. "Vince? That's a good name."

"I picked it," Vince says.

"So what's your real name?"

"Marty."

"Yeah, Vince is better. I'm supposed to be Ralph LaRue. You imagine? Ralph fuckin' LaRue? Come on. I tried it awhile, but I couldn't do it."

"You get used to the new name."

"I ain't changing my name for these fuckers." He thinks of something else. "Hey, what kind of training you get for that baking job?" Ray offers the bottle of Kahlúa.

Vince takes it. "Six months at the community college."

Ray cocks his head. "So what's that like?"

"Making donuts? I like it," Vince says.

"You takin' a percentage?"

"No."

"Laundering money?"

"No."

"Straight skim?"

"No," Vince says. "I just . . . make donuts."

Ray cocks his head. "I don't get it."

"It's . . . rewarding. What about you? What are you supposed to be?"

Ray eats an apple slice. "They got me in fuckin' diesel repair classes."

Vince smiles.

"Me. Repairing the fuckin' big rigs, right? Can you see that? *It's your fuckin' drivetrain, motherfucker.* Right?" Ray shrugs. "Turns out I ain't much of a student. My teacher said I got bad concentration. Gave me a fuckin' D." He takes the bottle back from Vince. "Guy was a prick."

Lenny has been standing with his hands on his hips. "Okay, if you two are done catching up, maybe someone can tell me what the hell's going on here."

"Sit down," Ray says, sliding a skinned apple slice into his mouth.

"No. You listen to me, Ray."

"Sit. Down."

"No. I don't know what you think—"

"Sit. The fuck. Down."

Lenny's face reddens. "Goddamn it, Ray!"

"Lenny," Vince says quietly.

"No! I'm tired of this. I brought you in on this, Ray. This is my thing."

Ray stalks across the room, puts his forearm in Lenny's neck, and pushes him backward, against the wall. Then he plants the paring knife against his shoulder and drives it slowly in, just above the collarbone. Lenny squawks and claws for the knife, protruding from his left shoulder. His legs kick at Ray's shins and he makes high-pitched peeps as he tries to get his hand on the handle.

Ray pulls the handgun from his waistband and points it back at Vince, who has started toward the two men. Vince stops. Then Ray puts the barrel of the gun in Lenny's mouth. "Shut the fuck up."

The squawking stops.

"Where is my twenty bucks?"

"Wha . . . Wha?" Lenny mutters with the gun barrel in his mouth.

"I give you twenty bucks, you come back with a half-gone bottle of chocolate milk from your house? Where the fuck is my twenty bucks?"

Lenny winces as he pulls the twenty from his pocket. Hands it to Ray.

Ray puts the money is his pocket. He pulls the gun out of Lenny's mouth. "Okay. Listen. You make another sound, I'll shoot you. You understand what I'm sayin'? I'm tryin' to talk to this man here. I'm tryin' to figure out this whole credit-card deal and I need you to be quiet."

Lenny looks down at the small knife handle sticking out of his collarbone. "What about the knife?"

"That's *my* fuckin' knife. You touch it and I'll carve you with it. Now shut the fuck up and sit the fuck down."

Lenny slides down, his back against the wall, the small knife handle sticking out of his shoulder. Ray looks sort of embarrassed by the whole thing. He chews his bottom lip. "You sit down, too," he says to Vince, who eases back in his chair. Ray walks back to the couch, pauses for a second, and tosses Lenny the dish towel. "You bleed on the carpet, I'm gonna peel you like this fuckin' apple." Lenny packs the towel around the knife handle, covering the bloom of blood on his shoulder.

Ray sits down across from Vince. "So what were we talkin' about?"

"HERE'S MY REAL problem. Lack of training. I got no diversification. Look at you. You got these skills. You can steal. Sell dope. Make donuts. And that credit-card thing, that sounds lucrative. I wanted in on that as soon as I heard about it. You're perfect for a place like this. Go out, earn yourself a living. Me, I just do that one thing."

Ray shrugs. "I'm good at it, but honestly, there ain't a lot of call for it. Even back there, I'd go months at a time without a real job. 'Course, some months, I can't hardly keep up with orders. It's seasonal, you know? Like in Philly, right before I left. Fuckin' worked my ass off. Everybody wants everybody done. I got people hiring me to do the guy just hired me to do the guy I'm supposed to do. You know? Crazy.

"But then I get busted and I'm supposed to go lay low in New York and I was goin' fuckin' buggy. I mean . . . I go a few months without workin' and I get—I don't know, *nervous*. My own fault, I guess. I work too hard. I get carried away. I want to *do something* and"—he leans forward, confessing—"between you and me, I end up doing the only fuckin' thing I know to do."

He looks over at Lenny, who is staring down at the knife handle in his shoulder and breathing in little bursts, like a woman having a baby. "And this guy . . . Jesus, *I'm* smarter than him. No, what I really need is a guy like you. Somebody else makes the money, somebody smart. I'm good at backing that guy up. You know?"

Vince nods.

"So . . . what do you think?"

Vince rubs his brow and glances to the bedroom door. "Yeah. I could see that."

Ray looks at the bedroom door and apparently thinks what Vince is thinking . . . Beth and the twenty thousand. He turns back. "Yeah. Well. We'll see how things go, huh?"

"Hey, Ray?" Lenny's brow is covered in sweat. The dish towel is about half red now. "I'm feeling kind of sick over here."

"Shut up," Ray says. But he stands up, goes to the kitchen, and gets a new dish towel. "Here." He takes the old one and tosses it into the sink. Then he goes to the window, parts the curtains, and looks out on the empty parking lot—gravel and a row of two-story rooms, painted doors without screens. It's after dawn, but the thick clouds make the light diffuse and Vince isn't sure of the time. Ray is staring out the window, too. "Pretty," he says.

It's the ugliest view Vince has ever seen.

Ray looks at his watch. "What do you say we try your mailman now?"

Vince nods to the bedroom door. "Will you let her go?"

"After she gets my money," Ray says. "You have my word." Ray opens the bedroom door. Beth is asleep, curled up against the headboard; she jolts awake. Her eye is swollen shut. "Get dressed," Ray says. "We're goin' to the bank."

Ray returns to the couch and pushes the phone across the table. "Call him."

Vince looks at the painting, those black green trees. That's how he feels, out of focus, unsure of his own lines. Finally, he leans forward, takes the receiver off the hook, and dials. Ray watches the plastic dial roll past the numbers.

"Hey. It's me. Vince. Look, that guy I told you about, he wants to meet."

Listens.

"I changed my mind, that's why."

Listens.

"The usual place. Say, nine?"

Listens.

"No, don't thank me. Really."

Listens.

"Right, we'll see you at nine."

He hangs up the phone.

Ray smiles. "What's this guy's name?"

"Clay," Vince says.

"Clay what?"

"Clay Gainer."

"So I call that same number, I'm gonna get this Clay Gainer?"

Vince doesn't answer.

"You better hope I get Clay Gainer." Ray picks up the phone and dials the same number Vince just dialed.

"Yeah, who is this?" Ray asks. "Clay who?" He looks up at Vince. "And what do you do, Clay?" Listens. "No, I'm the friend you're meeting later. I just wanted to make sure we were straight. So where's that meeting?"

Ray listens.

"No shit? They got good food there?"

He rolls his eyes. "Yeah, I suppose there's something to be said for cheap, you're right."

Ray shakes his head to Vince. "Okay. Hey, can we make it nine-thirty? Vince and I gotta swing by the bank first. Okay. See you then."

He hangs up. "Dicks fuckin' hamburgers? That's what's wrong with this town, right there. Everyone here is so cheap, they don't deserve a decent meal. You people would line up to eat gravel and tree bark if you could get two for one."

\*    \*    \*

THE WIND HAS picked up, streaming leaves off the shade trees and skipping phone lines like jump ropes. They brace against it as they walk to the car, in the full flush of morning—the sun blinking behind racing clouds. Ray walks behind Vince and Lenny, his arm around Beth's neck. She's showered and is back in black pants and a jean jacket; she has tried to put makeup on the black eye that Ray gave her. Her hair whips around her face. "You drive," Ray says to Vince, who takes Lenny's keys and climbs in behind the wheel.

Lenny slumps into the passenger seat, holding the bloody towel over the knife blade in his shoulder. "Can we take this out now?"

Ray looks at the wound. "You take it out now, it's just gonna bleed more. Don't worry. We'll get it in a little while."

"But I don't feel good, Ray. Maybe you could just drop me at home."

"Sure," Ray says. "In a little while."

Ray and Beth climb in the backseat. Ray pulls her close, his arm still around her neck, the gun nestled into her rib cage just below her breast. Vince catches her eyes in the rearview mirror and tries to reassure her, although of what he's not sure.

"You okay?" he asks her.

She nods.

"Drive," Ray says, and Vince does.

"So where's that house?"

"What house?" Vince asks.

"The house you two was gonna buy with my money."

"You want to see it?"

"Yeah. It's only eight-thirty. We got a little time."

Vince drives north, over the river, to the neighborhood where Beth's sad little bungalow sits, the paint chipped and fading, uneven shrubs on either side of the door. The "For Sale" sign—covered by a new sign that reads SOLD—shakes in the wind like someone loosening a tooth.

"That?" Ray stares out his window. "That's a fuckin' shack."

He turns to Beth. "I'm doin' you a favor. That place is one big shit from being an outhouse."

"It's nicer inside," Beth says.

"I hope so, because it's a fuckin' shack outside. What'd you give for it?"

"They were asking thirty-two," Beth says. "We offered twenty-eight-five."

Ray makes a face and looks up at Vince. "I wouldn't have give more than ten."

Vince drives away from the house, down a residential street, the leaves swirling in front of his car. He'd actually looked forward to living in this neighborhood. He looks up at Ray in the rearview. "So what are you gonna do?"

"What do you mean?"

"Once you get the credit-card thing rolling. And get my money. Then what?"

Ray just stares.

"I mean, are you gonna stay here? Get a crew together? What's your plan?"

"Don't worry about me. I got plans."

"What kind of plans?"

Ray shrugs. "Lay low here for a while, testify in a couple of things back in Philly. And then, when that's all done, and I've made a little money here, I'll just go back, pick up where I left off."

"To Philly?"

"No, I won't go back to Philly. I'll go to New York."

"You think they're gonna let you come back?"

Ray gestures with the gun. "Hey, I haven't said nothing about nobody who ain't already dead or in prison. I haven't given them shit about New York and I ain't gonna."

"They think you'll give up everybody eventually. One of the marshals told me you're an important witness."

"Fuck that." Ray looks out the window, chews his thick lip. "I never agreed to talk about New York. I'll give up a couple dead guys in Philly, then I'm goin' back."

"You really think they'll let you?"

"The feds?"

"No," Vince says simply.

"Who, the fellas?" Ray laughs. "Fuckin' A, the fellas gimme a fuckin' parade when I go back. Nobody does what I do as good as I did it. When they see I didn't rat nobody out, they'll throw me a fuckin' party."

Vince just drives. Ray is staring out the window and is quiet until Vince suddenly jerks the wheel, the tires squealing, and pulls into a small Catholic-school parking lot.

Ray looks around wildly, ducks behind Beth, and puts the gun in Vince's ear. "What the fuck are you doing?"

Vince turns off the car and holds his hands out to the side. "Voting."

"What?"

"I gotta vote."

"What the fuck are you talking about?"

"The election. For president. I gotta vote."

Ray stares at him for a couple of seconds, his anger becoming curiosity. "No shit? What's that like?"

"Voting? I don't know. I've never done it before."

Ray shrugs, waves the gun at the road. "Well . . . you're gonna have to do it later."

Vince catches Ray's eyes in the rearview again. He smiles. "Come on. We both know I'm not gonna do it later."

Ray pushes Vince's head forward with the gun. "Come on. Start the fuckin' car."

"No." Vince spreads his hands out to the side, head tilted forward because of the gun in his neck. "You'll have to shoot me." Outside, a woman and a man are walking in the parking lot toward the school.

"Goddamn it!" Ray says. "Drive the car!"

Vince speaks quietly, his head bowed, the gun barrel cold at the nape of his neck: "Look. I'm not crying here. I'm not begging, or pretending we aren't what we are. But I gotta do this first."

THEY SHUFFLE IN together, an odd and beat-up group. Vince is first, the cut on his cheek scabbed bright red, followed by Ray, his arm around Beth's neck in a way that doesn't exactly make them look like a couple. She uses her right arm to hold her left arm against her chest, folded like a bird's broken wing. Bringing up the rear is Lenny, who looks by far the worst, sweating and pale, his jacket zipped tight over the hump on his left shoulder—a bloody towel covering the three-inch knife handle.

They stand in a hallway outside the school, guarded by a fountain of holy water. Ray dips his fingers in and crosses himself. The polling place is down a short hallway, in the school's multipurpose room. Beth and Ray follow Vince down a hallway lined with pictures made by Sunday-school kids—two rows of bunnies across from some glue-and-leaf collages. They all turn their heads as they pass the cotton-ball bunnies; Vince imagines all those tiny hands drawing all those little bunnies and gluing all those cotton-ball tails. He looks over at Beth, thinks of Kenyon, and suddenly it's the only important thing: getting her out of this.

"That's cute," Ray says. "Cotton balls."

"I don't feel good," Lenny says.

The multipurpose room is half gymnasium, half cafeteria—the wood backboards cranked up against the ceiling, the lunch tables folded and rolled up against the walls. In the center of the room is a long wooden table, with three old women seated at the table, behind thick black ledgers. To the right of the women are four foldout voting booths, blindered on the sides, and a wooden ballot box padlocked in front. Vince stands just inside the doorway.

A woman is just finishing. She emerges from a voting booth and slides her ballot into the slot on top of the box.

Ray is at his ear. "So, how do you do this?"

"I don't really know," Vince says. He looks at Beth. She shrugs. Lenny opens the jacket, peels back the red towel, looks at his wound, and presses it all back against his shoulder.

One of the old women rises. She might be four feet tall, all gray, wearing the kind of shoes Vince's mom favored—the kind worn by nurses. "Is this your precinct, honey?"

Vince fumbles in his wallet for his voter registration card.

"That's okay. I don't need to see it. If you're on the list you get to vote. You folks in this precinct, too?"

"No," Ray says too quickly. "We're just waiting for him . . ."

She stares at him a minute, her mouth pinched like she's trying to keep something from getting out. "Okay." She points to the far wall. "I guess you can wait over there if you want." Ray, Beth, and Lenny move in a tight cluster.

The old woman takes Vince by the arm and leads him over to the table. "What's your last name, honey?"

"Camden."

She parks him in front of the first of the thick books. "This nice, clean-cut young man says that his last name is Camden. You got a ballot for Camden, Erlina?"

Erlina flips through the book, looking down through bifocals at the list of names. "Vincent J.?"

"Yes."

She turns the book to him and offers him a pen. Vince signs his name. They hand him a long, narrow card covered with several rows of numbers with corresponding tabs. Vince stares at it, wondering if he was supposed to have memorized the names these numbers represent, if maybe they ran some list in the paper while he was gone.

The first woman gestures toward a voting booth. "You got your pick of real estate over there, Vincent J. Camden." Vince likes the soft whistle of her voice through her dentures. "Slide that card inside the book and make sure you punch all the way down."

Vince looks back over his shoulder. Ray and Beth are watching him intently. Lenny is leaning against the wall, staring at the fluorescent lights on the ceiling.

Vince walks to the booth. There is a book attached to the frame of the voting booth and a small punch connected by a string. He slides his card down in the book, until the two holes on top line up with the two pegs on the book. Vince opens to the first page.

*Proposed by Initiative Petition*
*INITIATIVE MEASURE NO. 383*
*Shall Washington ban the importation and storage of non-medical radioactive wastes generated outside Washington, unless otherwise permitted by interstate compact?*

He skips to the next one.

*Proposed by the People to the Legislature*
*REFERENDUM BILL NO. 38*
*Shall $125 Million in State General Obligation Bonds be authorized for planning, acquisition, construction, and improvement of water supply facilities?*

He reads down the ballot. There are five of these questions, and all of a sudden it seems like a test he didn't study for: Does he want to pay $450 million for public waste disposal, does he want the state to disclaim unappropriated federal land, does he want to create a commission to discipline judges? What the hell? Vince stares at the first question. Reads it again. He turns to the elderly women at the table, who are giving a ballot to a man with a beard. The first woman sees the look on Vince's face, smiles gently, stands, and walks over.

"What is it, honey?"

"I wasn't expecting all this."

"What do you mean?"

"Some of these things . . . I guess I didn't prepare . . ."

She cocks her head.

"Like this radioactive thing. I didn't even hear about that."

She pats his arm and the vertical lines in her face spread into a smile. "Listen, honey. Just vote how you think is right. If you have to skip one, it's okay."

She returns to the table and Vince turns back to the ballot. He figures that it's a bad thing, bringing in nonmedical radioactive waste. He puts the little pointer in the YES hole, next to the arrow from the number one. He pushes down and he can feel the chad break through. It's a nice, small feeling. Water is good, too. Votes yes. But he votes No on public waste disposal, because $450 million seems a lot and he knows the mob is deep into garbage and will likely take a big whack into that money. He votes Yes on public lands and on disciplining judges (there are a couple he wouldn't mind seeing disciplined), and then he turns the page and there they are: the presidential candidates. He feels a quickening. Reagan and Bush are first, followed by Carter and Mondale, John Anderson and Patrick Lucey, and then a bunch of names he didn't expect to see. Clifton DeBerry of the Socialist Workers Party, Deirdre Griswold, of the Workers World Party; also Libertarians, Socialists, something called the Citizens Party . . . even a couple of Communists—Gus Hall and Angela Davis.

The guy with the beard is in the booth next to Vince.

"What'd you put for the radioactive thing?" Vince whispers.

He looks up. "What?"

"I had no idea there would be so many names for president," Vince says. "Women and Communists and everything."

The bearded guy shrugs and turns back to his ballot.

Vince looks around, sniffs, and settles back in his booth. He'll come back to the president. He flips the book until he finds Aaron Grebbe's name, in the state representative race, and pushes the pointer down. He reads the other names running for state offices, but he's never heard of any of them, so he turns to the page with the big congressman from the bar—Foley. He votes for Foley. He doesn't want to guess on the rest, or vote for someone who turns out to be an ass, so he skips them. That leaves the president.

Vince turns back to that page and stares at the names. He wonders about these men . . . what's at the center of them. What kind of men are they? Are they good? Wise? Tough? Have they risen from the rest of us, the best we have to offer? He wonders which traits he'd value most—the traits he has, or the traits he doesn't? You read the papers and watch the news and you think you have a sense of these men, but who are they, alone, at night? What would he do in their situation? What would *they* do in his situation?

Ronald Reagan. George Bush. Jimmy Carter. Walter F. Mondale. John B. Anderson. Patrick J. Lucey. He tries to connect the names to what he knows about these men, but they're just names on a page, and he finds himself filled with a cold panic; maybe this whole thing is stupid. He feels foolish. Maybe you build a thing up in your mind and believe that it connects to your own life and has some meaning. But what if you're just fooling yourself? What if it doesn't mean anything in the end?

Or is it enough to *believe* that a thing has meaning? He glances over at Beth, takes a breath, and bends over the ballot book, the whole world for a moment bordered by the cloth walls of a voting booth.

The pointer hovers above the names, and only then do you make the decision; a gentle push and the paper gives way in a kind of release that gives way to a vision of the house you bought for Beth, kids skipping rope while she watches from the porch—and you're embarrassed by the flatness of your dreams, even as you stare at the ballot and think that, if nothing else, for the first and the last time in this short, misguided life, Vince Camden has voted for president.

**LENNY IS SLUMPED** against the passenger-side door, out cold, his jacket still tight around his shoulder. Vince drives in silence, a half smile on his face.

"So what is it?" Ray asks. "Like a fuckin' wishbone? Or birthday candles? You won't get your wish if you tell?"

"No, I just don't want to say, that's all."

"What the fuck you don't want to say? What difference could it possibly make?"

"It makes a difference to me."

"Bullshit."

"Look, I'm not gonna tell you. And it doesn't matter anyway. I could tell you anything and you wouldn't know if I'm telling the truth."

The gun against his neck again. "And I could shoot you in your fuckin' head!"

"Okay. I voted for Reagan."

"You did?"

"No. I voted for Carter."

"Really?"

"Nope. Anderson. See what I mean? I could tell you anything."

Ray glares out the window as they drive through downtown. Vince angles in front of Beth's bank—red brick and glass double doors—and pulls into a metered space. He puts the car in park, reaches over, and feels Lenny's throat for a pulse. It's weak. He opens Lenny's jacket a little and looks at the bloody wound, the knife handle wedged just above his collarbone. "I really think we ought to take him to a hospital," Vince says. "He doesn't look good."

"He didn't look good *before* I stabbed him," Ray says.

Ray looks up at the bank, his eyes moving from the double doors to the windows and the pillars. "Okay," he says. "Here's how we do this." He grabs the wrist on Beth's broken arm. She shudders in pain. "You're gonna go in there alone. I'm gonna stand right there on the sidewalk with your boyfriend. If I see you point, or talk to a security guard or do anything screwy, then three things are gonna happen in quick order."

Ray holds up one gnarled finger, the nail perfectly clipped, the knuckle bent and swollen from too much work as part of a fist. "One: I shoot your fuckin' boyfriend in his balls. Right in front of your eyes. You're gonna watch him go down on the sidewalk and know that you could've stopped it. Number two: I drive straight to your apartment and I shoot that old lady that watches your kid. Three: I take that baby of yours and you never see him again. And know this, lady: I will be the angel of his fuckin' nightmares. I will skin that kid like an apple and mail you little squares. He's gonna be six before he finally dies. You hear me?"

Beth nods and he lets go of her wrist. The breath goes out of her.

They climb out of the car slowly. Lenny doesn't stir. As they walk to the front doors, Vince tries to catch her attention— (*Run!*)—but she won't look at him.

Ray and Vince stand on the cold sidewalk, hands in their pockets, squinting into the gusting wind, their breath steaming, watching Beth walk into the bank and up to a teller's window.

"She ain't gonna run," Ray says. "She ain't gonna get help. I know you think she will, but she won't."

Vince doesn't say anything.

"I know people. It's . . . a gift. I can see it in her eyes. She ain't got the juice for something like that. She's broken. She'll go get my money and she'll bring it to me, and when I finally shoot her in the eyes, in a lot of ways, it'll be a fuckin' relief to her."

Vince closes his eyes.

"You know what I believe? In my heart? I believe that I never did somebody didn't really want me to do them. I believe that. I do. Down deep, they all thought I was doing 'em a favor."

Ray shifts his weight, still trying to make small talk. "So come on, chief. Tell me. Who'd you vote for back there?"

Vince doesn't answer.

"You know what? You might as well tell me now. 'Cause in about an hour, when you're on your knees, pissing your pants and bleeding out your fuckin' eyeholes, begging me to finish you off . . . you'll tell me."

"No," Vince says. "I won't."

Ray snaps and steps up in his face. "You're such a cute mother-fucker! You have no idea what I can do!"

Vince doesn't answer.

Ray stares into his eyes for a moment, then steps back, seeming embarrassed that he lost his temper. He clears his throat. Pretends to laugh. "You know one thing I don't mind here . . . is the weather. It's a little cold today, but I do not miss the fuckin' humidity, that's for sure."

Beth comes out of the bank. The wind startles her hair like a row of birds. She hands Ray her purse. Catches Vince's eyes briefly. They walk back to the car. Vince squeezes her arm. "In front," Ray says. Beth climbs in front, between Vince and Lenny, who doesn't stir, slumped against the window.

Ray begins counting the bundles of hundred-dollar bills.

"You said we could go after we gave you the money," Beth says.

Ray smiles. Scratches his head. Seems amused. "I'll tell you what. If your boyfriend tells me who he voted for, you can go."

"No," Vince says.

Ray laughs. "I don't get what the fuck is the big deal with who you voted for."

"You really want to know?" Vince says.

"Yeah," Ray says. "I wanna know."

Vince adjusts the rearview mirror so that Ray's eyes are in the center of it. As good a time as any, he supposes. He pats Beth on the leg and she looks at him hopefully, as if she knew he was biding his time until he made some move.

"I got my first juvenile felony conviction when I was fourteen."

"I was nine," Ray says. "Big deal."

Vince continues: "My first adult felony conviction came two weeks after my eighteenth birthday. So I've been a convicted felon my whole life. You know what you lose when you get convicted of a felony? Two things: the right to own a gun and the right to vote. Every presidential election, I was either in jail or on parole. But I never heard anyone complain that they couldn't vote. Who cares about that, huh?"

Ray shrugs.

"Voting is for assholes, like paying taxes. Or having a job. And guns—big fuckin' deal. You can always find a gun on the street. Any felon can buy a gun. But just try to vote in jail. You can't do it. It's funny, you think about it, the only thing we *can't* do . . . is something we don't even care about doing.

"But lately I've been thinking." Vince glances over at Beth, who is watching him intently. He goes back to Ray's eyes in the rearview mirror. "Our old life, Ray? It wasn't about money or drugs or women or even power. It's about this hole we were always trying to fill. Big fuckin' hole. One more score, one more job . . . more booze, more broads, more money. But the hole never gets filled. We think we're so smart because we don't follow the rules, but tell me, Ray, you ever seen an old, happy crook? You ever seen *one of us* sitting on a porch with his grandkids? You know why you've never seen that? Because by that time, the hole is all that's left."

Ray is staring back at him.

"When they put me in this program, I was gonna be someone new. I was gonna change. But I just did the same old things. I was the same fuckin' guy." Vince pulls out his wallet. "Then, a week ago, I got this in the mail." Hands the crinkled voter registration card back to Ray. "And I thought, what if I don't *try* changing anymore? What if I just decide to *be this guy?* The guy on the card?"

Ray turns the card over in his hand, and then gives it back.

"What happens after you get this money, Ray? After you meet the mailman? How much money is enough? Fifty? A hundred? A million? Whatever it is, it won't be enough. The hole gets bigger. The more you put in, the bigger it gets. Kill me. Kill the mailman. Kill everyone in this town, Ray. Take everything they own. And then what?"

Vince turns so he's facing Ray. "*They gave us freedom*, Ray! Not from jail. From ourselves, who we used to be. They told us, 'Go be someone else. Go fix that hole' . . . you know how rare an opportunity that is? And how hard it is? It takes more courage than anything we've ever done. But it's ours if we want it, Ray. All we have to do . . . is get up in the morning. Go to work." He looks over and takes Beth's hand. "Come home at night and take care of our people." He looks back at Ray. "All we have to do is vote."

Ray stares off.

"You can't go back to New York when this is done," Vince says. "I just got back from there. I saw Johnny Boy."

Ray's eyes snap up to Vince's.

"I went to see him because I thought he sent you here to kill me." Vince shrugs. "Turns out he'd never even heard of me. Carmine. Ange. Toddo. I saw 'em all. Played cards with 'em over on Mott Street. They all wanted to hear about you. John wanted to hear about you."

Ray's mouth goes up in a half smile at the memory. He speaks in a whisper. "How is John? His kid—"

"Yeah. I heard. You took care of that for him, didn't you, Ray? The guy who killed his kid. You did that. Well . . . John sent me back here to take care of *you.*"

Ray stares. "Bullshit."

"He sent me back to kill you, Ray."

Ray's face is cold. "I don't believe you."

"You can't go back there," Vince says. "You can never go back. Ray Sticks is dead. Just like Marty Hagen. We died the minute they put us in the program. And we only got two choices now. We can be ghosts, running around thinking we're still alive. Or we can be somebody else."

Ray rubs his head.

Vince leans forward. "Let's go to the marshals, Ray. Tell 'em Gotti knows where you are now. Tell 'em everything. Start over. See if we can't make something with this life."

Ray looks down at the stacks of bills on his lap.

"Ray, if you take that money . . . if you go see the mailman, then you're the same stupid fuck you've always been. You'll never be anything but a ghost who used to be Ray Sticks, walking around thinking you're alive. And when everyone looks at you, all they'll see is the hole where you used to be."

Ray stares at him and Vince sees in his eyes a glimmer of recognition, of hope.

"Look at me," Vince says. "I might be the least productive person in this country. I'm thirty-six years old, and other than this baking job I've never worked an honest day in my life. But today I voted. And my vote counted the same as everybody else's. Now, maybe it doesn't matter to those assholes out there, but to me . . . well, it's something."

Ray brushes his fingers across his forehead. He looks over at Beth, and then up at Vince. He looks outside, where the wind is shaking down the sidewalk trees. But when he looks back at Vince he seems unchanged. "Turn around and drive," he says.

VINCE AND BETH hold hands in the front seat. They drive in silence down Third Avenue, the sign for Dicks Drive-in looming two blocks away. When Vince stops at a light, the wind rocks the car gently from side to side. Ray seems distracted.

"You know why I don't believe you?" he asks. "About John?"

Vince looks up in the rearview.

"Because you didn't do anything. If John really sent you after me, you would've tried something by now."

Vince looks back at the road. "At first, when Ange asked me, I sat there thinking about how I could do it. Where I could buy a gun. Maybe I could shoot you from a distance. Hit you with a car. Try to get you in some situation where I could surprise you. I even thought about hiring somebody. But who am I gonna hire that's better than you?"

Ray shrugs, accepts the compliment.

Vince pulls into the parking lot of Dicks Drive-in. "But the whole time I'm thinking that, I also knew I couldn't do it. Not if I mean the things I just said. So . . . I told 'em that I couldn't do it. And that's when I decided to try talking you into giving up and going straight."

"You told John Gotti no?" Ray laughs. "Now I know you're lying."

Vince puts the car in park and turns off the motor. He looks across the parking lot, to where Clay is waiting at the outdoor picnic tables.

"Look," Ray says, "nobody talks but me. Got it?" He starts stuffing the money in his pants pockets. He bulges with hundred-dollar bills, sick with money. "You try anything, I shoot the girl and then I shoot you. Got it, chief?"

Ray and Vince climb out. They look across the parking lot. Beth slides out the driver's-side door, the last one out of the car.

Across the lot, Clay sits alone.

"That your guy? The colored guy?"

"Yeah," Vince says.

Beth makes expectant eye contact with Vince—as if asking

*what now?* and Vince is glad they can't talk so that he can't tell her that he doesn't really have a plan, that the speech he gave in the car *was* his plan.

"Lenny!" Ray shouts back into the car. "Come on."

He doesn't move. Ray slaps the hood. "Len. Let's go!"

"Get Lenny," Ray says.

Vince bends down in the car, slides across the seat, and feels the side of Lenny's neck. His skin is cold, clammy. He can't find a pulse. He tries Lenny's wrist. Nothing. He looks at Lenny's shoulder. The knife is gone. Vince climbs out.

"Is he coming?" Ray asks.

"No," Vince says, and looks at Beth, whose face is set, determined.

Ray shakes his head as if he should've expected such weakness from Lenny. "Well, we'll take care of that later."

They walk across the empty parking lot to the picnic benches, where Clay sits by himself. As they reach the table he rises, reaches in his back pocket, and produces the brochure for the sports car he wants to buy. "Hey, Vince."

Vince points from one to the other. "Clay Gainer. Ralph LaRue."

Ray shoots Vince a glare. *"Ray,"* he says. "My name is *Ray.*"

All you can do. They sit, Clay and Vince on one side, Beth and Ray on the other. Vince holds his hand out beneath the table, hoping Beth will hand him the paring knife, but she just stares at him, that same placid look. Don't do it, Vince thinks. Jesus, *don't do it.* Clay opens the brochure, slides it across the table. "First thing, before we go any further, I gotta ask up front, do you have a problem with me buyin' this car?"

Ray takes the brochure, turns it over in his hand. "You bet your ass I got a problem. You work with me, you drive a Cadillac. Or a Mercedes, something with class. You can't drive this cheap Japanese shit. This ain't a car, it's a fuckin' wristwatch."

Ray hands the brochure back to Clay, who shoots Vince a told-you-so glance.

"Okay," Vince says to Ray. "You got everything you wanted. Let Beth go now."

"Maybe later," Ray says, smiling.

And that is when Beth leaps up, and the suddenness of her movement causes Ray to turn to face her, giving her the perfect angle, and Ray is so shocked he doesn't move or even get a hand up as Beth drives the small paring knife into his chest with all the force a hundred-pound woman can muster. All three men at the table gasp and jerk back as the knife slams into Ray's breastbone, and it takes a moment for Vince to realize what has happened, Ray staring straight ahead, unhurt, the broken blade clattering on the picnic table, and valiant Beth, wonderful Beth—driven now by instinct— flailing away at him with nothing but a plastic knife handle.

Ray hits Beth in the mouth, and she falls off the picnic bench to the ground. Ray leaps up, puts a foot on her throat, pulls the gun from his waistband, and points it at Vince, who has picked up the knife blade. "Gimme that fuckin' blade."

Vince stares at a spot over Ray's shoulder.

Ray holds the gun up to Vince's face. "Gimme the fuckin' knife."

Ray kicks at Beth, who covers her head with her arms. "You're gonna eat this knife now," he says to her. He waves the gun at Vince again. "Gimme that fuckin' blade, chief."

The wind stops, expectant, and for just a moment it's quiet— Vince still staring at the spot over Ray's shoulder, until finally he holds out the knife and Ray reaches for it, and just as he does, a shadow falls across his arm, a meaty hand lands on his shoulder, and another deftly plucks the gun from his hand.

Ray spins and comes face-to-face with Ange, wearing a dark overcoat and smiling warmly. Another guy stands a few feet away, in sunglasses. Vince doesn't recognize him.

Ray is confused. "Ange?"

"Ray. How's it goin'?"

"Ange?" They stand close, feet at shoulder width, everyone

tensed, the wind flapping their overcoats. Beth looks up at them from the ground. Without looking away from Ray, Ange hands the gun behind him to the second guy, who puts it in his coat pocket.

"What—" Ray swallows. "What are you doin' here?"

"Donuts told us where to find you."

Ray looks over at Vince, comprehension still a few seconds away.

Ange puts his hands in his pockets. "John wants you to come home, Ray."

"Yeah?" Ray shifts his weight, looks wobbly. "Well . . . that's . . . that's . . . Yeah. I mean, this fuckin' place. Yeah. Thank God." He laughs uncomfortably and turns back to Vince. "See, I told you they'd want me back."

"Sure," Ange says. "We need you back, Ray."

"You're the best," says the second man, as if reading from a script. "A legend."

Ray continues to stare at Vince, and then his eyes trail off and focus on a point behind him. It's odd the way Ray's hands just hang there, like he doesn't quite know what to do with them now.

"I'm sorry," Vince says quietly.

This brings Ray back and he blinks a couple of times, then wipes his mouth. "Fuck you," he says, and he turns to Ange with a big, almost-brave grin. "I was goin' nuts here. This fuckin' guy"— he jerks his thumb toward Vince—"thinks he knows everything." He looks down at Beth, who has crawled away. ". . . the broads here stab you in the back . . . and there ain't a fuckin' dime to be made . . . don't get me started on the pizza. You can't believe the fuckin' pizza here, Ange."

"Well, you won't have to worry about the pizza anymore," Ange says.

Something occurs to Ray, and he reaches in his pockets for the bundles of cash Vince and Beth were going to use to buy the house. "And hey, I got some money, Ange. For John."

Ange smiles. "That's unnecessary, Ray, but I'm sure it will be appreciated." He steps forward, takes the bundles of cash, and puts his arm around Ray. "You're a good man. Always thinking of the guys." He leads him away, like a guy leading his little brother from a baseball game. Ray goes willingly. Ange steers him across the parking lot and over the curb to another lot, next door, the second man falling in a few feet behind. They walk to the back of the lot, where a square, four-door rental car is parked. A third man climbs out of the car and motions Ray into the front passenger seat.

Just before he climbs in, Ray looks once more across the parking lot to the table, to Vince. He raises his hand as if he might wave, but it just hangs there, and Ange nudges him. Ray disappears into the car. Vince stares at the windshield of the rental, but it does nothing but reflect the gray clouds back at him.

Vince helps Beth off the ground and she sits next to him on the picnic bench. "Can we go?" Clay whispers.

"I don't think so," Vince says. "I think we'd better wait."

After a second, Ange climbs out of the car and walks back across the lot, the wind raising his black-and-silver hair like whitecaps.

"You were supposed to have him here at nine," Ange says.

"I had to vote."

"No shit? Who'd you vote for, Donuts?"

"I'd rather not say."

"Sure," Ange says. "I understand."

Ange looks around the parking lot.

"Ange, this is my girlfriend, Beth."

She waves her good hand.

"What happened to your eye?" He nods his head toward the rental car. "Did Ray do that?"

She nods. "He broke my arm, too."

"I'm sorry. The guy's an animal. You have my apologies."

"And this is Clay. My mailman."

Ange shakes his hand. "Your dentist here, too, Donuts?"

Vince smiles. "I gotta ask you, Ange . . . the money that Ray has—it's not his. It's mine. I was gonna use it to buy a house and if—"

Ange holds up his hand. "Come on, Donuts. You know I can't do anything about that. That's John's money now."

Ange looks around the parking lot, takes in the freeway behind him, and the streets leading toward downtown: covered with squat brownstones and a few taller office buildings, the whole thing surrounded on both sides by gently sloped, tree-lined hills, like a city someone started building and then quit. Cars move languorously on the surface streets. In front of the restaurant, a streetlight sways gently in the wind. "So this is it? This is the place you were so excited to get back to?"

"Yeah," Vince says. "This is where I live."

"It's not really what I pictured. It's less . . . I don't know." Ange shrugs. "Just less." He looks at the car across the parking lot, then back at Vince. "But I'm sure it's nice."

"So . . . are we square, John and me?" Vince asks.

"Yeah." Ange tugs on his shimmery slacks and seems to be searching for something profound to say. Finally he points a thick finger at Vince. "Be good." He walks across the parking lot to the rental car, the wind ruffling the edge of his coat. He opens the back door on the driver's side and climbs in.

They watch the car pull out onto the street and drive away. For a minute, the only sound is the wind raking the trees.

"I'm not gonna get my car, am I, Vince?"

Vince doesn't even look over at Clay. "No."


THEY LIE ON the couch all afternoon—Vince staring at the ceiling, Beth curled up on his chest. Kenyon toddles around the coffee table in a diaper, a sweatshirt, and slippers with bells on the toes. He jangles to his bedroom and brings out his toys one at a time to show

Vince, holding them up proudly. He brings out a stuffed frog and holds it for Vince to see.

"Frog," Vince says.

Kenyon looks at it, drops it, and ambles back to the bedroom. He comes back with a windup train.

"That's a train," Vince says.

The boy drops it and turns, all business, as if some little-kid handbook has instructed him that this is the proper way to act when you have a guest at your home.

"Football."

They don't talk about what happened, how Vince convinced Ange to come to Spokane and do the job himself, or what likely happened to Ray. They don't talk about the money they lost, or the house. And they don't talk about what happens now—although Vince thinks she must have some idea. They take turns sleeping, the other one watching Kenyon, who brings his toys back and forth from the bedroom in some frantic toddler inventory, pausing once to touch Beth's new white cast. She told the doctor in the emergency room that she was in a car accident, and they seemed to buy it. Then she and Vince went to the bank and canceled the home loan. "Oh, well," was all she said. They left Lenny in his car at Dicks and called the police anonymously from the bank.

"A top," Vince says.

Kenyon's expression doesn't change. He drops the top and simply scuffles off to the bedroom again.

Vince can feel Beth—her weight evenly distributed from his legs to his chest. He likes the feeling of having all of her touching all of him. He watches her back rise and fall with each breath. And her shoulders. He runs his hand through her hair and kisses the crown of her head.

She nestles into his chest. "Tell me again."

"Well," he says. "I'm going to borrow some money and we'll find a building and open a restaurant."

"And I'll be the waitress."

He speaks barely above a whisper: "You'll be the waitress. I'll be the chef. It'll be called The Picnic Basket and we'll serve everything in picnic baskets and the walls will be painted like trees and some of the tables will be blankets spread out on the floor. We'll serve cold fried chicken and sandwiches and whole pies. And there'll be kids everywhere, slides and swing sets . . . it will be like a park, but inside."

Kenyon toddles out with a toy bear.

"Bear," Vince says.

"And we'll live in a house?" Beth whispers.

"We'll live in a great house, with a barbecue and a front porch, and while I'm gone you and Kenyon can wait for me there with a big glass of lemonade."

ALAN DUPREE WINCES as he grabs his suitcase from the luggage carousel.

Phelps is still laughing. "You're the only cop I know goes to New York and gets himself mugged."

Dupree lets Phelps take the suitcase.

"So what, this guy just jumps you, out of the blue, gives you a black eye and breaks your ribs?"

"Something like that," Dupree says.

"Tell me you chased him."

"I chased him."

"Did he get your wallet?"

"No."

"Well, that's good, at least. That's a little less embarrassing."

They walk out the doors of the white, swooping jet-age airport, to Phelps's car. Dupree moans as he settles in. Phelps drives them back toward town, curls onto the freeway, and descends Sunset Hill into Spokane, the sun breaking through the clouds behind them— just in time to set. Phelps updates Dupree on everything that's happened—the diesel repair instructor over at the community college they found stuffed in the trunk of his own car, and just today, a stereo-store owner found stabbed to death in the passenger seat of his car at Dicks Drive-in. With Doug, the passport-shop owner last week, that makes three bodies in eight days.

"And no connection between any of them?" Dupree asks.

"Not that we can see," Phelps says. "Don't hold your breath, rook. Sometimes you just get a streak like this. Who knows why? Something in the water, maybe."

Dupree stares out the window.

Phelps says there's been no sign of Vince Camden since he popped in at the marshals service. "Probably left town again."

Phelps exits the freeway into the neighborhood just below the South Hill. He turns onto Alan and Debbie's street and into their driveway. The lights are all on. "You taking tomorrow off?"

"No," Dupree says. "I'll be in."

Phelps jumps out and tries to get Dupree's suitcase, but Alan shakes him off and carries it himself. He's halfway up the porch when Phelps calls after. "Hey, good job, by the way. Figuring out Camden was in witness protection. You did good, rook. You can't always catch the guy."

Dupree says, without turning, "Yeah."

Inside, he buries his face in Debbie's neck, and repeats the story about being mugged. She rubs his back and then goes to make him something to eat. Dupree eases into a dining-room chair, pulls a number from his wallet, picks up the phone, and dials.

"Fair Oaks Treatment Center."

"Yeah, I wanted to see about a patient I checked in there this morning."

"I'm sorry. We can't release information on clients."

"Please. I dropped him off there myself. I just want to know if he's still there. His name is Donnie Charles. He's a cop."

"I'm sorry, sir. I can't."

"Please. It's important."

"Are you family?"

"No. I'm . . . his partner."

The woman on the other end is quiet for a moment and Alan can hear the pages ruffling. "He's here," the woman says.

THEY EAT DINNER quietly. Dupree has just lowered himself in a bath when he hears the phone ring. He hears Debbie say, "I'm sorry. He's in the bath." And then he falls asleep and the next thing he knows he jerks awake in cold water and sees Debbie standing in the doorway of the bathroom. "Alan. I think you better come out here."

Dupree comes out in a robe and sees Vince Camden, his back to them, sitting on Dupree's couch, drinking a cup of coffee, and watching the late election returns. Dupree looks over at Debbie. "I'm sorry. He said he had something for you. I didn't want to disturb you." He pats her reassuringly on the hand and she goes back into the kitchen.

On TV there's a square-jawed guy, his arm around his wife, waving to a roomful of supporters at a downtown hotel, shaking hands as the numbers on the screen tell the story: *60% of precincts: Grebbe 61.4%; Thomas 38.6%.*

Finally Vince Camden turns. "Hey." He holds up the business card Dupree gave him days earlier, his home number on the back. "I'm sorry. I called and got your address from your wife. I didn't want to wait until tomorrow."

"Are you—"

Vince Camden nods. "Turning myself in."

"For—"

"What've you got?" Vince asks. He smiles. "I've been stealing credit cards. Dealing pot." Vince shifts on the couch. "And I can tell you who killed Doug, the passport guy. And Lenny, the guy in the car at Dicks today. And maybe more."

Dupree just stares at him.

"It wasn't me," Vince says. "It was this guy, Ray. He was at my house the day you came by. He did it."

"How do you know?"

"Well, I saw him kill Lenny. Stabbed him in the shoulder with a paring knife."

"Do you know where this Ray is?"

"No," Vince says. "I don't. He was staying at a motel on the west side of town. But he's not there now. The last time I saw him he said he was going back to New York."

"By himself?"

"I couldn't tell you."

Dupree isn't sure about the inflection—if Vince can't tell him, or won't.

Vince turns back to the TV. Dupree stands behind him, in his robe, unsure what he's supposed to do now. Or what he wants to do. He's just so goddamned tired. Finally, he sits down in his easy chair, next to the couch and across from the console TV.

Debbie returns from the kitchen, sets a plate of sliced banana bread on the coffee table, and fills up Vince's coffee cup.

Vince takes a bite of banana bread. "This is very good, Mrs. Dupree."

"Thank you." She looks at her husband for help.

"Oh, I'm sorry," Dupree says. "This is—" He stops. "Is it Marty, or . . ."

He smiles. "Vince. Please. Call me Vince."

"Vince. This is my wife. Debbie."

They shake hands, and then Vince goes back to his banana bread, breaking off bites above his little plate. They sit together like a family, watching the local returns. The Republicans are making major gains; even heavyweights like Warren Magnuson and Tom Foley are in danger of losing. The presidential race was called hours ago, with Reagan winning by nine points and four hundred electoral votes. There's some anger directed at Jimmy Carter for conceding so early, when the polls were still open in the West, and the news anchor cuts to a tape of Carter's concession, flanked by huge red and white stripes, brace-knuckled at the podium, Rosalynn and Amy standing shamefully at his side like co-conspirators, their arms dead at their sides, the three of them resembling nothing so much as a poor Southern family being turned out of their home. His eyes are puffy and red—*I promised you four years ago that I would never lie to you, so I can't stand here tonight and say it doesn't hurt*—and his face seems different in some profound way from the face of the man who arrived just four years earlier, as if time and pressure have conspired to sever the muscles and allowed the familiar features to drift—*I call on the new administration to solve the problems still before us. And to bring Americans back together.*

Dupree looks over at Vince Camden. His mouth is open a few inches and he's watching as if this were all happening to him.

"I'm gonna get dressed and then we'll go," Dupree says quietly.

Vince nods without looking away from the screen.

Dupree comes back out in jeans and a sweater. He keeps his handcuffs at his side, hoping Vince won't notice them, unsure why it even matters. Debbie sees the cuffs and raises her eyebrows. On TV Reagan is ebullient, confident; he belongs—*I am not frightened by what lies ahead and I don't think the American people are frightened by what lies ahead*—jet-black hair hard-parted on the right, cuff links peeking from the sleeves of a pressed white shirt, beneath shoulders built to fill a dark suit, and already he looks more presidential than the man he beat, and Nancy beams skeletal at his elbow—*Together we're going to do what has to be done. We're going to put America back to work again*—and he raises his thumb to the throng of supporters and the Reagan signs bounce and confetti rains on the hotel ballroom.

History is just the memories you haven't had yet. History is this cycle of arrogance and fall, arrogance and fall, and as soon as something happens, you can't remember when you didn't know it would happen, when there was any other outcome than the one in front of you. Reagan waves. *Even if it had been the cliffhanger we were expecting, it would have been the same. This is the most humbling moment of my life.*

And finally, Vince sits back on the couch. Looks up and smiles.

Dupree can't quite read the look on his face—a kind of bemused surrender, the recognition of irony, perhaps. "What is it?"

"I just realized: I'm going to be convicted of credit-card fraud."

At the very least, Dupree thinks. But he doesn't want Vince to clam up, so he says, "Look, if you cooperate, if what you say is true about your friend Ray, who knows—you could be out in a year or two. Maybe even less."

"No, I know," Vince says. "But it'll still be a felony." Again that ironic smirk.

"Yeah," Dupree says, waiting. "So . . ."

"Nothing . . . Nothing." Still smiling, Vince turns to the TV—the screen a blur of confetti and balloons and bunting, and at the center of it, an almost seventy-year-old man vowing to free his people of their fears and insecurities, to make them stop feeling puny and vulnerable, boldly promising to lead them into the past.

Vince turns away. "So was I the crow or the lake?"

"I don't know," Dupree says. "Both, maybe."

"Yeah, that's kind of what I thought," Vince says. "Ready?" He stands, offers Dupree his wrists, and begins his life.

AUTHOR'S REFERENDUM # 672

The following shall be thanked for their contributions relating to this book, including but not limited to: editing, support, over-service and patience, in accordance with grammatical law and authorial appreciation.

---

## DEPRESS FIRMLY

| (INSPIRATION PARTY) ANNE WALTER | ➡ ◯ |

| (PEOPLE FOR THE ETHICAL TREATMENT OF LANGUAGE) DAN BUTTERWORTH | ➡ ◯ |

| (MANUSCRIPT LIBERATION FRONT) CAL MORGAN | ➡ ◯ |

| (KNOB CREEK PROGRESSIVE PARTY) DANNY WESTNEAT | ➡ ◯ |

| (LIFE OF PARTY) JUDITH REGAN | ➡ ◯ |